THE

Tears

WE NEVER

Cried

THE
Tears
WE NEVER
Cried

Ryshia Kennie

Black Lyon Publishing, LLC

THE TEARS WE NEVER CRIED
Copyright © 2019 by RYSHIA KENNIE

Our books may be ordered through your local bookstore or by visiting the publisher:

www.BlackLyonPublishing.com

Black Lyon Publishing, LLC
PO Box 567
Baker City, OR 97814

This is a work of fiction. All of the characters, names, events, organizations and conversations in this novel are either the products of the author's vivid imagination or are used in a fictitious way for the purposes of this story.

ISBN-13:   978-1-934912-89-8
Library of Congress Control Number: 2019953027

Published and printed in
the United States of America.

Black Lyon
LITERARY
FICTION

In memory of my dad whose battle with Alzheimer's inspired this story. For my mom who cared for him over all those years. And, for every family and caregiver, who have wrestled with the challenges of dementia each and every day.

Prologue

From the diary of Jessica Jane McDowall

I'd always thought that death should come quickly. There's nothing humane about lingering. But nature is cruel and there's no finer example than what happened to Mama.

Mama's illness was the worst of a string of bad luck that only brightened once with the birth of my daughter, Cassandra Lynn. But life is a fickle thing. You give life and then you have life taken away.

Mama and Dad have been gone for almost a year, my husband, Tom for quite some months. It's only me and Cassie now and that part feels right. What feels wrong is the fact that my parents are gone. I know I'm too old to feel like this. After all, I'm the mother of a nine-year-old, but I feel like an orphan. I have nothing left of Mama but the pearls she so loved.

I plan never to tell Cassandra what happened to Mama. I know it's about as useful as collecting good luck charms. I feel if I don't talk about it, then it has become rather like Pandora's box, safe as long as it remains tucked away ... unseen ... unknown ...

Chapter One

December 6

I remember the moment it happened. I had barely pulled away from the curb, done a quick shoulder check, and that's when life broadsided me.

I was thirty-nine, coincidentally exactly forty weeks from my fortieth birthday. I've lived forever since that moment, or so it seemed. Even though it was really only a year and change out of my life, that day that began it all.

It was a day like any other except … I swear the ring on my phone was louder than normal. And Mother's voice was strident and demanding.

"Cassie, you best get over here now. I've lost my best pen and they've taken my Christmas cards away."

I had no idea what she was talking about, but the panic in her voice was real and like nothing I had heard before.

"Cassandra McDowall?" The disembodied voice was no longer my mother's, but instead one that was male and full of authority.

"Yes." Somehow my fingers were already knotting in trepidation of what he might want.

"This is Tod Rushinski, staff sergeant with the Regina City Police."

My palms began to sweat.

"Your mother is Jessica Jane McDowell?"

"Yes." Fortunately it was the only word required for it was the only word I could choke out. The police never phoned for a *good* reason.

"We have your mother here at the station."

"My mother? Is she all right?" Images of my tiny mother, cuffed and chained, surrounded by burly police officers poised to pounce at her slightest move sent shock waves through me. I imagined the terror on her face, her usually neatly coiffed hair askew. Horror reels played through my mind. Mother hurt, injured, attacked by unknown thugs.

Elder abuse, rape, mugging.

Mother, her coral pink lipstick smeared across one crinkled cheek, swinging her purse and being taken down and left bruised and alone by a dumpster.

Who could have done this to her? What had happened? I couldn't choke out the question. Instead I had a chokehold on the steering wheel.

"She was detained at a department store. Store security stopped her for shoplifting."

"Shoplifting. No. Not Mom."

"Two boxes of Christmas cards. I'm sorry. I'm not meaning to frighten you. The store security called us because she appeared confused." There was a short silence and I could hear Mother say something in the background. "Miss McDowall, I'm sorry to say this, but we were only called because your mother wouldn't give more than her first name. I suspect she'd forgotten. We didn't get her full name until after we brought her to the station."

"That can't be," I finally mouthed. I wasn't sure if those words were actually audible. Mother knew her name and the names of each of her ancestors back five generations. My heart hammered as I thought of how frightened Mother was and how alone she must have felt.

"We have her here because no one knew where she belonged. We're obviously not going to book her for anything. But lost seniors aren't issues that department store security deal with."

"She's under arrest?" I still couldn't focus on the other word: *lost*. Not Mother. That was impossible. And yet something told me, some quiet little voice, that it was completely possible. Mother hadn't been herself lately. Something wretched deep inside me—something I couldn't identify that was taking me to a dark possibility I couldn't comprehend.

"No, of course not. Normally I'd get your address and we'd drive her home. But there's been a rash of traffic accidents. The weather has every spare officer I have on the streets." He hesitated as if he were oddly reluctant to indulge me with further details. "Could you come down?"

"Of course she'll come down." Mother's voice insisted in the background, a note of frustration in her clear-pitched voice that had once been lead soprano in the local choir.

"Right away."

I ended the call without waiting to see if the faceless Tod Rushinski might have more to say. The entire conversation took all of a minute to turn my life on its head and have me charging through rush-hour traffic like the speed demon I wasn't.

Speed didn't adapt well to a prairie winter that was sheeting intersections with ice. I put my foot on the gas, ignored the brake and fishtailed through the intersection to a concerto of honking horns. I swung a wide right and wrestled the car out of a skid that threatened to take the bumper off a parked car. Ten minutes later I was parked and sweating outside the broad, nondescript police station, its austerity relieved only by a layer of sleet and snow, its bland cinder-brick exterior coated like a badly frosted cake.

I charged up the wide span of concrete steps, skidded to a stop in front of the commissioner who, although his age might match my mother's seventy-five, seemed determined to stop primary clearance to the rest of the building. From the looks of the rednecks around me, I doubted his effectiveness.

One rough-edged man with a faded black leather biker jacket stared at me morosely from a corner of the slightly crowded and chilled entrance.

In the opposite corner a rather sulky looking youth slouched against one wall, his arms holding more tattoos than muscle. His glossy gaze traveled a slow, insolent path over me and I gave him my best glare. He winked at me.

I turned away. The last thing I needed was the attention of a sixteen year-old smart ass.

"Miss." The security man motioned for me to approach

his desk. As I did, I focused on my one and only purpose for being there, finding and obtaining Mother, freeing her from incarceration and wiping the record clean.

Cleared by the elderly commissioner, I slowed only at the receptionist who pointed me to a span of stairs as utilitarian as the outside of the building. On the second floor, the door opened and a slightly familiar face smiled and motioned me in where he immediately took me to a corner office. The familiarity blew right by me. All I could think of was Mother.

"Have a seat."

He motioned to a hard-backed chair and I sat only because I wasn't sure if my legs would hold me.

I know him, I thought, and tried for a minute to place him.

"Cassie. I can't believe it's you."

"Russ?" His identity, despite the official police uniform, came to me in a rush. It was surreal facing who had once been the fuzzy-lipped Russ Thomas. Last time I'd seen him he'd been wearing a suit one size too big and a tie one knot too tight. It had been high school graduation. He looked different now, better — much better.

"I've thought of you often through the years, Cass."

I didn't know what to do with that information but whether it was purposeful or not, it was rather calming to focus on something else. I glanced to the corner and saw a duffel bag with a telltale hockey stick propped against it.

"A hockey player," I murmured. Not a surprise in a town that sees snow almost six months of the year.

"Men's rec league. I play whenever my shifts allow." Russ shrugged.

I remembered Russ had played hockey all the way through school. In fact I'd been to a good number of his games — not because I'd been into Russ but because he'd played on the best hockey team in the city and I had been completely into hockey.

"You always wanted to play in the NHL."

"Me and half the guys in this town."

"But you were good." In fact there had been rumors of a talent scout out to watch a few of his games. I wondered what had happened.

He shrugged. "Even drafted, good doesn't make a career."

"I don't understand."

"I was too far down in the draft and there was an issue or two with the farm team I was sent to." He looked down at the papers on his desk and then back up at me. "But look, this isn't about me."

I almost shrank from the sympathy I saw there and my heart did a triple skip as reality slammed into me one more time.

"I saw your name and thought I'd take over for Tod," Russ explained. "I hope you don't mind. But a friendly face …"

"Yes, no. I don't mind." I blustered not exactly sure what I minded or didn't, only one thought reeling through my mind. Where was Mother?

"Your mother went with Tod to get a coffee. She was seeming a little agitated."

"What happened?" I blurted out and it seemed I forced the words passed a mouthful of memories. Faces and connections dashed through my head—mine, his, Mother's—I couldn't focus, couldn't think. I stood up and clutched the desk with two hands as if preparing myself for an execution.

"The call came in about two hours ago. Initially the store security thought it was a simple shoplifting situation. Then they discovered it was a bit more complicated than that." His hands folded on the desk and he leaned forward.

His eyes seemed to lock with mine and I willed him not to go any further. He missed every silent cue I threw at him. "She's here as a lost person."

"Mom just has some memory issues." Then I realized Mother had tried to shoplift. Straight-as-an-arrow, church-once-a-week Mother, who had once made me return a pack of bubble gum when I was five. I'd lifted the gum from a local convenience store and she'd made me go directly to the manager with an apology.

"I was told she didn't know her name." I took a deep breath after I said that and my fingers ached from my grip on the edge of the desk. "I find that impossible to believe. What was said to her? She must be terrified. That's the only explanation."

Mother rambled and repeated herself often enough.

But this? He obviously had no idea what he was talking about.

"I can only tell you what the store security told our officers. It seems she was stuffing a box of Christmas cards into her purse. She wouldn't give either the box in her hand or the one in her bag back, and she was reaching for more. In fact, the store security said she was getting quite belligerent."

"Mom? I can't believe it."

"I'm not telling you this to upset you, Cassie. But it's obvious your mother needs help. She refused to leave the store and was repeating the word *mine* over and over."

I couldn't think of any of it. I couldn't fathom it. Instead I thought of Mother's purse. It was the size of a mid-sized shopping bag. She loved having, as she said, something with substance hanging from her arm. It would easily hold a box of Christmas cards or two or even three.

"We'll pay for the cards."

"Look, Cassie. That's not the issue. Really, the Christmas cards were returned to the store. Except." His smile was not one of happiness but rather one of resignation. "For this one." He held up a single card with the traditional snow scene and a nativity front and center. "It was still in her purse."

I could hardly look at that card. The nativity was like a glaring light for all Mother believed. And it only reminded me of Mother's moral backbone and her strict religious beliefs. "I can't believe it." I remembered how that word—can't—stuck in my mind.

"You might want to have her examined," he replied gravely.

"Definitely," I agreed. McDowall women were not quitters. Whatever was impairing Mother's memory and affecting her behavior would be dealt with. I wouldn't let this continue.

He looked at me sympathetically. "It's a tough road, I know. I just lost an uncle to Alzheimer's."

"Alzheimer's?" I squeaked.

"I'm sorry, Cassie."

I was unable to speak. The possibility was so overwhelming, so devastating, as not to be contemplated. Mother had needed help lately, more than usual. There had been a disturbing phone call or two, but she was still able to take care of herself.

"My Uncle. I don't know if you remember him but ..." Russ's voice droned on as if telling me the story of his uncle would make whatever was going on with Mother that much easier.

I nodded blindly while my mind hit rewind on Mother's disturbing phone calls. I had to admit our conversations had begun to get a little thin around the edges. Mother didn't have much to say about much of anything. I attributed that to the fact she needed to get out more. But sometimes she'd had quite a lot to say and I remembered those conversations with trepidation. Only last fall she'd told me the neighbor had stolen her tea towels. It had been a ridiculous accusation and one I was able to resolve quickly after I found the same tea towels in the bottom drawer of her dresser.

There had been other instances, similar ones, as well as the conversations that involved numerous repetitions of stories and events. But every time there was one strange event or phone call immediately or shortly after, Mother had bounced back, into the land that I considered normal. At that point no one had said she had dementia. Even her general practitioner had assured me there was no need to worry when I had dared to mention the subject. Normal senior moments, nothing else, and if one wanted proof—well, she was still able to function, still doing her thing. But then she'd never done anything like this.

"I'm sorry to say this, Cassie, but your mother gave us her first name and that was all. That was actually more than she'd told the store security. She couldn't tell us where she was or where she lived." He cleared his throat and his next words decimated me. "Or what year it was. That's a standard question we employ when we suspect mental confusion."

He looked at me with concern. "Would you like a glass of water?"

I nodded and sat down. My legs were officially rubber. The lack of knowing a year—that was the fact that drove the reality home. Not Alzheimer's, but definitely memory issues that needed to be addressed and resolved. The glass of water arrived in my hand and I didn't remember him placing it there or what he said next. Mother's voice brought reality back like a backhand out of nowhere.

"Cassie! Where have you been? I want to go home."

"Mom!" I stood up and in the process knocked a familiar pink pen to the floor, Mother's pen. She had carried it like a talisman everywhere over the last few years. I hadn't thought anything odd about it, it just was. But what my gaze fixated on was the strand of pearls around her neck. They'd belonged to her mother and for as long as I could remember they weren't worn on anything but what she called an occasion—and definitely not for a shopping excursion.

"You've found my pen, sweetie," Mother said as she reached for it. But in the process of reaching she stopped.

"Mom?" I croaked, my voice giving up in a maelstrom of conflicting emotion. I watched as she moved in slow motion, seemingly caught by something else on the other side of the desk. I held out my hand, meaning to offer her my now vacant chair.

She ignored me as her eyes lit up when she spotted another pen. This one with a purple swirl down its side, her second favorite color. She reached and in that moment, all her odd little behaviors, her forgetfulness, her childish lapses combined into one possibility and again it was all I could do to stay on my feet.

"Mom, no." I took her by the elbow.

"Cassie, sweetie." She pushed me none to gently. "Let me get my pen." There was an emptiness in her eyes that I hadn't seen before, or maybe I hadn't wanted to. The only thing that held her interest was the pen with the purple swirl I had just denied her.

I glanced at Mother who was holding her pen and caressing it like it was a lost child while longingly eyeing the other.

"No, Mom. It's not yours."

"Mine."

I almost burst into tears. Instead I took a deep breath. Just hearing the word she'd repeated in that store when she'd been alone and confused ripped an emotional gully through me. I'd never felt so emotionally divorced from my mother. It was as if a physical rift had ripped between us. I should have reached out to her, touched her in some way to bring her back to reality and I couldn't do it. Instead, I watched as someone else stepped in for me.

Russ smiled, picked up the pen and handed it to her. Mother lit up like he had offered her part ownership in the Taj Mahal.

That's when I knew she needed me. There was no one else who did—need me that is. I'd buried the dog over five months ago. There wasn't even a house with my name on the mortgage, just one beaten Toyota in a negligible shade of blue and an apartment full of nothing worth mentioning. And Dad, well he had left long ago and good riddance. Or so Mother always said.

It was just Mother and me. I dashed a tear from the corner of one eye.

"Sweetie?" Mother wrapped her wiry arm around my waist, her breath laden with garlic and the remains of whatever she might have had for lunch.

When she dropped her arm as if she'd forgotten her original intent, I took her arm. "C'mon Mom, let's go home."

On that snowy Monday our lives had changed, but even then I couldn't define how much.

Chapter Two

December 13

"The car is stolen!"

Mother's voice sliced through the swirls of sleep.

I leapt out of bed, glanced at the clock and tripped over the unfamiliar flannel sheet. On the wall was a poster of a rock band I'd loved at fifteen. I was back in the room of my childhood.

I'd brought Mother home to live with me for that first night after the Christmas card debacle. One night was about all either of us could tolerate. My apartment was too small. It had taken me only a few days to get my stuff together, notify my landlord and move in with Mother.

"Hang on, Mom." I fought to catch my breath as I reached for my housecoat.

"Cassie!" Her voice cracked across the layer of frost that collected on the window frame overnight and slammed through the partially open window. I have a penchant for fresh air. Sleeping with a window open even in the midst of winter is normal for me, and made it easy to hear Mother's shriek outside as it erupted a second time loud enough to roust the neighbors. Her screech had me excited but not panicked. Not until my conscious and my unconscious married those two thoughts together—outside and Mother.

"Cassie!" She hollered an octave higher this time.

The alarm clicked on, an old-fashioned clock radio. More remains of my childhood.

"It's thirty-eight below today and that's without the wind

chill. It's officially the coldest day of the year," the radio announced with good cheer.

The alarm clock's red glare reminded me it had just turned eight in the morning. I was only half-awake and partially rational. How could the car be lost at this hour of the morning? I didn't realize that unlike Mother, I used the word lost rather than stolen. Instead, I made the final leap into action, tied the belt of my housecoat and ran in bare feet across the worn linoleum.

I shoved the door open and saw Mother dressed up like she was going somewhere. Her hair was neatly combed, her hands were encased in fake fur trimmed gloves but her eyes were panicked and she was clearly not seeing me.

"Cassie!" Mother shrieked as if I wasn't standing right there, not six feet from her. Something sounded like fright in her voice.

I resisted the urge to take her in my arms and hug her and never let her go, as if that would change everything. Instead I asked, "What happened?"

I was finally fully awake and cognizant as the wind danced lightly through my housecoat, and my unshaven legs quivered in the cold. The delicate hairs brushed over goosebumps as if celebrating the fact they hadn't been mowed under. Don't get me wrong, my legs used to be baby soft. I even creamed them like it was a religion every night. When was the last time I'd shaved my legs or for that matter, my underarms? It was strange. Maybe all beginnings are. But thinking about something so mundane in the face of the other possibility, Mother losing her mind — what did any of the rest of it matter?

"The car was stolen," she repeated with a thread of impatience in her well-modulated soprano tone. "Call the police."

I shivered and wrapped my arms across my chest. "Come inside," I said and gestured with one arm that had begun to shake. "The cold is killer."

"A skiff of a breeze."

"It's wicked, Mom. You'll freeze to death. The temperature is a nick under forty below, and that's without the wind chill. Let's go inside."

"We're wasting time, Cassandra." But she followed me into the house. She even removed her boots without further comment. But she refused my request to divest herself of either her coat or gloves. "We have to get going. Call the police, search the neighborhood."

"Mom," I began, considering how to phrase my thoughts. As had happened so many times those last few days, I thought of nothing appropriate.

"Where were you this morning?" There was an edge in my voice—some might call it anger, but if you knew me, you'd hear the worry.

"Why—at church," she replied, her eyes were murky and focused somewhere over my left shoulder. "It was locked, and on a Sunday. I couldn't believe it. So I banged on the priest's door."

Her eyes met mine with full force and the murk was gone. She was angry. She'd found her stride, her purpose. It was beautiful to see that return to the Mother I knew. But there was another reality I had to face. She was driving and anything could have happened. It was thirty-eight below zero—what if the car had stalled? What if ... No, I wouldn't think of the other what if—the possibility that Mother or someone else might have been seriously hurt.

"And a church no less," she continued. "Such behavior, lying. The audacity of him claiming it's not Sunday, probably wanted to sleep in." She let out a scoffing little breath.

"Mom, it's Monday."

"Monday." A frown flitted across her porcelain-pale forehead. "Are you sure?"

"Positive. You went to church yesterday. Remember? Helen picked you up." I referred to her friend that lived only a few blocks away.

"Well that explains it."

"What?"

"Nothing, sweetie."

"For God's sakes, say it, Mom." I lost my patience but really I have to say it was a good chunk of fear and a tentative amount of grief speaking.

"Cassandra Lynn, I will not have you cursing in this house!"

Mother's hands were on her hips as she faced me off.

"Shut the door," I took a long breath. "Please."

"Hmmph!" The door banged shut as if to emphasize the disappointment on her face.

"I'm sorry, Mom," I said as my goosebumps quaked despite hearing the furnace kick in.

I touched her arm as if that would seal the apology. "Explains what, Mom?"

"The priest was a little testy. Dear man, can't remember his name. What's for breakfast?" She pulled off her coat and gloves, slung the coat over her arm and strode past me, the scent of lavender trailed in a wave that smelled like she had used half the bottle. Since when did she use lavender? That was Grandmother's scent, an old-lady scent—I distinctly remembered Mother saying not that long ago. I closed the inside door and tried to shove back the wad of emotion that seemed to clog my throat.

The car.

Something knotted in my stomach. I should have taken the keys away from her.

But driving, the independence to go wherever, whenever you please was not something to trifle with. Neither was a life, I reminded myself. Because there was no denying it was dangerous, not to mention ludicrous, for someone to drive who couldn't remember what year it was or that she went to church only yesterday.

"Do you still have your keys, Mom?"

"Keys?"

"Keys for the car," I replied. "I'll need them to bring the car home."

"Oh, yes. Right," she agreed seemingly forgetting that only a few minutes ago she had pronounced the car stolen. "Do you want me to drive you?"

"No!" I said a little too forcefully and Mother jumped and her lips thinned. "No," I repeated with slightly less force, not mentioning she had no car to drive and I wasn't lending her mine. "You'll be okay for a few minutes?"

"Of course. I'll just make some toast and watch the news. I don't need a babysitter." She scowled at me.

"No toast. Don't touch anything." I looked at her sternly. "I'll make breakfast when I get back."

She folded her arms across her chest and gave me that look I remembered from when I was late getting in as a teenager.

"I mean it, Mom."

"Okay."

I should have known then that her answer was too meek.

"I'll be back shortly." I was dressed and bundled in as many layers as I could find not five minutes later. I could barely see through the swirl of wool scarf that covered my face but I'd rather be warm than fashionable. Besides, the wind was starting to kick up and a prairie winter wind at those temperatures was nothing short of brutal.

"Cassie!"

The shout knifed through a half an inch of wool covering my ears.

"Yeah, Mom." It was an effort to turn around. With all the layers I felt rather like a kid sent out to play, that Mother should be waving at the door.

"It would do you good to go to church once in a while."

I looked at her and knew that for now the car was forgotten. I needed to get her on medication and quickly, before this thing progressed any further.

"Maybe this Sunday?" she said hopefully.

"Maybe," I agreed. It had been many years since I'd set foot in a church. There'd been no need. No weddings, no funerals. Those two events were really the only reason I felt a need to attend anymore.

Not so with Mother. Church was a lifeline, a social gathering, a meeting point. I'd thought sometimes that it was more about the coffee after the service than the service itself. Of course, maybe that was a thought that made me feel justified in my own lack of devotion. "Look Mom, I've got to get the car."

She looked at me blankly.

"Remember, the car? Your lost car? Stolen car?" I was being unnecessarily edgy about it, but my patience, well back then, it needed work. Besides, it was frustrating and disheartening dealing with Mother when she was like that, not to mention bitching cold out there.

"Oh my, yes. Well for heaven's sake, Cassandra get with it. Get this reported and resolved immediately." She wavered in the open doorway. "I'll just get the coffee on."

It was a short walk to the church where I was baptized and where I learned the fine art of daydreaming. I'd lost track of how many Sundays Mother had brought me there as a child and I'd sat on those hard pews thinking the monotony of the rote prayers would never end.

She'd led me safely into the adult world and now she was beginning to rely on me. A wave of sadness washed through me at the thought of my mother getting old, more dependent and possibly losing all the pizzazz I'd so admired about her.

The parking lot was empty except for Mother's car. I unlocked the door with a heavy heart as I realized Mother would no longer be taking the helm of her own ship. And while I would get her back on track and independent again, the car was more than likely a thing of the past. I flicked the ignition switch on the late model vehicle and the car started easily, surprising considering the cold. Mother obviously hadn't left it long.

A bubble of panic almost choked me as I realized she walked the six blocks in the cold to get home. What if she hadn't made it? Was she wearing a pantsuit or a dress? What kind of caregiver was I not to notice those things? For the first time in a long time I looked at the church's frosted spire, and I sent a prayer of thanks. If there was a God he'd hear me and if there wasn't … If there wasn't, then maybe we were all doomed.

"Found it in the church parking lot, Mom," I announced as I finally arrived home to the pervasive smell of overcooked bacon, and stopped with one hand poised to take off my boot. "I told you not to cook."

"They're under arrest, I presume," she said primly. "The perpetrators."

"No, Mom," I began. "The car was in the church parking lot."

A plate of bacon sat on the counter.

"Parking lot." She giggled. "Imagine that. They gave the car back to the Lord. It must be retribution of some sort."

The Lord? Retribution?

"I guess, Mom." I shrugged and began peeling out of my layers.

"Breakfast in five minutes, Cass. Make sure to wash your hands."

"Why are you here, Cassie?" She scowled when I returned to the kitchen. "It's not like you to get up this early."

Despite the opposition of those two sentences, the first comment hit hard and true. I dumped coffee into the filter and tried to catch my breath.

"Cassie, what about work?"

And that statement confirmed everything I knew. Mother didn't have Alzheimer's she was just forgetful, confused only when she was overwhelmed. Otherwise, she was fine.

"I phoned in and have the next two weeks off." My boss had been amazingly accommodating but then I had the bad feeling both he and I might be glad to see the end of one another. My being absent for a while allowed him to pop in his replacement of choice, or so I imagined.

"Wonderful, dear. When are you going home?" She dusted her hands on her apron. "Not that I don't mind having you here but ..."

"No worries, Mom. I'm not here for long." The words I said had no real meaning. Despite telling myself this was temporary, a good chunk of my belongs were parked in one half of Mother's double garage.

"I hope not. You're too old to be living at home."

I looked at her over one shoulder as I flipped the eggs. Had she forgotten why I was here? I couldn't ask. I flipped the eggs unnecessarily for a third and then fourth time and turned the burner off.

It was almost midnight when I realized as I sat wrapped in a cozy housecoat with my feet tucked beneath me and the latest romantic fantasy in hand, that Mother and I were in this together and from the looks of it, for the long haul. I tried not to think what the long haul might mean.

I preferred to stick to my original version — a month maybe two.

I'd be back to work shortly, maybe I'd buy rather than rent, and everything would return to normal.

Chapter Three

December 20

I awoke to soft humming and was drawn into distant memories of my childhood. I'd fallen asleep on the couch and sometime while I slept Mother had covered me with a blanket. I listened to her humming softly, her knitting needles flashing and each click weaving another stitch on a patch of baby blue wool.

I looked at her through half-closed eyes and I saw Mother as she used to look. Her hair was swept up neatly in what she called a French twist. Her blue eyes were alight with enthusiasm over some new project. I always admired her elegant hairstyles and her ability to sweep through life with grace and verve. I'd read books on how such style was accomplished and I'd never been able to replicate it. My hair was the color of chocolate pudding when I'd prefer caramel; it was also thin and wispy. I'd finally given up any attempts at styling and cut it off into an easy wash-and-wear, just-above-the-shoulder bob that suited me and had pleased me so much I'd worn it like that for the last five years. Style—that was Mother.

"What are you knitting, Mom?"

"An outfit for Dell's baby."

"Dell?" My cousin Dell had popped the most recent addition to the McDowall clan a number of years ago. "Mother, Dell's baby is almost two. He's walking." I pointed at her project. "That's newborn size. It's too small."

"Oh, oh dear. What was I thinking?"

"I'm sorry, Mom. I didn't mean to be short."

"That's okay, sweetie." She set the knitting aside and

stretched. Aside from her hair being in a slightly crooked updo, she looked nothing but normal. But she'd forgotten when Dell's baby was born. And that wasn't a fact easily forgotten as Dell sent almost monthly updates on his progress.

Was it my fault? Was my being here making everything worse by making her dependent? Maybe it was time for me to back off and find alternate support, one of the nurse-on-the-go agencies to assist me in checking in on Mother from a distance.

"It's a big birthday for me next year, Mom." I stuck that thought out there in the hope Mother would connect my age and the year.

"They're all big for you, Cassie. You always were a party girl."

"Party girl?" I had no idea what she was talking about. She seemed to be referring to me as if I were decades younger than I was. "I missed all that, Mom. I got married too young instead."

"You were twenty years-old, Cassie. More than old enough."

I remembered that wasn't what she'd said then and the divorce had only proved she was right. "Do you know what this year is?"

"What do you mean?"

"Nothing. I was just thinking about my birthday."

"September second."

She remembered my birthday and maybe not my age, that was enough.

But there was no denying something was terribly wrong. Besides the terrifying incident with the Christmas cards, there'd been other things she'd said that had worried me and made me doubt what she was aware of and what she wasn't. Did she think I was grown up Cassie living here or was she thinking of me decades ago?

"Maybe I should think about getting my own place, Mom." I didn't mean it, I was only testing to see what era Mother was in.

"Why?" Her beautiful blue eyes lost their sparkle and the knitting lay forgotten in her lap.

I'd inherited her eyes, big and wide, but green. I think it was the only thing I inherited from Mother. She certainly didn't have either my full lips or my size.

"Don't you like it here? Where would you go?"

"I'd get an apartment. Maybe nearby," I said as if that was some kind of consolation.

"There's no rush, Cassie. I like having you here. Young people are staying longer and longer at home these days. I saw that on a talk show just recently."

Something wretched deep within me. She wasn't getting better. What was I doing wrong? Maybe I'd done too much for her these last few weeks. Maybe I'd taken away the need to think for herself. I resolved to do less. And at the same time I resolved to do more. To stimulate her memory—buy more crossword puzzles, take her to museums.

Mother picked up her knitting and began to knit another row like the discussion about Dell's baby had never occurred. She looked up as the needles clacked expertly and the baby blue patch swung with each twirl of the needle.

The phone rang and Mother looked puzzled before dropping her knitting needles. The phone rang, once, twice, three and then four times before she finally got it on the fifth ring.

When had she started moving so slowly? Was it before or after I moved in?

"Cassie, telephone."

"Cassie?" A deep, vaguely familiar voice followed my tentative hello. "It's Russ Thomas. I hope I haven't caught you at a bad time."

"Russ. No, of course not." I picked up the old-fashioned, pastel pink landline and moved slightly away from Mother, out of her hearing range.

"Look, it was good to see you the other day despite the circumstances." He cleared his throat as if he were interviewing for a job rather than having a conversation with an old school mate.

"How is your mother?"

"Mom. Fine." I glanced over my shoulder and saw she was oblivious to the conversation as she leaned forward to catch the National News. And my next words were ironic considering her choice of television viewing. "She's a little more confused than I'd like to see her."

"Have you taken her to a doctor?"

"Right after Christmas. I have a referral to a specialist."

An uncomfortable silence drifted through the line. I doodled and considered what might be said, what shouldn't be said. The seconds of silence seemed to last forever.

"The Alzheimer's Society has quite a bit of information."

"She doesn't have Alzheimer's." My whisper had a gritty edge. "She just has memory issues."

"It's called denial, Cassie. But denying it isn't going to help you deal. Look, I could be wrong but we both know your mother has memory problems."

I cracked my thumb knuckle and wished I could will everything back to normal. I wanted to transport myself back to the days when Russ was only a vague memory of my childhood.

"Would you like to go for coffee? We could talk more," he suggested.

Problem was that I didn't want to talk at all, not about what Russ wanted to talk about. It was enough I was seeking professional help for Mother. Second-guessing the issue beforehand was pointless. But whatever Russ could tell me might be helpful. Maybe I would meet him for coffee. What would it hurt?

Russ. I hadn't thought about him in years and here he was twice in my world within a matter of weeks. I still blushed at the thought of my arrogant turn-down as his date at grade twelve graduation. My seventeen year-old self would never have believed the boy I'd found unattractive then, would eventually grow into his feet. But even then with his sharp-edged pubescent face, there had been something about him. Unfortunately, I'd been too young and shallow to see it.

"I'm not sure. Mom …" I trailed off lamely. Could I leave her alone? She lived alone only three weeks ago.

"We can meet right after lunch. Maybe there's a friend your mother could visit for the afternoon?"

I appreciated his thoughtfulness. "I'll see."

"Who was that, dear?" Mother asked after I returned to the

family room.

"Russ Thomas."

"Oh, that boy you stood up in high school. I hoped you hadn't scarred him for life, rejecting him like you did." She laughed, the sound rich and warm. She didn't stop. Her laughter became a grating scratch against my nerves that were a little raw.

"Mom," I warned.

I might have saved the effort. She laughed so hard that tears came to her eyes. Her laughter finally made me smile. It had been a long time since I'd seen her laugh like that. In fact, I couldn't remember the last time. Her laughter used to come so readily, unvarnished and easy.

"Don't tell me he's asked you out?"

Before I could answer she chuckled again.

"I hope you don't stand him up this time," she called as I headed down the hall.

And with those few words she made my decision. There was no way I could say no without looking like, as she would put it, a complete horse's ass. Besides, I had no right to turn down anyone's offer of help especially when I hadn't come up with a lot of ideas of my own. I wasn't going to consider that my need for help was vying with my attraction to the man I'd never believed the boy would become.

•

"Russ," I acknowledged him two days later as he stood up and moved like he was about to hug me. I dodged back and pulled out a chair, one the safest distance from him rather than the one right beside him. It was a game that said as long as there was distance between us, that would make him play ball by my rules.

"I'm glad you agreed to meet me," he said. His voice was deep and easy.

We ordered coffee, exchanged pleasantries and then Russ leaned forward. I instinctively leaned back.

Russ got right to the heart of the why we were there. "Have you and your mother talked about her memory issues?"

I shook my head.

"Why not?"

"Mom says there's nothing wrong with her. I hate to suggest otherwise."

Russ was quiet but I knew he was watching with those damn caring eyes of his.

"Don't look like that." I smacked my hand on the table, making the coffee cups jump.

"I'm sorry."

"No. It's me, Russ. This whole thing has me on edge."

"Admirable."

"What?"

"Moving home like you did. I don't know if I could have done it."

"There wasn't a choice. She would have done the same for me." And I thought of her years of raising me as a single mother and all the sacrifice that had entailed. Never mind the devotion I'd always felt for her. "I'll get her some help and back on the road to independence."

The words fell flat between us.

"What?" But I knew what. He thought I was still in denial—and he might be right. He thought it was worse than I was admitting.

"I brought some pamphlets with me." He pushed them across the table until they lay like a minefield in front of me.

"Thanks," I muttered and then met his look head-on. "How long did your uncle have Alzheimer's?"

"Two years that we know of. A year in a nursing home." The words were even softer. "It was fast moving. In fact they suspected there was an underlying condition, that it might not have been Alzheimer's at all. We'll never know without an autopsy and we passed on that." There was sorrow in his look.

"That's tough." But his uncle's fate wasn't Mother's.

He looked at me sadly. "I don't envy you, Cassie. It's not an easy road."

"It could be anxiety, artery blockage, any number of manageable or even reversible things." I bit my lip as I immediately held the worst-case scenario at bay.

Silence sat between us for a full minute as both of us

digested what may or may not be.

"Would you be interested in a movie one night, maybe supper?" Russ asked.

I see him standing awkwardly in his oversize sneakers. The gangly boy was an image slow to fade in my mind but here was the voice of a man, a man who had grown very well into his sneakers. And, a man I wasn't unattracted to. "I'm sorry, Russ. I don't know if I can. I've Mom to consider."

"I understand. We'll play it by ear."

"I don't think you do," I murmured. The unknown lay dark and dank ahead of me. What I knew was the new Russ had more than my interest. Unfortunately what I couldn't give him was my time. My reality and my time were tied to Mother for as long as she needed me. I had to forget about Russ as anything more than the friend he was quickly becoming.

We talked for a long time after that, never saying the word *Alzheimer's* again, but discussing the research, current treatments and where the best avenue for information on memory-related issues could be obtained. Because that's what I so hoped it was, a memory-related issue that would respond to therapy and medication.

I definitely wasn't putting Mother in any nursing home. I'd seen too many relatives sucked into that black hole and forgotten. I think that was the only promise that I made in those early days I was able to keep.

Chapter Four

December 27

The date with Russ Thomas was already a week in the past. I'd have loved to have seen him again, but I hadn't told him. In fact, I wasn't sure what I'd told him. Right then, romance fell a short second to Mother and the reality of my day-to-day existence.

That said, I thought we'd see each other again. He'd traveled to places as remote and even more remote than me, and there was an edge of daring in how he lived his life—from his career in law enforcement to his penchant for out of the way destinations that attracted me. I could have talked all night but he also had a sense of responsibility that was stronger than mine. He had me home at seven sharp. Not before dark—you can't beat that in a Saskatchewan winter. He'd have had to bring me home before five in the evening to beat the curtain of darkness. But I was home early enough so Mother spent little time alone. I wish I could say I appreciated his thoughtfulness. Instead, my inner child grumbled about the early hour and the fact he didn't kiss me.

I pushed thoughts of Russ and yearnings for romance and, if I were truthful, a normal life, aside. It was tough, as resentment creeped in at odd hours in the day. That was why I tried distraction techniques like holiday decorating. A week ago I'd been ferreting around the basement in search of Christmas ornaments and found a diary Mother had written. I tried to give it to her and she'd waved me off.

"Take it if you want, Cass."

Normally I wouldn't have taken her up on it but, all things considered, my curiosity wouldn't let it go. If Mother didn't mind, then I was going to read it. I had a desperate urge to learn everything I could about her before it was too late. But with preparations for Christmas keeping me fully occupied, I only thumbed through it.

Christmas went by without a hitch or at least much of a hitch. On Christmas Eve, I'd left the turkey in the fridge to finish its final thaw. I half-woke Christmas morning to the delicious aroma of roasting bird and turned over and fell back asleep. I woke again to see the glow of my alarm clock suggesting that it was just shortly after eight. My internal clock seemed to be set later than normal. I would have slept well past eight o'clock if I hadn't been aroused by the smell of cooking food, twice. It was the second time that drove the nail of panic straight into my gut.

"Damn it! The turkey!"

By the time I got to the kitchen I found Mother working a crossword puzzle. I could see through the oven window that the turkey was turning a too-crisp brown. As I stood with tussled hair and my worn fuzzy housecoat and viewed the tableau before me, I considered what to address first—the turkey or Mother. In the end I addressed both.

"Mother, what were you thinking? It's too early to begin cooking. That turkey is beyond done. Probably ruined!"

Her face dropped as she sat in her nightgown, a pair of bright red slippers on her feet and *Winter Wonderland* belting from the beaten digital clock/radio on the counter. She stood up and that only made it worse. She was tiny and defenseless, both mentally and physically. I silently cursed myself and my inability to temper my words as I watched them take the Christmas joy from my mother's face.

It took a cup of cappuccino-flavored coffee and one of her famous homemade rhubarb muffins along with a rousing sing along to put the Christmas joy back on her face. I quietly took the turkey's slightly burnt remains and slipped them, when Mother was bathing, into the garbage bin. In the end we opted for roasting a duck I found at the Chinese grocer, the only open grocery store in the city.

The day went smoothly after that, right up until afternoon when we sat down in front of the little tree Mother had put up before I'd arrived.

"Here sweetie, open this." She handed me a package that I turned over with due reverence before opening it. I remember sitting for a moment staring at the cellophane-wrapped item. Mother's gift to me had me at a loss. It was a set of drawing pencils and paper.

The stark white paper glared at me. I looked up, caught her anxious gaze and looked back down at the assortment of thick pencils and paper. I have no aptitude for drawing. Why had she gotten me a drawing kit? Then I remembered when I was twelve I had thought I could be the next Picasso, and had sketched anyone and anything within ten feet of me. Back then I'd longed for a real drawing set. Ironically, I'd never gotten one.

"Fabulous, Mom!" I gushed. "Thanks."

"You're welcome," she replied, already shrugging into the new pink robe I got her. Pink was her favorite color and she confirmed that as she stroked the fuzzy material. "I just love pink. Don't you?"

We ended the day with a glass of brandy, laughter and a nostalgic look at some of Mother's old photo albums.

•

From the diary of Jessica Jane McDowall

There's trouble in my family. I phoned Mama the other night and her voice was off. I can hear the worry in her voice and how she speaks of Dad. I think Dad is sicker than she admits. I want to go home to help her out but I know there is no money for a trip. And, I can't talk to Tom about any of this.

I never realized when I married him that he was such a morose man. Of course, I did realize it early on in our marriage but I never talked about it, not with anyone. I didn't want to tell Mama for she would worry. And my friends? Well, it's silly, but I felt like I had failed. Their marriages were mostly happy. I can see now why diary entries once began with Dear Diary. It's like you finally have a friend you can trust with everything.

I tire of coming up with excuses for why our payments on the utilities are late. But every month it's the same because for all his penny-pinching, the excess goes to his beer. If he drank the occasional rum, a social drink, rather than the beer he guzzles, we wouldn't have a problem. I think we are the only family who barbecue hamburgers for only as long as it takes to drink or chug, as Tom calls it, two beers. The drinking bothers me but the lack of laughter in this house, that is what is killing me. I dance with Cassandra whenever I can, because it's the only bit of fun we have.

The next entry was only two months later:

Dad is worse. I took an extra job at the grocery until I had bus fare. I leave this Saturday and the only thing I regret is that I can't take Cassandra with me. I have to trust that Tom will know how to take care of her. It's only a few weeks but still I worry.

And three weeks after that:

I am so worried about Cassandra. I've been gone longer than I planned but I never thought Dad would die while I was here. Tom doesn't communicate well and while he's not an affectionate man I can only hope he's done his best by our daughter. I come home next weekend, after Dad's funeral.

We were in the lull between Christmas and New Years. It was that time of sleepy mornings and quiet days.

When I opened Mother's diary that morning and began to read, I discovered that it was all written over a one-year span— the year I was eight turning nine.

I had never guessed the heartache that had combined with the drudgery of life Mother had endured with my father. I remember some of his taciturn nature and I remember Mother's comments about his drinking. I imagined by the time she was over ten years into the marriage she was pretty much at the end of her rope.

"Cassie!"

I was drawn out of my musings by Mother's call for my

attention.

She was wearing a summer dress over a pair of what she would call, dress slacks. "We're going out for supper."

"Out for supper?"

"It's tradition." She frowned at me. "You forgot."

She was right. "Give me a minute to get ready." I'd picked her up and taken her out on that day every year since I'd moved out over two decades ago. How could I have forgotten? It was a tradition we both loved.

"By the way, have you seen my car keys?"

"We'll take a cab." I knew I was dodging but how did I tell her that her keys were revoked—for good?

"Well, hurry up and get ready. We'll be late."

"Give me a minute." I stopped, remembering the summer dress. I turned back and headed down the hall. "Mom?"

"Yes, sweetie."

How should I broach her choice of attire? I glanced over and saw last year's church picture and the sleek pantsuit with the bolero jacket she had worn for the sitting.

"I love that outfit, Mom," I said, pointing to the picture.

"Do you?"

I could see I'd piqued both her interest and her vanity. The one thing Mother has always been was fashionable. She looked down at her outfit and frowned.

"I suppose I should change." She looked at me with a bright smile. "Should I wear that outfit, do you think?"

"That would be fantastic, Mom. You look fabulous in it." And she did. It showed off her petite and still sleek figure. For her age, Mother was still a picture of understated elegance.

The restaurant Mother mentioned was popular but not one I was familiar with. Fortunately, despite the popularity of the day, we only waited for fifteen minutes before we were given a choice seating in a quiet alcove.

"My, isn't this lovely, sweetie?" Mother said as she accepted the server's help in seating. Her eyes sparkled.

The dining area had muted lighting, the setting warmed by a crackling fire in the corner. Bing Crosby's version of *White Christmas* filtered softly through the sound system and the clink of china drifted over the blended rise and fall of other conversations. I'd always thought the song slightly ludicrous, especially hearing it from the unseemly vantage point of a prairie winter. I'd only known one Christmas ever that wasn't white—thick with snow and cold. The blissfully brown Christmas was the result of a fluke weather system.

"It is," I agreed as I took my attention from the song's grating lyrics and looked around. "I've never been here before. It was a good choice."

Mother was solely responsible for picking out the restaurant. It was one her friend, Helen, had mentioned to her a number of weeks ago. It was amazing the things Mother remembered and again, the things she didn't.

I looked over at her and considered how to broach the subject. I wanted to know more about the Mother I'd just discovered in the pages of the diary.

"What were your parents like?" I began hoping to wend my way back to what I really wanted to know. I dodged the words that would be more direct but would upset Mother— her parents' illness and death. Still, I desperately wanted to pursue the newly discovered other side of the woman I called Mother.

"Don't you have to go to work soon, sweetie?"

"No, Mom. I was let go." It was apparent there was no point pushing the issue. Mother's mind was working in another direction.

"Let go?"

I realized there had been a lot new those first few weeks. I'd partnered up with Mother, reconnected with Russ and lost my job.

I'd phoned only last week for an extension on my leave from work. That's when my boss had offered me my official layoff. I admit it wasn't much of a job. Managing the books at one of the larger convenience stores wasn't looking for glory in the employment lines, but it paid the bills. At least it had until my boss decided he had a nephew who was more in need of employment than me.

"Oh my." Mother shook her head. "You'll have to start pounding the pavement."

"No, Mom. I think I'm going to take time off. Enjoy some

time with you."

"Sweetie, really. Won't you run short of funds?"

"I'll be fine." I'd always been an arduous saver, what others might call frugally cheap. Or at least, that was what one misguided date had the misfortune to call me. I'd dumped him quicker than he could finish that sentence.

Mother pursed her lips and turned her attention to the menu.

I glanced down at the menu but it wasn't holding much interest. I looked at Mother.

"I think I'll have the fish."

Mother snapped the menu closed.

"Fish?" I asked. "That might be good. What kind?"

"Kind?" Her face crinkled and she interlaced her long fingers, the nails polished in a silver-grey shade that only enhanced the elegant artistry of her hands.

"Trout, salmon, what?" I picked up the menu and flipped the pages. As I did I realized that Mother had not really read the menu. She was ad-libbing as she had a tendency to do when things became too much. I considered the fact that at just over five pages of fine print, the menu was not only unreadable to aging eyes, it was overwhelming.

"Why don't we both have the grilled salmon," I suggested. "And a glass of their house Chardonnay."

"Perfect."

Her smile made me feel like I had just climbed Mount Everest barefoot.

Supper arrived and our conversation was easy. Mother regaled me with the exploits of both her church group and the summer antics of one of her neighbor's children. I wasn't sure if they were antics from last year or years prior, but it didn't matter. We both enjoyed each other, the ambience and our time together. In fact it was that which caused me to table a thought that I'd had for the last week or so.

I'd felt the need for a vacation since that day—the day of the Christmas card incident, almost a month ago. If I was in need of a vacation, then Mother could only be more so. For no matter what she wasn't saying, I suspected she must have some worry about what was happening to her mind and her independence. I had to will myself to stop thinking along those lines as my eyes did that now too-familiar double-blink, and I could feel the damp beneath my lids.

We both needed a vacation. Maybe a weekend shopping excursion to another city.

"What do you think of a vacation?"

My last vacation had been four years ago when I hiked Machu Picchu.

"Cuba," Mother said.

"What?" I really had to learn to focus.

"I've always wanted to go to Cuba. Palm trees, sand," she said dreamily. "Fidel."

I wasn't sure how Fidel fit into Mother's dream of sand and palm trees but that, and who was really in power in Cuba, were not a discussion I wanted to pursue.

"You'd have to get on a plane, Mom."

"Oh my." Her hand went to her cheek. "I think we should go," she said decisively.

She lifted her wine glass to her cupid bowed lips. They were lips I would have sold one or both of my back molars to inherit and, of course, I hadn't. I guessed my over-sized lips came from some long lost relative because they weren't in my father's genetics either.

"Sweetie!" Mother tapped her palm delicately on the table. "You're not listening."

Now that she had my full attention, she proceeded. "We need a vacation. It will be good for both of us."

"Maybe." I couldn't give my full-hearted agreement. International travel with Mother was craziness, but there it was, the thought that maybe it was possible.

Cuba. It meant getting Mother a passport. It meant a lot of things. But the idea of a vacation, a real vacation, had me hooked. Cuba was a long way away and Mother was a long way from completely lucid. Although, I had to admit if you'd seen her that night you would never know there was anything wrong with her. Maybe I'd been right all along. Mental stimulation was all she needed. She'd just been spending too much time alone. It was denial, a little part of myself kept saying, *You're living with false hope but it's better than the alternative, the truth.*

"Let's see how it goes," I suggested. "Maybe I'll get some pamphlets and we can see about locations and things." I made a note to ask the neurologist whether it was a viable plan. Cuba wasn't a big place and the flight was by no means arduous.

"Cuba it is then." Mother giggled and pushed her empty wine glass at me. "I think this calls for a toast. More wine."

"You're right," I agreed and flagged the waitress who refilled our glasses.

"To Cuban rum and Cuban men!" Mother chortled and chugged back half of her wine.

Cuban rum? Men? Where did that come from? I was left to ponder those huge tracts of a parent's life of which a child, adult or not, are never privy to.

Chapter Five

January 10

"Alzheimer's more than likely. Of course it's hard to confirm. Dementia of some sort," the neurologist said with good cheer as if he'd just handed out a clean bill of health and not a sentence of imminent insanity.

Anyway you looked at it, as Mother would say, it was a bitter pill to swallow.

"No known cure, but there are trials that may slow the disease. In fact, with Alzheimer's there seems to always be a new drug in trial phase especially in the middle stages." He tapped a pencil in short raps against the desk. "Middle stage. You more than likely didn't notice the initial signs. Most people are very adept at hiding the symptoms."

"How are you feeling?" he asked Mother as she re-entered the room. She'd spent the last twenty minutes relaxing in the outer room under a nurse's watchful gaze while he delivered the news to me.

Mother settled into the chair beside me with a smile at the doctor and a perplexed, slightly annoyed look at me.

The neurologist leaned forward as if to close the distance between us. His unnecessarily grandiose oak desk that he perched behind combined with his small stature and cherubic face made him look like a boy playing at doctor. But he came with all the qualifications. Besides, in a mid-size prairie city it wasn't like there was a great deal to choose from in the specialist area. I prayed he was as good as others had claimed, or as he seemed to portray. If confidence meant anything, I should relax. He positively reeked of confidence, from his posture, to his lush leather furniture, to the multitude of academic accolades on his wall.

"So. You've been forgetting some things lately."

"Me?" The word came out in stunned denial. "No. My mind is as sharp as a tack."

"Mom," I began. "You have been forgetful."

"Well," she agreed. "Some. But that's normal for my age. Isn't it?"

"Sometimes, but in your case, Jessica Jane, you have some memory loss and there are signs that things aren't normal."

"Just Jess," Mother said as if everything that had preceded her name had not occurred.

"Yes, well, Jessica Jane. As I said, some memory loss," the neurologist continued and it seemed like Mother wasn't the only one suffering from selective hearing.

"I suppose I do have trouble remembering phone numbers. That's not serious, is it?"

"All perfectly understandable. Now we have treatments …"

"Treatments for what?" Mother cut him off.

"I suspect you have Alzheimer's."

"Ridiculous!" Mother cut him off again. But there was an edge of doubt in her voice and she looked to me with something almost imploring in her eyes.

I put my hand over hers. "That's why we're here, Mom. To see if there's something that can help your memory."

She was quiet at that news as she digested something bigger than she'd anticipated.

The news was not what I wanted. It's not what either of us wanted and it lay between us, a wide uncharted territory that we were only beginning to learn how to navigate.

"How are you feeling?" the neurologist asked.

"I feel fine," Mother said, her voice muted. "I'm perfectly fine," she repeated. Her tone was that it was an imposition to make the effort to respond to what was clearly obvious.

"Well, you're definitely doing fine right now. There is some noticeable memory loss. But there's a possibility we can slow it down."

"Ridiculous!" Mother's tone changed as quickly as a prairie winter and about as welcoming. Now her tone was full of enraged hauteur. "I can tell you what I had for breakfast today, yesterday and last week for that matter."

"What was that?" he humored her.

"Frosted Flakes," she replied. "And bacon and eggs on the weekend."

Frosted Flakes? I couldn't remember the last time Mother ate Frosted Flakes.

The neurologist smiled at her in a bemused manner before glancing at me. I shook my head. Beside me Mother was perched on the edge of her chair.

"Well, that is impressive. I can't remember what I ate three days ago," he placated her.

"See!" She turned her annoyance on me. "I told you this is a complete waste of time."

"Mom. Let's just hear what he has to say."

"The memory test is fairly conclusive," he said to Mother. "It's best to be proactive."

There was a stubborn look on Mother's face and I was almost afraid to consider what she was thinking.

"Some of the trials may delay further memory loss. None of them will stop or prevent it—not that we know of, yet." He focused on me as if assuming that already Mother couldn't understand. "There's one about to start in a few weeks that I think would be a good fit."

He explained the combination of drugs or placebo they would be using. "I think it's well worth your consideration. I'll have my receptionist get the necessary information and you can let me know by the end of the week."

"Perfect," I responded with enthusiasm. It might not be a cure but at least it was a faint, if frayed rope of hope.

"Don't be ridiculous, dear," Mother interjected, glaring at the neurologist who interlaced his fingers and sat back in his chair. She turned her full attention to me. Her delicate nose flared and if eyes could spit, hers would have been spitting darts straight at me. "I will not be involved in a trial of any kind. I'm not a, a …"

She struggled with the word and some of the fire slipped as

she stumbled.

"Guinea pig," I suggested with a heavy heart. I was willing to get her into a trial, any and all, if only she'd agree.

"A pig of any sort," Mother agreed. The anger left as suddenly as it came. It was as if even her emotions wouldn't hold long in her faltering memory banks. She stood up and turned to me. "Come dear, let's get going or we'll be late. Your father likes supper on the table at six sharp."

"Dad's gone, Mom."

She bit her lip. "Yes well. Six o'clock. We best get going."

Her lucidity seemed to have vanished.

"Too much all at once," the neurologist said softly, the words unheard by Mother. She had her back to us.

She whirled without a moment's warning and marched over to the neurologist's desk. "I remember now why we're here," she said. "You're to help me."

She spun in a reverse direction, her movements remarkably agile for a woman her age. And I remembered her stories of her early years of dance lessons, her practicing in the kitchen alone and, when I was little, with me. It was all part of that dream to perform that she had never really let go. She pointed at me and the anger was back. It flared her dainty nostrils and arched lines over her brow. My head pounded double time and I hoped this appointment ended before I was completely overwhelmed by a migraine that had us taking a taxi home. It was ironic that my ability to drive was the thing that popped into my head, considering what Mother's next words were.

"She." She stabbed a finger in my direction. "Won't give me my car keys back." And the look she gave me was cold and disconnected, as if I was a complete stranger. Not her daughter but instead a thief who had entered her home and stolen her car. A thief who refused to leave—maybe I'm embellishing, but that's what that tirade made me feel. Every emotion in me hit standby and I looked to the neurologist for help.

We both looked to the neurologist but for different reasons.

The car keys had been a point of dissention between us for days. Ever since I finally admitted her keys weren't lost, when I was caught red-handed and Mother saw them lying in the bottom of my purse. I'd hidden them since then.

"She lost the car three weeks ago. Forgot it was in the church parking lot."

"I did not," Mom argued with a stubborn and slightly hurt edge to her voice. "You took them, my keys."

I felt horrible but I wasn't backing down. "Mom, you couldn't remember where you parked the car. You thought someone stole it."

I reached for her hand.

She backed up.

"Mom. Please, quit being difficult."

"Difficult!" Mother spewed and turned her attention to the neurologist who had been listening quietly. "My own child has stolen my car from me."

Relief poured through me, ridiculous, pathetic I knew. But Mother had finally acknowledged I wasn't a stranger, a thief who entered her house unannounced and stole her things.

She reached into her purse for a tissue. Her lower lip trembled and I remembered how Mother had loved to act in local productions and the church Christmas play every year. She'd once told me if she hadn't met my no-good father, she would have gone on to be a dancer, possibly even an actress.

"Well, Jessica Jane. I think for the time being you let your daughter drive. At least until you get your cataracts addressed."

"Cataracts?" Mother squeaked and looked truly mystified.

The man was brilliant. It might be a lie but it saved Mother's pride and I was beginning to realize that in the end that might be all she had.

"I have a report here that says you have some difficulty seeing at night."

Mother nodded.

"That's often a symptom of cataracts. A correctable condition but one you should probably have checked out shortly."

"Of course," Mother agreed immediately. "It would be foolhardy to drive under conditions like that."

And that was that.

"Thank you, that was brilliant," I said as I shook his hand later, after Mother had been led away by his nurse. "And something I can remind her of later."

"I've learned sometimes a lie, if it means preserving a patient's dignity, is not a bad thing." He sighed heavily. "Besides cataracts weren't much of a stretch. It's common in people as they age. And in your mother's case I could see a bit of a film over one eye." He shrugged. "Not that I'm an eye specialist."

"Something I never would have thought of, and it smoothed over a rather difficult situation."

"None of this is easy," he agreed. "It's a devastating disease and I don't envy you going through it. On a personal level, I ushered my dad through a decade with the disease."

"A decade?" I could only think of how short a space of time that was, for a life. My breath seemed to stop because I wanted more than that. I wanted as many minutes with Mother as I could get.

"Sometimes it's more fast moving. From what you told me, and the results of the MRI, that might be the case with your mother. It's hard to tell at this point."

"How long?" It was the question I least wanted answered.

"They can survive anywhere from two to twenty years after onset. I'd guess your mother has had this for a few years, possibly longer." He held the door open for me. "I'll have to report the driving."

"It was a mistake." I'd barely gotten over the last truth and now my heart pounded at the humiliation Mother would feel at having her inadequacies highlighted and bolded for the authorities. "Can't we just go with she's not driving anymore."

He smiled. "No, I won't report the incident, just that her license should be revoked. Your mother need never know. There just won't be a renewal sent out this year. If you have any interest in the trial I mentioned—phone me. Otherwise, we'll see her in two months."

"One other thing." I paused in his open doorway. "I've been thinking of taking a trip with her."

"That would be a good thing. Stimulation, new environment. I can't encourage that enough."

"To Cuba," I added.

"Oh." He pinched his chin between thumb and forefinger.

"You'll have to keep her close. There'll be some confusion before she's settled into the hotel and the plane ride might be stressful. All in all, it's not un-do-able."

"Advisable?"

"I can't give you a yes or no but your mother is still in the earlier stages of a disease that may be progressing faster than normal." He smiled with continued good humor. "Your mother is healthy otherwise, and would enjoy the trip. And if you think you're up to it ..." He let the rest of his sentence dangle. "There may be no further opportunities. Alzheimer's in later stages is probably not something you want to manage in a foreign country."

In the waiting room, Mother got up as soon as she saw me. Her purse was clutched in front of her. The purse was white and matched the piping on her navy blue suit. "Ready, dear?" she asked brightly and took my hand. That too, was a first.

A resolve settled inside me like I had never felt before. I would do everything I could to slow this disease down and I would be there every step of the way for Mother. There was no need to clear out my stuff from her garage because I wasn't going anywhere. This time might not be the best of her life but I'd make it as special as I could. It was a silent promise I made to myself and Mother. I wouldn't fail her anymore than she had ever failed me. I could only squeeze Mother's hand reassuring her as I led her outside and into the brilliant sunshine of another achingly cold winter day.

Chapter Six

January 17

If I played one more seek and search word game with Mother, both of us might run into the yard screaming. I pulled out the well-worn book anyway. I'd read word puzzles were good mental stimulation. Maybe I'd gone into overkill but I wanted so badly for Mother to not get worse. The neurologist had confirmed while there was no cure, the jury was still out in regard to the slowing ability of mental activities. They might help. I was all over that *might*.

Mother held up her hand in a stop-sign position. "No, Cassie. Don't you have something else to do? I'm going shopping."

Shopping? I wasn't sure how she planned to get there. I was only going to assume the bus wasn't one of the options. I wasn't going to suggest she couldn't drive. She'd already asked where her car keys were one too many times. Obviously she couldn't go alone and just as obviously I couldn't say that. I went for the roundabout option.

"Would you like company?"

"I'd like that, Cassie. It's been a long time since we shopped together."

It wasn't a bad idea. Mother was in need of a new winter jacket and if we were going to consider a vacation, a swimsuit was in order. And even if we didn't go, I read that swimming—physical exercise of any kind—was good for the brain. I'd thought about signing Mother and me up for the new swim sessions at the local pool in March. Swimming was not something I loved or even liked, but I'd do it for Mother.

"I'll meet you in the garage," I said.

Ten minutes later I was getting impatient. I glanced to the house. Mother was taking a long time considering all she needed to do was freshen her lipstick, grab her purse and lock the door. The first two were tasks she'd said needed to be done and the last was what I reminded her to do as she left. But Mother was pretty good at locking the door. She'd admonished me about it enough times growing up. She'd always said if the door weren't locked, someone would get in and ransack the house.

I heard the door slam and saw Mother double-checking to make sure the lock was snapped in place. I turned back to the garage and slid the key into the lock. I'd just unlocked the garage when Mother came sailing up behind me. Her face was flushed and a drink sloshed in her hand.

She handed me the glass. "Take a healthy swallow dear. It's the best rum and coke I've mixed yet."

Something twisted inside me. This wasn't normal, rational behavior. In fact it was about as rational as the Christmas card debacle. Was Mother worse? It couldn't be possible.

I stood and stared at her, and willed it to all go away.

She pressed the glass at me, oblivious I was about to get behind the wheel of a motor vehicle. "Do you think the Cubans have better rum?"

"Mother, what are you doing?" I knew I looked appalled. I was. "You don't drink and drive." In fact I hadn't seen her with a drink in hand since going out for supper over three weeks ago.

"Who said that?"

"The law, sane people in general. It's illegal."

She looked at me and a small furrow formed over her right eyebrow. She wasn't getting it. I went for what she would get.

"You did. The year you decided Dad was going to kill us all if he insisted on drinking before getting in a vehicle." She'd told me that story many times in my early teens as if that would hammer home the dangers of alcohol and motor vehicles.

"Hmmph," she snorted and swirled the glass as the ice cubes clinked.

I switched tactics. "Besides, it's ten o'clock in the morning. That usually suggests a problem. You know, a drinking problem."

I'd never seen Mother drink more than a cocktail or two, a glass of wine, and all at socially appropriate times. Not this early in the morning, not before shopping. It was only later that I cringed at the words and how I said them.

"You left Dad because of his drinking. You don't want to be like him, do you? A drunk, like Dad." I added the last as if my previous words hadn't been insensitive enough. Besides, it's not like I was the first to reference my father in that context. Mother had done it for most of my childhood.

I immediately realized it was a bad move from the devastated look on Mother's face. I had to be more sympathetic. How terrifying was a faltering memory? All I had done was upset her.

I reached out to her and she drew back. Her bottom lip quivered and for a horrifying moment I thought she might cry. Instead she took a deep breath and fire lit in her eyes. She was mad. I'd stepped over the line and I took a step back from her delicately enraged figure.

"Are you suggesting I have a problem?"

I shrugged but kept my eye on her. Mother and angry—the combination was never predictable. She might be half my size but that wouldn't stop her from giving me a good whack with whatever she might have handy.

"I'm just saying it's too early in the morning and the wrong time for a drink."

She ignored what I said and took a giant swig of her drink. Then she shrugged and said, "I don't drink. You know that. If everyone else is having an alcoholic beverage, I prefer to stick to rum."

I bit back the comment that was now edged with a smile. I'd forgotten that momism. Rum, in her book, was not considered alcohol. I'd learned not to question some of her beliefs.

She eyed me with determination. "Let's get going, shall we?"

"Can I ask that you leave the drink behind?" I watched Mother like she was a rattler poised to strike. When she looked like that, anything could happen.

"You can," she replied, clutching the industrial size glass that was still over half full and reeked like she might have poured the entire liquor cabinet into one glass. "But I'd prefer you didn't."

I slouched back against the garage door and waited. Open liquor and a moving vehicle was another problem. There was no way I could let Mother off on this one. I had no desire to pay the fine that might result.

Besides, if she finished that drink, she would be lucky if she were still walking. Forgetful and drunk did not make for a good combination. I didn't intervene further, only watched as she entered the garage and set the glass carefully down on the workbench. She positioned it between a hammer and a pair of vice grips. She dusted off the bench with a dainty swoop of her hand and repositioned the glass.

Only after five minutes of that was she satisfied.

Finally, she got in the car, shut the door with an annoyed little snap and looked at me. "I didn't leave your father because of his drinking you know. Your father left me, because of you."

My hand dropped from the gearshift that was about to hit reverse. The car remained idling in park, and I stared at Mother.

"What do you mean?"

"Mean about what?" She looked perplexed.

Sometimes things just dropped from her memory. Immediate sentences, whole paragraphs—and other times she remembered things even I had forgotten.

"Dad left because of me?"

"Don't be ridiculous, sweetie." She laughed softly and patted my arm. "It's the only child syndrome you know. I read about that. What happened between your father and me had nothing to do with you." She sat back in her seat, her hands on her lap with fingers interlaced and gazed straight ahead.

I was left with a huge unanswered question as I put the car in reverse.

"Look, dear. Flo hasn't shoveled her driveway. I think she may have gone away."

"Mom, Flo doesn't live there anymore." In fact Flo had died

over ten years ago. I didn't have the heart to tell her because it would make her grieve all over.

Needless to say, we didn't get either the winter jacket or the bathing suit that day.

•

"Your father loved this time of day," Mother said unexpectedly over breakfast two days later.

And if I hadn't responded I would have remained oblivious and maybe that would have been better. But that's me, give me the bait and I'm sure to bite. I wouldn't have lasted long as a fish.

"Do you ever think of him? Wish it had been different?" I'd always wondered what it would have been like if my father had stayed. I was eight the day he left. Old enough to remember him and young enough to forget much of who he had been. I remembered his face only because of an old photograph I still had. Truth was, I hardly thought of him after he left.

"Think of him, of course. Didn't I just mention him?"

"It was the affair, wasn't it? That's why you asked him to leave." I already knew the answer. Mother had put up with the drinking for a lot of years. The affair was a one chance and you're out ordeal. Old news. But I asked anyway, more to make conversation than anything. I poured a cup of coffee and waited for the familiar answer. Mother had given me her reasons many times always emphasizing she could have dealt with the drinking. There was AA after all. But the affair—that was the final blow. He'd never apologized and that had been the ultimate insult.

"What if he'd apologized? Would you have taken him back?" I wondered, as I always had, who he had the affair with or for that matter why. It was a moot point but I still pondered the unanswered questions. I pulled out a chair across from Mother and sat down, the coffee warm in my hands as I took a sip.

"Your father didn't have an affair, sweetie. It was me."

"You!" I almost spat out my coffee as I looked across the breakfast table at my mother's gleaming snow-white hair cut at a precise shoulder-length bob, her nightgown buttoned to her neck, her fork held in exactly the proper angle, her elbows hovering inches from the table—just off, never on—as she finished off the last of her scrambled eggs. My mother, who never went anywhere without a jacket or sweater, in case of bad weather and I suspected, to cover her upper arms—had a secret.

Unbelievable!

So unbelievable I knew it was no fantasy. My mother would never fantasize about something like that despite the state of her memory.

Before I'd even had a bite of breakfast she had just blown one of the truths of my existence completely out of the water. That wasn't how it was supposed to be. The truth was supposed to be that my father was a philanderer—it was common knowledge Mother divorced him because of it. It wasn't the other way around.

Or was it?

"Oh yes, dear. Maybe I should have told you sooner. But you weren't even his to begin with."

"What!" That time I put the coffee cup down with a small bang. "What are you talking about?"

"Sex of course, sweetie."

Sex! Since when had Mother ever talked about sex? When I was ten she refused to discuss the facts of life, even when I prodded her. And when I was twelve, a box of feminine necessities, as Mother so tastefully called the box of Kotex, had arrived on my dresser. It was up to me to figure out what to do with the box and follow the cryptic instructions she had given me over a month before that. In fact, there was a time I had blamed her for my own screwed-up approach to sex that had taken me years to finally sort out.

Sex and that I might be a love child from the woman who could not even deal with a Kotex box—wasn't that ridiculous? Unbelievable! Impossible.

"Love child?" The question was uttered in an incoherent squawk. I couldn't have put together a coherent sentence if I had tried. My reality had just been swept out from beneath me along with a sense of identity that was all pinned on the perception my mother was a delicate and sophisticated woman who had found herself married to an alcoholic philanderer—my father. And no matter what Father was, he gave me a sense of belonging. He was a man with a background—Scottish, a history and a family. I'd lost half of who I was in the space of a minute.

"You mean, did I love your father?" Mother giggled. "He was very debonair."

Now I was confused and had no idea if she was referring to the man she married, the one she'd often referred to as a rotter, or to another man, a man who may have fathered me.

I leaned forward and headed in for the long haul, the truth was somewhere and I'd find it.

"Why did it take you this long to tell me?"

"Tell you." A furrow appeared between her eyebrows, and her mouth turned down. "Why on earth would I tell you? You were a child."

"Then. But I haven't been a child for quite a few years."

"Sex is private," she said primly and pushed her plate aside.

"Who is my father?" I asked hoping that the bluntness of the question would push past any resistance she had.

"Your father," she repeated slowly. "Good heavens, Cassandra Lynn." She never used my full name unless she was very stressed or very annoyed. "Have you lost your mind? You know who your father is, even though he was never much of one."

"But the affair?"

"I think I've had enough for one day, Cassandra. There are certain things better left behind closed doors."

"I don't think the name of my father is one of them," I said to her retreating back. But I had a feeling Mother had just opened a chasm for which there would be no backfill. I feared the secret to my father and thus my oversized lips that seemed at odds with the plane of my face would be buried with Mother.

I wished I hadn't thought of the secret of my paternity in quite that way. In the way of it being buried with my mother—that was too close to an eventual reality. A reality that I was beginning to suspect would arrive sooner than I could ever be prepared.

My coffee was clutched in both hands and my back was to the hallway. I didn't hear Mother approach but there was no missing what she had to say.

"I'd suggest, Cassandra Lynn, you return my car keys. That's my car you know. Not yours. And I'm not putting up with any more of your shenanigans."

I twisted around to address a comment that seemed to come out of left field but she'd disappeared down the hall. Within seconds I heard her rummaging in the back room.

That outburst only shook my already unsteady emotional state.

"Get a grip, ninny," I muttered, furious with myself. But the stress of it all had caused my eyes to water. It took two tissues before I got myself under control. Mother could chastise me all she wanted, she was not getting the car keys back. But that's not what upset me—it was the thought of Mother's voice vanishing from my life.

I took a scalding slug of coffee as if that would wash every unwanted thought down.

Chapter Seven

January 24

"You've made up your mind, haven't you?" Russ asked.

We'd been talking by telephone for a few minutes. He called me every other day, sometimes every day. I relied on those calls. In fact, I more than relied. If I wanted to be truthful, whenever I saw his name on the screen, my heart sped up just a bit. And, at the same time, relief flooded me—no matter what kind of day I was having, he was my rock. I wasn't sure where I'd be without him.

"I am. I had my doubts about going to Cuba but I think we'll both go stir crazy if we stay here. I just hope Mom is able to enjoy it."

"Do you think she'll remember it was her suggestion or even that she wanted to go?"

"I hope so."

I loved the sound of his voice; it rolled with an easy confidence tinged with that gentle caring, that was so uniquely Russ. Some things hadn't changed. They'd only matured and gotten better.

"Have you booked it?"

"I will. First thing, as soon as I get off the phone. I expect there'll be a dozen deals this time of year."

"And you may be leaving with only two or three weeks notice."

"The sooner the better," I stated firmly and I meant it. We needed out of here and we needed out of here soon. Not that going away would fix anything, but I'd read emotional health was necessary to slow any degenerative disease and if anything was good for emotional health, I assumed, it was a tropical vacation.

"I didn't tell you I found Mother's diary." I went on to describe the few things I'd read about her parents and the fact that it encompassed only the scope of one year, when I was still a child.

"Sounds like she had a tough time," he said.

I took a breath but somehow the time didn't seem right to tell Russ my suspicions regarding my paternity nor the insights I'd gleaned of my mother. I wasn't sure if the time ever would be right to tell anyone.

An hour later, I found a trip for two to Cuba, flight and hotel for ten days—it would be good for both of us. Never mind that it was an all-inclusive. I'd always had an aversion to them. In my mind, it's not a real way to see a country. But there was no other option, not with Mother. I was on the phone to book the package later that morning.

I told Mother what I'd done that afternoon.

"I don't know, dear. The last time I went anywhere I was sick for a month." Mother jiggled her earlobe with her thumb and forefinger, and her knee bobbed up and down.

"It'll do us both good to get away. Enjoy some sun."

"I suppose," she said doubtfully.

She got up and headed down the hall. I was left alone to daydream about the upcoming trip. But despite Mother's confusion and complete lack of interest, all my doubts had suddenly vanished. I imagined nothing but relaxation, great weather and a chance to see another country. It was our winter escape and it was going to be great.

Cuba.

It was a place neither of us had been. At least I thought that Mother had never been. But her mention of Cuban men and Cuban rum just wouldn't leave me. The statement was a mystery that niggled at me along with the mystery of my father, a man I thought I had known. A man whose only picture lay hidden in the bottom of a stack of pictures in the back of Mother's closet, and had since the day he left. But that man wasn't my father.

It was turning out exactly as I had feared. Mother refused to speak further on the issue and seemed to have forgotten we had a conversation at all. I was desperate to get a bit of something that would tell me the name of the man whose genes I carried.

But after the diary, which I had flipped through again and again, reading snatches here and there in a desperate grab for information, there was nothing.

The only men in Mother's photo albums were assorted relatives. The one picture of the man I once thought was my father was all that remained of my skewed heritage. That lone picture I guessed was an oversight on her part. I remembered the bonfire she lit days after he left. Anything he had not taken with him ended up in that bonfire.

As a kid I'd been confused when he left. But I'd never been overly close to the man I called Dad. He was a man of few words and little affection. The bonfire had been more exciting than the man.

Who do I call Dad now? I thought. Somewhere was there a man with slightly oversized lips, an olive tint to his complexion and a solid frame. Did he pinch pennies like me? I doubted it. I suspect my beginnings with money savvy were rooted in what I'd seen of the only man I'd called father.

Of course from there I differed. I might have his aversion to sticking with a job but that hadn't hurt my investment portfolio. While I'd done books for a variety of small businesses, I'd still managed to create a healthy stock portfolio. Stocks were a game I'd played since I'd first gotten an allowance, and Mother had enrolled me in a junior investor's class. I'd been manic for investing ever since.

•

"Cassie!"

There was an edge of excitement to Mother's voice as it drifted through the narrow hallway in a search and seek tone.

"Look what I've found." She lifted a dusty, drab photo album and clutched it to her pristine white sweater before dropping it on her bed.

She patted my hand and gestured that I should sit down. I

perched on the bed on the other side of the album.

"Where did you find it?"

"Hard to believe," she said. "But it was wedged under a pile of clothes I had ready to go to charity."

"Really?"

A tingle of excitement coursed through me. It was almost like it was hidden. This could be the key to all my questions, the key to so many things. For my mother it might be memories of the events that had shaped her adult years, events that could now trigger memories for her. Despite the neurologist's pronouncement, I wasn't giving up.

I speculatively eyed the photo album. My heart did a little rush. Was this the album that would finally reveal what half of my heritage looked like?

I was sure this was it. It would answer all the questions. I was almost shaking.

The first few pages were nothing but a mishmash of age-distorted images. When I glanced at Mother, I saw she had that dreamy somewhere else kind of look that took her into a world that didn't engage well with me. I turned my attention back to the album. It was a dull, black-paged style of photo album where the photos were held in black corner pockets—four to a photo.

I leaned on my elbow so I was half-laying down. The pictures were all black and white, the subjects dressed in styles of days long past.

"When was this, Mom?"

"Before I met your father." She looked puzzled and her finger grazed over a man's image. "I don't remember him."

I leaned over and looked at the man she was pointing at. The man in the picture was leaning heavily on a cane. He was ancient—possibly a relative long forgotten. Like my father.

"Do you suppose this is a picture of my father?" I was close to the hundred percent zone that it wasn't but I tested the water anyway. If she had said yes, I wouldn't have believed her. A long time ago Mother had mentioned how most men looked completely unattractive with grey hair.

"Cassandra Lynn."

I looked up, caught by the flicker of annoyance in her voice.

"You never listen. I told you these pictures were taken a long time before I met your father. In fact, these were my party days."

"Party days?"

I sat up. The album was suddenly a dusty impasse between us. Since when did Mother have party days?

"Don't look so stunned, dear. I went out and had fun just like you did when you were young."

Ouch. With forty looming just over the horizon, that one hit close to home.

"I even had a drink or two, and I was popular with the men."

I bit my tongue on that statement. This wasn't quite the time to repeat the paternity question. It was a treacherous road that could take me to many possibilities. I skittered backward, mentally and physically. I was perched on the edge of the bed putting what I considered a safe distance between Mother, the album and me. I didn't want to know everything about Mother, at least not the stuff too intimate to be left anywhere but with her. I leaned forward and turned the page.

"Who is that?" I pointed to a young woman I'd never seen.

"My good friend Aliza. She found herself pregnant at twenty-two and without a man. And her family." She bit her lip. "They threw her out. Terrible thing. Could have happened to any of us."

I froze at that comment. But the possibilities were floating everywhere.

She fingered the page. "I still miss her."

She turned to me and I could see sorrow film her eyes, a light mist that she dashed away with one hand. "A real scandal. Unwed. People talked about that for years."

"What happened to her?" I'd never heard of Aliza and Mother wasn't one to friend hop. The friends she had now, she'd had for years. Admittedly, none of them were from her girlhood and I'd never thought about why.

"Aliza died shortly after."

"Died? An accident."

"Yes," Mom nodded. "An accident. Didn't read the prescription. Sleeping pills."

"Sleeping pills? At twenty-two?"

Suicide flashed in neon letters across my mind. She was part of history now, Mother's history, and how she wanted to remember her was up to her.

An hour later, I was disappointed. I'd examined every picture to the point Mother became slightly miffed.

"I don't see why we have to scour each photo, Cassie. I enjoy going through these pictures as much as you but I can't see your ..." She fumbled for the word.

"Persistence," I offered.

"Exactly."

"I just love history. You know that."

"I suppose."

She gave in and we spent the next few minutes going over the last pages, and an enjoyable half-hour after that reviewing the exploits of Mother's youth. But none of it revealed that one lone man, the man who might be my father.

He was a man who had disappeared into the shaky mists of Mother's mind, and I feared I would never discover who he was or who he might be.

It was like it had always been, just Mother and me.

Family was what you made it.

Chapter Eight

February 7

I went down to the soup kitchen today while Cassandra was in school. She's too young to be in contact with such hardship. It often breaks my heart to see people brought so low that they can't even meet my eyes as I fill their plates. They're not all like that of course, but those that are ... Well, it's humbling.

This place is like nothing I have ever seen before. The other day I saw a man refuse the last biscuit so that a boy barely into his teens could have it. The poor man looked like he hadn't eaten in days, too. His clothes hung on him. I wanted to help him in the worst way and there was nothing I could do but give him a dollar out of my own pocket in the hope what little it was might help him in some way.

I'm looking forward to next week. I've signed on for once a week. That seems to work best at least now while Cassandra is still so young. I hope Tom's mood is amenable and I don't have to fight with him about the cost of bus fare to get here. It was close this time, but his buddies called him for a jaunt to the beer parlor and he forgot all about it.

When he got back we had a big blowup. For once I stood my ground. He didn't want me going near the shelter, swore I'd get bugs or worse. But I know it was all about control and that he likes it best when I'm at home. I suppose I can't blame him, considering everything that happened. But maybe if he'd never been non-stop drinking like he does, or loved me like he promised, maybe I wouldn't have gone to Toronto that year by myself. Maybe it would all have been different. But then I wouldn't have Cassandra.

I had opened the diary that morning, desperate to bring myself closer to the essence of Mother before I lost her all together.

Toronto. My eyes were drawn back to that entry. Was that where the secret of my father was hidden? It was a mystery becoming thicker and more enticing with each new piece of information.

I looked suspiciously at the entry. The letters were blotted slightly, a few words indistinguishable, like mother had cried over the diary. My hand trembled and I wanted to cry myself at the thought of her pain.

Dark thoughts were impossible when Etta James was rocking out bluesy and gravel-edged. I could hear Mother singing along, her clear soprano weaving pleasantly through the song.

I thought about what she might have become if she hadn't had the burden of raising me as a single woman. She was a decade or two too early for the time when a woman could do anything, children or not, husband or not. After the divorce, she had again laid whatever dreams she had aside to take back-to-back jobs—all at minimal wages—to raise, house and clothe me. It hardly made what I sometimes considered a sacrifice, caring for Mother, much of one at all.

I expect that you'll make something of yourself, Cassie.

I remembered her words as clearly as if she were speaking them all over again in that tiny, worn kitchen. She had told me I needed a flight path, as she liked to call a career. Economics had been the logical choice. I'd always been good with money.

It had been my early marriage and subsequent divorce that had prematurely ended my university education. I'd always planned to continue but real life seemed to keep standing in the way.

Mother sang at top volume along with Etta James belting out, *Trust in Me.*

I hummed under my breath. There was something that had always been peaceful about Mother. I wished I could say the same about myself. I don't know if it was her unswerving religious beliefs, as she had told me years ago, or something else. Whatever it was, it was a serenity I couldn't seem to acquire.

I moved on to the mirror in the hallway and picked up a can of glass cleaner. I put it back down. I didn't want to see myself reflected in a smudge-free mirror because even the glass couldn't tell me what I was or what I believed.

Mother sailed into another rendition even though the song had ended.

Mother's voice lilted soothingly through the house and it was another thing I would remember about her long after she was gone. Why did her being gone seem to press so heavily on my mind? Especially now when we were living together in harmony with a trip in the immediate future? Mother was still fine, still functioning so well that she might be able to go on for years.

Might.

It was another word with a powerful impact that could go one way or the other. It was a crapshoot of odds, and I'd never been good at odds.

The neurologist had said most patients lasted two to twenty years after diagnosis. He'd also said twenty years was rare, ten the average. He had also implied Mother's condition might be progressing rapidly and that there was a clear possibility she wasn't in the early stages.

I was noticing things lately. Like Mother's balance; it was off. I saw her just the other day stop and waiver on her heels as if she'd forgotten to put her feet down flat. I decided there would be a physical just as soon as I could get her in to see her regular physician, the same man who had announced after her regular exam over a year ago that there was nothing wrong with her.

Quack was a word that hovered on the periphery of any reference to that man. But I was a charitable woman and general practitioners were scarce. Once you acquired one you hung on or took your chances queuing up in a medical clinic.

"I made a doctor's appointment for you, Mom," I said over tea.

"Whatever for?"

Her spoon rattled as it dropped and landed in the china saucer. The swirls of soft pink and vibrant red flowers that were painted generations ago on occupied-Japan china glared at me. I kept my eye on the saucer and avoided eye contact. I knew Mother was angry when she treated her good china in such a manner.

"I thought it was time for a physical."

"Cassandra Lynn," she said slowly. "If and when I need a doctor, I'll phone one. If I were you I'd think more to your own health. That." She pointed at the cinnamon bun in my hand. "Is nothing but fat and sugar. In fact I heard on television that food like that kills. Kills, Cassandra Lynn."

I put the cinnamon bun down. Somehow it had lost all of its appeal. Instead I agonized over dragging Mother to yet another appointment that she had no liking for even if that appointment was almost two months away. I wanted to make our time together more than just a nightmare of doctor visits and memory games. I wanted her to have fun.

"Didn't you heat one for me?" she asked with a small frown as she pointed at the bun.

"You want one?"

"Of course. I love cinnamon buns."

"You just said they were nothing but fat and sugar that will kill."

"Cassie, do you believe every word I say?" She picked up her spoon and twirled it lightly between her fingers before setting it down. "You always were such a gullible child. I always said …"

She was on to one of her Mother rants. It was as if the time between childhood and now didn't exist. Even when Mother's memory was good, sometimes her memory of me was firmly fixed at when I was thirteen or fourteen years-old. For her, my likes, dislikes and even my emotional maturity, had stalled there. It's times like that when I shut her down and retreated to the land of my thoughts.

I took a cinnamon bun, put it on a plate and slid it into the microwave. Seconds later, as the microwave dinged the bun's readiness, I popped open the door. It seemed that was the signal for my brain to trigger back on to Mother's very one-sided conversation.

"Do you remember the time when …"

"I found a deal to Cuba," I announced. That day I just couldn't take another foray into the past so I interrupted with a reminder of the upcoming trip, as I was fairly certain she'd forgotten last week's announcement.

Mother looked up at me momentarily puzzled. Then her face lit up.

"Cassie Lynn, I can hardly believe it. That talk we had so long ago, well I thought it was just that, talk." She clapped her hands and the teacup rattled in its saucer. "I never thought the day would come that I would stand on the sands of Cuba or walk on the seashore with Fidel." The end of that sentence dropped with a kind of dreamy longing.

Okay, she'd surprised me again. Despite forgetting the trip we booked, she remembered our talk, the agreement that we might go on a trip. Hope raised my spirits a notch. Mother's memory wasn't that bad—and if we could slow the disease's progress in time for a cure …

Thoughts like that kept me afloat in those early days. But there was something else troubling me—Mother's reference to Fidel. But fortunately there was no mention of either rum or men in general.

As usual, I was premature.

"I do love Cuban men," she murmured before lifting the teacup with thumb and index finger, her baby finger pointing out as she took a sip.

It meant nothing, I told myself. But there was a darker thought that lurked in the corners and whispered maybe Mother's hang up with Cuban men wasn't as innocent as I'd like to believe.

•

We were going to Cuba

I was counting the days.

But within that bubble of excitement lurked doubt. I knew that despite what the neurologist had suggested, it wasn't going to be easy. Traveling with Mother was insanity. But I feared something even worse than the real or imaginary threat of international travel. I feared the winter more. I feared the long dreary days and the tendency for life to cocoon as it counted days until spring. Mostly, I feared that the social isolation, the weather, all of it would drive us both insane.

We didn't discuss the trip a whole lot until later that week.

"I can't believe it. I've always wanted to go to Cuba." Mother's eyes were glossy with excitement as she held a travel brochure and looked at me like a child who had received a long awaited dream.

"Can you believe this, Cassie Lynn?"

Then, my name had been interchangeable, first and second, even only Cass at times. Except when she was angry. Then she called me by my full given names, first and second. If she were furious, that only meant she'd add the surname. Fortunately, she hadn't come to that yet. I was never sure which variation to expect. But as long as she remembered my name, a sad little hiccup formed in my throat at that thought. That's the worst reality, the day when there would not even be that.

We're not there, I reminded myself and pushed my shoulders back as if straightening my posture would make it all so much better. We might never get there.

Mother hummed a little tune that was unrecognizable to me but seemed to make her happy. It made me happy just hearing her sing like that. Liquidating part of my already dwindling savings account seemed like a small thing in comparison to her light the world smile. I hardly thought of that trip to Iceland, once a next-year dream that had just jumped further down the timeline of my life.

Mother took out a thick sweater and plopped it into her suitcase. It was almost as if she could read my thoughts.

"No, Mom." I touched her hand. "You won't need that. We're going to Cuba."

"Cuba? I thought you said we were going to visit Aunt Em."

"No. Not this time."

It was the second time she'd mentioned Aunt Em in a week. She didn't remember Aunt Em was dead. She'd signed the card and walked with me to the mailbox. We'd attended the funeral service, and none of it jogged her memory. I put up with the questions because I didn't have the heart to have her relive that sorrow again.

We were swamped in the nightmare of the disease. My friend, Leah, had added to my worries by suggesting a genetic link. I'd considered the specter of Alzheimer's that might be my destiny but it wasn't that that bothered me. I'd researched the disease as far as you could without being presented an honorary doctorate. I knew heredity was indelibly meshed and linked with a lifetime of choices, experiences and personality traits before being married up with chance. But what I wanted worst was for all that research to fix Mother!

It was strange. In some ways the disease was more of a nightmare for me than Mother. I knew what was happening. I suspected she didn't, and I feared the worst, that she knew but she would never say. And as she did so often lately, she interrupted my thoughts with happier ones.

"Where are we going?" she asked and she squinted at me.

Her mascara was smeared, her blue eyes were slightly bloodshot but her lipstick still plumped her lips in coral perfection. I made a note to locate her reading glasses. She obviously couldn't see close-up clearly.

As I thought that, she adjusted her dress that perfectly fit the lines of her still slender figure.

"Cuba. In one week."

"I suppose I'll need a new wardrobe then. It's hot in Cuba."

It's hard to describe how sweet that relief felt. She hadn't forgotten everything, not yet.

"Yes, it's hot. Shorts."

"Dresses."

"Of course, dresses and maybe a bathing suit or two—and sandals."

By the end of the week, Mother had packed and unpacked dozens of times. I finally packed the previous night and was just sitting down with a book when the phone rang.

It was Russ. I held the phone just a little tighter and somehow all my doubts vanished at the sound of his voice.

"You're ready to go then?" he asked. "Sure you don't want me to take you to the airport?"

"No. We'll be fine." It was a lie. I would have loved to take him up on that offer, for his to be the last face I saw before setting off on that trip. I wanted to say yes in the worst way but I had to think of Mother. Instead I said, "We'll be fine. I've already scheduled the cab. The plane leaves early, 7:15, and we'll have to be there a few hours before. That's too early in the morning for anyone to be getting out of bed to pick us up."

"So 7:15 and you're Cuba-bound. Excited?"

"Excited and anxious all at the same time," I admitted. "I'm not sure how all of this will work out with Mom."

"I'll miss you, Cass," he said in that soft, yet firm voice of his.

When I hear my name like that, when his voice shifts into that gruff oddly sexy, masculine tone I know he could be more than a friend, and even while I entertained the thought, I knew it could never be. My plate was full and no one, no man wanted to volunteer to be part of this.

"Maybe I could take you both out for supper," he suggested as if my thoughts had meant nothing. "When you get back."

I didn't respond right away. Russ Thomas was not who I painted him to be.

"That sounds fine," I finally replied and I know the comment was staid but it was all I could offer, at least then. My life wasn't my own. I'd given up control, not to Mother, but to the disease that had invaded her.

"Well, take care," he replied. "I'll be thinking of you. Have a good trip."

"I will."

Seconds later I looked longingly at the silent phone. Maybe I'd speak to him when I returned and tell him how I felt. Problem was, I wasn't sure quite how I felt.

If I was honest, I wanted more than just a phone call. But my emotions were all mixed up and woven through with the pain of what was happening to mother, and I feared untangling even a single thread. But even without analyzing those emotions, I knew I wanted him in our life, mine and Mother's. But, mostly, I wanted him in mine. And as much as I wanted that, I wasn't ready. I might never be.

Chapter Nine

February 21

Bon voyage, snow. Hello, Cuba.

Traveling with someone newly diagnosed with dementia was heroic. Or so a good friend said. But then, Leah never had to worry about such things. She'd lost both her parents years ago.

"Doesn't matter that I'm not in your situation. You're still nuts!" Leah had emphasized a little too loudly.

"Maybe."

"I'd go with you if I could get the time off."

"It's okay. We'll be fine."

At three-thirty in the morning I woke up, showered and roused Mother. In her words, she was bright-eyed and bushy-tailed. Me—I blinked sleep-grit from my eyes, popped an aspirin and then two more for good measure, and dragged our bags to the door.

I rushed around checking windows, shutting off the water, double-checking locks. The last thing I did was empty the garbage. I remember I knotted the black plastic and reached for the blind that I left just slightly open.

"Hold this," I said to Mother as I handed over the mid-size bag of garbage. She took it and swung it in her hand like a child's toy. She was humming and dancing a kind of one-person tango.

"Maybe run it out to the outside bin," I said. She disappeared outside and when she returned I didn't even give her more than a cursory glance as I bolted the back door and checked the blind for the second or maybe the third time.

Thirty minutes later there was nothing left to do but wait. That was the one thing I hated about travel, the waiting. Mother was sitting on the edge of her pink, age-tested suitcase. I scoured the street for signs of life, for the cab I had booked last evening. I glanced at my watch. Outside the snow reflected the streetlights' whitewashed light and snowflakes drifted lightly across the artificial glow. The other houses were in darkness, but then it was only 4:15 a.m.

Light skipped across the hard crust of ice and snow that coated the street as a car pulled up. I handed Mother's coat to her. "The cab's here," I told her, and my attention was immediately diverted to ensuring that all suitcases and Mother got out safely with the door locked behind us.

The run to the airport went without a hitch. The streets were snow-packed silence at that time of the morning, the traffic lights unnecessary as we sat alone at almost every intersection. We made the airport in record time and I realized we could have slept in an extra half-hour. But you never know. Better to be safe than sorry. That had been Mother's favorite phrase while I was growing up, and now it was stuck in my head.

I figured we might as well clear security and then we could settle in with a coffee and a bit of breakfast. Besides, at that moment there were no line-ups, no pressure and nothing to distract Mother. It was a relief to think only this security check and one at the Cuban end. No flight transfers, no second security check, nothing. I tried not to extrapolate too far into the future and imagine any of the potential possibilities—I refused to think of them as problems.

Our passports and boarding passes were clenched in my hand. Mother stood quietly and I relaxed slightly, not quite so afraid of what she might do or not do. She followed the custom officer's instructions and was looking completely calm.

I held Mother's elbow as we waited for the final clearance. They'd allowed us to go up to the check-in desk together. I'm not sure why. Maybe it was because they could see something in Mother's slightly rheumy look. Maybe it was because I was hovering over Mother like a bear with its cub.

She'd been fine the whole drive there. When we stepped

into the airport's fluorescent glare I think she became slightly overwhelmed. I could see that in the way she rubbed her index finger against the palm of her hand and when we stopped her feet seemed to do a little shuffle dance. It wasn't just Mother who was nervous. I was running on little more than nerves and I admit to feeling slightly delusional as I glanced around the airport looking for a familiar face. Looking for Russ.

You're being ridiculous, I told myself. *Why in the world would he be here? You're on your own, a grown woman off with her slightly confused mother.* No one was going to bail me out. And that was it really, I wanted a friendly face to take my elbow and take charge.

"Cassie, sweetie." Mother interrupted my thoughts. "This lady would like you to give her your suitcase."

"Of course," I came back to the moment with a bang as I noticed a familiar black garbage bag sitting primly just ahead of Mother's dusky pink suitcase.

There was no denying that perched on the conveyor belt ready for international travel sat our household garbage. I'd been too stressed wrangling all the small details and mother, to pay attention to what she was carrying. But now that bag was glaring at me so obvious that I don't know how I missed it. It was the bag I had given Mother to dispose of and she'd dutifully carried it all the way to the airport. I don't want to imagine what might have happened when that bag of empty soup cans and denuded bones and coffee grounds hit the airport scanning equipment.

"Excuse me." I leaned over as I tried to be as discreet as possible and to spare Mother's feelings by getting out of the range of her hearing. "There's a bag there that shouldn't be checked."

"Excuse me?" The customs office repeated as she looked puzzled and took a step back. She followed my line of vision as she glanced at the silent conveyor belt where the black garbage bag sat primly jockeying for space against Mother's suitcase.

"My mother brought a bag by mistake. We don't want to check it. It's …" I fiddled with the edge of the counter. "Garbage," I whispered.

"Garbage?" She said in a voice that carried.

"Cassie Lynn!" Mother's hands were on her hips. "Don't ask questions."

"She has Alzheimer's," I whispered. "It was a mistake. That bag is our garbage."

She looked suspiciously at me. "What kind of garbage?"

"Food scraps, paper, that kind of thing. You know, garbage." My head was beginning to pound despite the aspirin overload. "She brought it here by mistake."

It took a moment of frowning puzzlement before the custom's officer's face cleared. "I see."

I wasn't so sure she did. It was more than likely a first for the airport. But she turned around and removed the bag from the conveyor belt. I heard something clink and rattle as she set it gingerly down. She motioned for another official who came over and after a whispered conference he opened the bag. After that things went fairly quickly as the bag was taken from the area.

"I'm sorry," I said. My heart was pounding at the thought of what such a bad beginning could mean. I glanced at Mother and she was smiling and watching a young family wrestle with two children and eight pieces of luggage.

"Where are you headed?" The custom's officer asked and actually smiled.

"Holquin, Cuba."

She looked up, her eyebrows raised and surprise clearly in her eyes. "I'm impressed. I have an aunt with memory issues. I can't imagine traveling with her."

I smiled. It was a tight smile.

"Well, have a good trip," she said brightly and handed our passports back to me.

It was a bit of a rough start but so far nothing major had happened. It was all fixable, little glitches, and maybe a few I should have caught before we were even out the door, like the garbage.

Things went downhill an hour after that.

"Attention passengers. Boarding for Flight 243 to Holquin, Cuba has been delayed."

"Crap!" I said more to myself than anyone.

"Sweetie, what is it?" Mother looked at me with that

worried look she had bestowed on me so often through my life.

"The flight is delayed."

"What does that mean?"

"That we wait," I said with resignation. But a check with the assigned boarding gate didn't look hopeful. A storm had settled in. Low visibility was impeding takeoff.

"We'll have to wait out the storm," Mother said matter-of-factly.

We found a bench in a quiet corner of the airport and Mother nodded off. I remained awake listening vigilantly to the endless announcements of changed flights and rescheduled arrivals. We ended up spending the day in the airport. Mother slept off and on, at one point curled up on the bench.

It was almost midnight before we boarded that plane. We'd had both lunch and supper in the airport and Mother had napped off and on through the day. So far, considering the arduous wait, she'd held up amazingly well.

"We're going home now, Cass?" She frowned up at me as she tried to wipe away wrinkles in her blouse.

"No, Mom. We're going to Cuba."

Her face lit up. "Fidel." She clutched her purse and took my hand.

Boarding was completely without incident. Mother was quiet. Maybe she was concentrating, as was I, on getting us to the right seat and getting the carry-on luggage stowed without incident. And maybe she was just enjoying the swirl of faces and activity around her. It was hard to tell.

"Isn't this delightful, Cassie Lynn?" Mother asked as she settled into her seat.

As we hit cruising altitude, I was feeling beaten down and groggy. I'd survived one airport and there was one more to go. I considered how dragged out I'd feel by the time we arrived in Cuba. I looked over at Mother and was amazed at how youthful she looked. Her eyes sparkled and her cheeks were naturally blushed. And her skin, well it glowed like she had just come from a spa.

"I never thought the day would come when I'd go back."

References like those, and of course the bigger question,

my paternity, had me puzzled. "You've been to Cuba before, Mom?"

"Of course not, dear," she said. "Why ever would you ask that?"

"No reason."

Doubt niggled in my gut at these obscure references to some sort of tie to that far-away island. I would have liked to believe it was my imagination. Mother had never left Canadian shores—or so she has always said.

"You've never been out of the country have you, Mom?"

"Of course not, sweetie. I've told you that many times. Your father didn't like to travel. So really, for all my married life I stayed home." She looked up at the overhead panel.

I realized she never talked much about her life post-marriage. "What about after Dad?"

It was as if I hadn't spoken.

"I see the seatbelt light is out. I think I'll go to the ladies room."

"I'll come with you."

"Ridiculous. I'll just ask that nice young lady the way." She pointed to the flight attendant, unbuckled her seatbelt and got up like being on a plane was second nature to her.

I held back the urge to follow. Instead I let her pass me and make her way carefully down the aisle. I watched as she whispered to the flight attendant, who smilingly took her arm and led her to the restroom. *Bless you,* I sent my silent thank you at the retreating back of the flight attendant and thought there were more angels in this world than I had once believed.

Mother returned safely five minutes later. I realized then that as much as she needed me, there were times when I had to learn to let go.

Hours later as the plane descended over Cuba and Mother's attention was riveted to the window, I felt the return of excitement for this adventure. Up to now worry had sucked any pleasure I might have had during the flight.

Now with Mother humming a tune with a salsa-like flavor I couldn't name, I began to relax. I looked out the window where a span of blue that wasn't sky pierced the cloud bank and then I caught a glimpse of land.

Below I could see palm trees and golden stretches of sand.

"I love the water," Mother said dreamily as she looked down at what seemed an endless stretch of sun-kissed water.

Cuba—we were there. Finally.

In my purse I had a note outlining Mother's condition in both English and Spanish. Some days it paid to get the right doctor. Talk about a stroke of luck to have one bilingual in Spanish. I had that note ready to produce at a moment's notice. As we disembarked directly on the tarmac and filed across the warm pavement into the airport, I kept a close watch on Mother. I barely noticed the aged Russian missile launcher that shadowed the entrance to the arrival area. I can't say I didn't see it. But I'd never been good with weapons or history. Instead I acknowledged the launcher's presence with just enough attention to rekindle my already jumpy nerves. But historic relics of conflicts gone-by were not that day's mandate. My sole purpose was Mother. This was my watch, and my mission was to get her through Immigration quickly and easily.

It turned out my watch was not good enough.

Chapter Ten

February 22

The Cubans were not as accommodating to my request to go through the customs checkpoint with Mother as officials had been at home. A squarely built man with a rather pleasant face held us back as I tried to explain.

"Stay," he said with quiet authority.

He brushed my hand aside when I tried to give him the note that explained it all. But I wasn't panicked yet. We'd work things out. In the meantime I followed instructions and slipped the note back in my pocket. Except for the rusting missile launcher, there was no show of weapons, few military uniforms and the geriatric spaniel employed as a drug sniffer was hardly threatening.

My attention swerved back to getting Mother safely through customs. I listened to our current roadblock as he spoke to some of his co-workers, and as another passenger addressed him. I soon realized his English was pretty much restricted to four or five necessary words. Stay being one of them.

He motioned with one hand like he was a traffic cop. Fear almost shut me down as I saw it was Mother he was motioning to.

"No!" I blurted the word out and moved forward with Mother.

"Señorita. Stay."

It was the most he'd said so far and already it was way too much.

The fates were definitely against me as Mother moved

ahead of me.

I could have taken her arm but then I would have created a scene. Mother would have balked for sure. And a scene, that was the last thing I needed on foreign soil. I couldn't appeal to Mother. She wouldn't understand. I knew she was already on the edge, over-stimulated from the excessive wait at home followed by a long flight and new surroundings. Her eyes had that kind of glazed look that told me she was muddling along, not connecting the dots of reality. She was a walking time bomb just ready for the proper stimulus to set her off.

Bomb in any reference at an airport was bad news. I felt like there were lights and signs pointing at Mother, that my thought had just become public knowledge and made us both suspect. My stomach flipped upside down.

Mother was an arm's length ahead of me as she was motioned forward by another official without a please or thank you. In fact, that time there was only a silent sweep of his right arm, while his left was held up at me as an obvious deterrent.

Mother only swept him with a disdainful look. I imagined that the look was a silent assessment of his manners or lack thereof. He pointed to an area behind him and Mother nodded. Mother was acting like she had done this before. That this was familiar and she knew exactly what she was doing.

I had to trust her in some situations and maybe, like the jaunt to the airline bathroom, it was another of those times. But I wasn't so sure. My jaw was locked and my head was beginning to pound as I strained to see around the man who stood between Mother and me.

I tried to imagine that everything would work out just fine. And for exactly two minutes there was peace before Mother's outraged tone hit me.

"Unhand me right now, young man!" Mother's voice carried across the thirty-foot space that separated us. I saw her stiff stance and my upper palate vacuum-sucked to my lower.

I could see the official motioning at Mother and talking fast, too fast. Mother was shaking her head and clutching her purse. Panic began to well in a stiff bitter ball that I feared I might choke on. I had to get to her before the worst—whatever that might be—happened. But it might as well have been an ocean between us, or a roadblock, or whatever you wanted to call the uncommunicative man who stood between Mother and me.

"She has Alzheimer's," I said and pointed at Mother. I don't know why I bothered considering I'd told him that before. I clutched my carry-on and felt the stares of fellow passengers heat the back of my neck. I wanted to scream at someone, anyone.

I tried to peer around the roadblock. For all my height, and his lack thereof, he was an effective block. Mercifully, seconds later, he stepped out of the way while holding his arm out to keep me contained. That gave me a clear view. It was a slim relief but at least I could see as well as hear what was going on.

"Señora," I heard the official ask.

"English," Mother commanded.

I imagined that her lips were pursed and she was looking at him none too kindly. There was a pissed tone to her voice that didn't bode well. Anger, upset of any kind, can wreak havoc with memory—it would send her into confusion quicker than anything I've ever seen. I had to get up there and I had to get there fast. I don't know why I couldn't stop thinking about getting to her when it was pretty clear that wasn't going to happen.

Despite his position of authority and Mother's precarious position as a tourist requesting access in a foreign land, he didn't push her. "I'm sorry, ma'am."

"You have beautiful hair, young man," Mother gushed as if she was not the focal point of an impending international incident. "The ladies must love you."

But this was completely her personality and not the disease speaking. Mother always had an eye for men—and Mother could be charming. The men, no matter what their age, always liked her.

"Your purse, please." The official reached for the purse as if it was a given Mother would give it up.

I froze. I knew this was the moment where it all slid south. It was the moment when, with any luck, we would be sent back from whence we came. That was the best-case scenario. Visions of jail cells danced in my head, and I remembered there were brutal penal colonies on this island. Colonies I didn't want either of us to see.

"I will not relinquish my personal effects," Mother replied. "Release my purse. Immediately."

In another situation I would have been impressed at her clear command of language especially under duress. She hadn't shown that broad a vocabulary in days. Instead, I had only one focus and that was getting her attention quickly.

"Mom!" I burst out unable to be quiet a moment longer. "Let him see your purse."

Mother didn't turn. Instead, she did an unscripted dance as she attempted to wrestle her purse free from the official. The roadblock wasn't looking at me. His attention was fixed on Mother. And that distraction allowed me to slip past him just long enough to drop the note in front of the official now in charge of Mother.

Mother wasn't paying attention to anyone but the man insisting on seeing her purse. My heart dropped when I saw his youth and considered he might have no familiarity with dementia. I was learning, but not as quickly as I'd have liked, to never make assumptions. Suddenly a light seemed to dawn and his expression lightened even as he picked up my doctor authorized note. His other hand dropped the grip he had on Mother's purse. He had barely glanced at the note but he looked at Mother now with affection and his next words reeked of nostalgia.

"You remind me of my grandmother," he said softly.

My fists unclenched even though I was still prepared to go in and do battle. But the battle lines seemed to have shifted. If Mother didn't cooperate I was tempted to go in and battle not the official, but Mother.

"She had a purse like that. She was classy, like you."

"Did she, dear." Mother gushed.

There was a tap on my shoulder and I turned around to face my personal roadblock. He shook his head, his mouth a straight line of disapproval. He pointed to the line. I glanced back at Mother.

"Do you carry Chiclets," the official asked Mother and there was a note of hope in his voice. He spoke with perfect, careful English. I was impressed, not so much with his language ability but his sudden and obviously instinctive reaction to Mother. For, he'd yet to read the note. I was impressed even when he looked up and winked at me.

I could have kissed him myself for his empathy, never mind he was every bit as good-looking as Mother had intimated minutes earlier.

I allowed the roadblock to show me back to my place in line. By that time I could feel the avid attention of the entire lineup. We, Mother and I, were the entertainment. I couldn't have cared less. Everything was going to turn out fine, provided my roadblock didn't have me deported for noncompliance.

Meanwhile, Mother was successfully diverted. She opened her purse and the official took a quick, cursory look as she handed him a box of Chiclets.

He opened the box, took one out, slipped a piece into his mouth and handed the box back.

"Keep it," she demanded. "They get stuck in my teeth. Can't chew like I used to."

The roadblock, darned if he didn't wink at me as he motioned me forward. What was with these Cubans?

And Mother? With those last words she sailed right through customs. By the time I was screened, I found Mother being entertained by the young man, still holding the box of Chiclets and now obviously off-duty, and a young woman who turned out to be our tour director. Both appeared to be enthralled with whatever Mother was telling them. I wasn't sure if, at that point, I wanted to know. I was just relieved we had both made it through customs. We made it despite what Mother would have called, her shenanigans.

The trip was going to be easy, at least easier than I had thought. I'd worried for nothing. I was almost jubilant as we got into the well-organized line to the bus that would take us to our resort thirty minutes away.

"Darling young man."

I smiled at Mother. I couldn't disagree there.

The brash young man had earned a gold star in Mother's books. Maybe things would turn out okay after all.

Despite my attempt at good thoughts, it took me almost the entire bus ride to wind down and begin to appreciate Cuba.

I noticed the air first—plump and warm, it soothed winter dried sinuses and reminded me of other trips. Trips I'd taken in the past to other tropical climes that were just as laced with heat and humidity. That they were trips slightly more adventurous than this didn't matter. I knew even then none would match this one for importance.

I let my attention drift. Mother was dozing and safe. There was nothing for me to do. No timetables to keep track of. Everything was out of my hands. I could appreciate the appeal of the all-inclusive to the majority of travelers. And while I couldn't say I was a convert, it was good to sit back and relax and let someone else handle the details.

I leaned against the seat and looked out the window. The road was narrow, roughly paved and liberally rut-pocked. Cinder brick houses sprouted sporadically along the countryside. They mirrored each other in two or three-room sameness. Goats were more numerous than houses, and we passed the occasional flock of chickens and a few cows in the ditches. They were all death-thin with ribs as harsh as the horns that pierced either side of their skulls.

Despite the state of the cows, unlike many tropical islands I'd seen, there were no shantytowns marring the landscape. Yards, roads and ditches were swept and clean, and the homes were simple but they were in good repair and as immaculate as the yards that surrounded them. The land was lush, rolling slightly as land does when mountains begin to close in, and while these mountains were small and set back, they were still making their presence felt.

The tour guide perched on the edge of a seat mid-bus as she provided sporadic narration throughout the trip. She stood up, holding the seat for balance. "If you look to your right you'll see people by the side of the road. They'll be picked up by one of the collective rides." She lurched and caught her balance as the bus downshifted into a turn and the elevation began to change.

I stretched to look around Mother, whose mouth had dropped open as she softly snored. I was fascinated by the glimpses I'd caught already and, despite the early start, ready to hit Cuba at a run. But I reminded myself it was Mother's trip. We'd take it easy and, even if it killed me, we'd stay close to the resort.

It was an easy promise to keep, at least that first day. By the time we'd made it through the lineup of tourists at the hotel check-in, gathered our key and assorted information, and provided requested identification, we were still in time for breakfast. We'd been over twenty-four hours in transit. I took Mother down to the bar, and we enjoyed a coffee in the open air.

Looking at her then, I saw the Mother I remembered. The Mother of quick wit and youthful zest who had pushed me easily out the door, off to live my own life. I wanted that Mother back in the worst way. I wanted that trip to be the cure—the cure for both Mother and me.

Mother raised her mug, winked at me and said, "Told you the men are beautiful."

So far, from what I could see she was right. Not overly tall or largely built, but their features were anywhere from pleasant to handsome. I knew it was sexist, but I figured considering everything, my next thought was allowed.

I was thinking it wouldn't be a bad ten days. In between entertaining Mother, there was always window shopping—for men that is. As enticing as that thought was, it was dominated by the thought of one man—Russ.

Chapter Eleven

February 23

Mostly—yesterday evening at the resort had been a wash. We'd cruised the resort and toured every nook and cranny before crashing early. As a result, I woke early. The sun was streaming through a crack in the blinds. My watch said six-thirty a.m. I sat up and looked over at Mother. It had been a long time since I had looked over and seen Mother first thing in the morning. I might have been nine the last time it happened. Nostalgia hit me like a volleyball to the gut. If you've ever played volleyball and if you're not that athletic, you'll know exactly what I mean.

Mother was still sleeping like a baby. The analogy was rather disturbing for lately I projected too many times after she'd gone to bed how I was destined to become the parent and she the child. In those moments I considered if that was my destiny, that I might never have children because I now had Mother. Unfortunately, to me that thought was no more than a brutal cosmic joke. I would prefer children. I was sure Mother would have preferred grandchildren to her current situation. But neither of us had a choice. The universe had spoken and hadn't even waited for the answering nod before turning over the ball and buggering off.

I brushed the dark, contradictory thoughts away. We were in Cuba. Ten days of fun and sun, no dark thoughts allowed. Besides, the doctors weren't always right. Mother might have dementia and that might not be reversible, but maybe it was stoppable. I wasn't letting go of that dream—not yet.

I got up and did a cursory wash, having showered the night

before. I slipped into a pair of shorts and a tank, wrote a note on a yellow sticky note with a thick black marker, and stuck it on the dresser mirror. She couldn't miss the note that made it clear where I was. I'd also left firm instructions for her to wait.

I was only planning to go down and get a coffee. I'd be back in fifteen minutes. I wasn't worried about Mother. She was still able to stay alone for brief periods of time. Besides, I was fairly confident in the confines of the resort, Mother was safe even if she did slip out and walk on her own. I'd alerted many of the resort staff to Mother's condition and they'd all assured me they'd watch out for her. It was not a complete security blanket but enough for fifteen minutes of freedom. Besides, other than a few incidents here and there—minus maybe the shoplifting, the car and I stop myself there—Mother was still fairly functional. If I didn't tell you something was wrong, odds were you wouldn't know. So getting around a small resort, piece of cake.

I was heading back to the room with my cup of coffee a half-hour later. It took longer than I had thought and I remembered hoping that Mother was awake and ready for breakfast. I basked in the velvet feeling of all that luscious humidity against my skin. The concrete path wound just enough to appear mysterious. The addictive rich scent of roses intertwined with the scent of dew-laden mulch. I sucked it all back and recorded it for all those winter days that would follow. When I looked up, Mother was on the path in front of me.

"Cassie, sweetie!" Her sundress floated lightly around her ankles as she hurried over to me. Her winter-pale bare feet gleamed starkly in the bright sun.

"Mother, your shoes."

"It's the tropics, for heaven's sake. I'm treating myself to some nakedness."

I didn't even notice her strange phrasing, not much.

"Where'd you get the dress?" I moved closer. My heart did a little race as if guessing at the possibility that this might be a complication. This was no off-the-rack dress. I'd kill for a dress that luscious. The dress was too big for Mother. I could see part of her white cotton bra as the bodice settled a little lower than it should. The color was too vibrant for Mother. The brilliant yellow swath that cut through the cream washed Mother out. All of that came to me in a rush as we stood facing each other on a path that was still quiet, in a resort where it was still early. Many had done little more than migrate to the restaurant for breakfast, and some hadn't even done that.

Problem.

Now that my mind had admitted the possibility of the problem it was flaring in neon colors across all synapses. I could barely think as I tried to comprehend the enormity of what may have happened.

"Let's get breakfast, Cass," Mother suggested. "I'm starved."

I'd never seen that sundress before. I squinted against the glare of the early morning sun.

The possibility merged with the probability and I began to think of opportunity and method of entry.

Did Mother break into someone's room?

Impossible, I realized as I looked at Mother's slim arms and small, fine-boned figure. She had neither my frame nor my strength, and even I would have difficulty taking down some of those hotel doors. They were better built than many places I'd lived in.

"Breakfast," she suggested again as she smiled at me. I couldn't smile back.

My head was beginning to pound and my stomach was clenched and screaming for an antacid.

"Mom, where did you get that dress?" I repeated the question slowly.

My heart pounded and I set the coffee on the sidewalk. I reminded myself this wasn't Mother's fault. I took a deep breath and turned around.

There was fear in her eyes, like she knew she'd done something wrong and couldn't figure out just what. Now the person I wanted to shout at was me.

"I'm sorry I was short. But Mom, where did you get the dress?"

"This?" She looked down blankly. "I've always had it."

I knew well what was in her suitcase, having packed and unpacked it three times before we left home. There was no sundress there. There had been no sundress in our room last night. In fact it had been in the back of my mind to visit one of the shops here at the resort and get her one. Yesterday I'd been too exhausted to remember that pledge.

"That isn't your dress, Mom." The words were like the brush of tinfoil against a filled tooth, sharp and jarring.

"What do you mean?" But her face crumpled slightly as the possibility inserted itself on her reality. She looked down at the dress. "It's a little big."

A couple was walking along the path toward us, twentyish and chatting brightly. I took mother's hand as the couple passed by completely locked in their own world.

"What's wrong, sweetie?"

"Shhh," I told her. I dropped her hand but my fingers clung to her elbow and I pushed in front of her as if that would be enough to hide her presence and more importantly, hide the dress.

"Cassie Lynn," Mother's voice had that pissed edge. She didn't like being pushed anywhere. Most especially she didn't like not being front and center.

The couple glanced back and nodded graciously before carrying on. I blew out my breath in one relieved rush. I could see the scene so clearly that I was surprised it hadn't occurred. I was surprised that the woman hadn't stopped, looked at Mother and shouted, "You stole my dress!"

In our room, Mother slipped out of the dress and into a matching pair of shorts and top that were completely hers. I folded the dress up and slipped it into a dark plastic bag that had been left by the hotel for laundry. I took a cursory look around the room, just in case there was something else Mother might have acquired in her travels, but everything in the room was legitimately ours. On the way to breakfast I dropped the package off with our concierge. I'd explained Mother's condition to him yesterday and he too had a parent in the same situation. He took the package and promised it would be returned to the rightful owner.

"When the señorita reports her dress missing I'll be able to slip it back into her room." He winked at me. "It will be our secret how the dress disappeared and reappeared again."

I thanked him profusely and wrestled the knot of relief that combined with his unexpected generosity. It made me want to weep on his shoulder.

"Have a good day, Jess," the concierge said with a last smile for me.

Everyone called her Jess. Here she had demanded it the instant she met someone.

"Let's get breakfast, Mom." I gave a final "I can't thank you enough" wave to our savior, and headed for the open-air restaurant where a buffet style breakfast was set up.

Mother slipped in ahead of me and led the way. She scanned the restaurant, quickly got a plate, and handed me one. She was moving through the line as I stood watching her. My hands were a little shaky but I was grateful to see Mother was back to being Mother. The episode was left only in my mind and my rattled nerves. Maybe the round of medication the neurologist had prescribed that replaced the trial Mother had refused had finally kicked in and curbed the disease. I clung to that thought. For now she didn't need me to be anything but a companion, her daughter. Thank goodness, because right then it was all I could do to keep my plate from dropping, my hands were shaking that bad.

Ironically it was Mother who kept me on track and took me safely through the buffet. Without her I might have just grabbed cereal and a coffee and retired to a distant table to lick my wounds and calm my nerves. Instead I found myself directing a small, wiry man who smiled easily at me, on what ingredients I might like in my omelet. I followed blindly behind Mother and was even tempted into dusting icing sugar on a small stack of waffles.

As we exited the line, I headed for an isolated table in the corner. Mother rerouted me immediately.

"No sweetie — wait. Look, it's Jeff and Nancy. Let's go see if we can join them."

"No," I began, but I was talking to air as Mother headed over to the couple she mentioned. I was left to either stand directionless and look slightly anti-social or follow behind her.

I followed and I considered the vast dichotomy of the disease. I don't know why I thought of it then, that disease

I hated to reference. But it affected Mother in so many unexpected ways. That she would remember the names of two people she had just met and yet she'd lost all sense of where she was or what she had packed less than an hour ago. But the dress was a moot point for at least one of us. As far as Mother was concerned, the incident was forgotten.

Breakfast turned out to be an enjoyable and informative affair. Mother was beyond charming. It seemed Mother had returned to the present and I was still struggling with the recent past. I barely heard much of what was said in the first five minutes. I think I just smiled and nodded and allowed Mother and her new friends to lead the conversation. In fact, I know I did.

"Snorkeling." Mother clapped her hands together. "Let's."

"What?" I felt like I should shake my head. Like I was coming up for air and had arrived in a room of aliens. Snorkeling? Surely I'd heard wrong.

"I was just saying there's a good rental agency on the beach. You can rent flippers, masks, and life jackets, and try your hand at it," Jeff said good-naturedly and smiled at me. "Did it yesterday. And if you head farther down the beach nearer the coral there's a lot to see."

"Let's do it, Cassie." Mother's eyes lit up like a kid at Christmas.

It was insane. Water sports were one thing, floating on an air mattress in the pool, possibly—but snorkeling?

"It's quite safe," Nancy inserted. "Everyone does it. Young. Old." She shrugged.

"Sounds like fun to me," Mother said. "What about you, Cassie?"

And it was in that moment I knew I was not making the decision for both of us. Mother had just drawn the line. She was going whether I was or not. She was an adult. I supposed there was nothing I could do to stop her.

I shrugged before agreeing. I had to quit worrying.

•

On the beach two hours later, I shifted my bathing suit as discretely as possible. It was beginning to ride upward in places we won't mention. I wished I'd visited the gym more frequently so I could have comfortably worn a bikini. As it was, like Mother, I was in a one-piece and that comparison just made me feel so much closer to that mark—forty—middle-aged.

I shivered despite the heat that seemed to wrap around me like a warm-weather massage. How could one be depressed on a Cuban beach with the sun beating hot around them and good-looking men at every turn?

A tiger-striped cat strolled across our path. Mother stopped dead and dropped to her knees in the sand. The cat was obviously used to strangers admiring it; it leaned up against Mother and began to purr.

It was on the tip of my tongue to remind her she didn't like cats. I believed *loathed* was the word she'd used long ago. For whatever reason Mother had decided to like that cat or maybe she'd forgotten she disliked cats. I preferred to think it was the first option.

"Buenos dias," a young man called cheerfully as he strode past, long-legged, sleekly muscled and barefoot.

"Good day," I choked out.

I tried not to stare, at least not obviously, but I couldn't help it as my attention strayed after that golden physique as the young man carved distance between us.

"Cuban men, sweetie. Didn't I tell you?" Mother looked up at me from her place on her knees in the sand where she still stroked the cat.

"You did. And how did you know about Cuban men?"

"Really dear, I'm seventy-five years-old. I've learned something in my time. Hemingway spent a great deal of time here. Before the revolution, you know." She got up and dusted sand off her knees.

"He did," I agreed.

"Fidel. I wonder if we might see him."

"I doubt it," I said.

"Oh, really. That's too bad. Such a vital man." She wrapped her arms beneath her chest as if suppressing a shudder. "I can hardly wait to try scuba diving."

"Snorkeling," I corrected her and was happy to see that

she'd shifted the topic from thoughts of men that always seemed to turn strangely to Fidel. My curiosity was getting to me but I just had no idea how to ferret the information from her.

The sand rolled a warm, gritty massage along the bottom of our bare feet. I could have walked like that forever. Instead I stopped and looked out to sea where small wooden fishing boats bobbed on the horizon.

On the shore a group of Cuban children of staggered ages splashed in the water. Further ahead I could see a couple spotlighted by the sun that reflected against their sun-starved skin and marked them as tourists.

I don't think they cared as they held hands and gazed out to sea.

Briefly and rather reluctantly, I thought of Russ.

We began walking again, and as we did we breathed the subtle flavor of sand, salt, sea and sweat—and something else. Something that smelled like a combination of forever and ambrosia and made you ache to never leave.

"There." Mother pointed.

She was pointing at a small bamboo-framed shack that sat on the edge of the sand. A Cuban couple smiled and waved hopefully at us. They were dressed in matching board shorts and white T-shirts that were faded like they had seen more than a season or two worth of sun. I saw snorkels and masks hanging from one rough-hewed wall that listed in a ridge of sand.

Thirty minutes later we'd had a brief instruction and each had a snorkel, flippers and mask. The life jackets were on, belted up and unbearably hot.

"Let's get into the water," I said to Mother, and took her sweat-slicked hand. That sentence went against everything in my being. I was trying not to think about what we were about to do. I knew how much Mother loved water. She'd forgotten how much I hated it. Not hated it, as in its very existence— it was more like I was scared of it. I doubted my swimming ability and the ocean was a vast place. Now I was responsible not only for myself but for Mother. The thought, despite the life jackets and Mother's excellent swimming abilities, was beyond daunting.

Mother grinned up at me. "Let's go."

She yanked me forward and I balked, my heels grinding into the sand.

"C'mon," she persisted and excitement vibrated from her. Her smile could have lit up the beach at night.

I wouldn't disappoint her. Somehow I must move forward and smile, I reminded myself. But the thought of sticking my head into unknown water to see unknown alien beings that others might call fish, was slightly unnerving.

Mother squeezed my hand and then let go and almost skipped ahead. She'd gotten her mask on and was struggling with her flippers by the time I reached the water.

"I'm not sure how to do this, sweetie." Her snorkel was hanging half in and half out of her mask and was completely useless in the position she had it in. It was a good ten minutes before I had both her and me ready to make the last plunge into the depths of … my mind flitted to an appropriate word. *Hell* came to mind. I tried to discard it.

"C'mon, Cassie Lynn, quit dilly-dallying." Mother was slopping ahead already knee deep in water and doing a rather awkward hopping walk as she waded deeper.

Mother had always been the swimmer in the family. She'd tried to get me to swim, and I can swim enough so I don't drown. Other than that, water to me was a foreign entity. The ideal day near water was a blow-up lounge mattress in a crystal clear pool. I fought back images of what might be lurking in the water and tried not to look out to sea. Out there I knew true sea monsters lurked.

"Are you sure about this, Mom?" I stood with the warm and deceptively gentle Caribbean caressing my ankles, and stared out to sea.

"It'll be fun, Cassie. You'll see." Mother reached behind her, took my hand and led me farther out. We were up to our waists in water. I looked down. I could see sand and rocks on the bottom. Somehow that was slightly more comforting than the endless water that stretched ahead of us.

Mother was the ultimate water baby. And because of that, no matter how uncomfortable this made me, I'd do it. I took a big breath as another doubt stabbed me. There was no option. Mother couldn't snorkel alone.

We kept walking, gingerly for me, eagerly for Mother. I was being ridiculous I knew. A senior was about to show me up—a senior with dementia. It wouldn't happen.

"Okay, let's do it," I said with a forced smile as we slid face-first into the water. I was churning my fins as if they alone would keep me afloat. Every now and then I looked over at Mother whose eyes were wide. She looked utterly blissful and totally unaware of me. That made it all worthwhile.

A few minutes later I poked her just to remind her I was there and not to go out too far.

She scowled at me and pointed down.

It was an effort to tip my face straight down and look at the bottom where shards of coral sculpted the ocean floor. A netting of lace green waved gently in a slight current. A conch shell with a gorgeous hue of pink had me considering how beautiful it would look on my coffee table when suddenly it sprouted legs and walked across the sandy ocean floor. I was reminded that seashells were not just ornamental entities but once—living beings. I pointed the conch shell out to Mother and sucked water.

Bubbles shot out around me and I flopped around for a minute before I got my snorkel back in place, calmed myself and realigned my bearings. But I didn't bolt and that was a good thing. After that first mistake, it got easier. The saltwater was as buoyant as the travel brochure had promised, and besides we had the life vests.

We floated there for a long time as we watched life on the ocean floor saunter by us. A school of rainbow-striped fish, not much bigger than mid-size goldfish, passed by, and a crab stirred up a sand storm on the ocean floor.

When the grouper arrived, I realized we had floated a little further out but I couldn't help staying just a moment longer. I held Mother's hand as we watched the large grey fish that looked at us with what might be intelligence. I never thought you could interact with a fish. But that grouper hung around doing that "get to know you" dance for the remainder of the time we snorkeled. But grouper or not, after forty-five minutes we were both done, Mother was exhausted and I'd had my fill of seawater—literally. I snorted salt for a good hour after that.

Our first week went like that, lazy and languid. We snorkeled more, toured the resort, met a few more tourists, and lounged with Jeff and Nancy. It turned out they had met in Cuba. Nancy was British and Jeff was Canadian. The logistics of geography on a new relationship was daunting. But in Cuba, a resort that had us isolated from the world, logistics just didn't matter. For me the specter that haunted both Mother and me was not mentioned. In fact I hadn't thought of it for days. I even dreamt about the possibility of Russ, forgetting about the impossibility of it all. After the incident that began the week, life had slipped into normal.

Late one afternoon, with a tropical drink and the water lapping at my feet, I wanted to think that all Mother's troubles had gone away, that Cuba was the miracle cure. I even thought maybe if we never went home we would never have to face the truth of Mother's awful diagnosis. I fantasized a lot in those early days. That was what kept me sane.

Beside me, Mother had dropped off to sleep with a book in one hand and a bottle of sunscreen in the other.

The last few days in Cuba had been so peaceful they were like a dream or maybe even paradise. I was determined to enjoy every moment.

But even then, I knew that paradise couldn't last forever.

Chapter Twelve

February 28

Paradise officially ended today at 11:45 a.m. Central Standard Time.

Mother was in a snit. I hadn't seen anything like it since my childhood when my father used to antagonize her at every turn. One of his favorite moves was to declare the Pope's infallibility to be a hoax. Now for any good Catholic, those words could start another crusade or at the least, a good war. They had always worked on Mother. Words of a similar bent raised her fury an extra notch and ensured our house was always three steps shy of a war zone.

Not my father, I corrected myself. The man who Mother married, who played at being my father, played badly I might add and then left. "Good riddance," I said as I shadowed Mother's oft-repeated phrase and turned my attention back to her and the current issue.

"I will not, I repeat, will not, Cassandra Lynn, stay here a moment longer."

I envisioned her stamping her size-five feet to emphasize her point. Size five unlike my size nine—everything about Mother was petite.

"Mom."

"Home!"

We couldn't go home. Not *couldn't*, of course we could—but I wasn't willing to do what it took. I might be all about Mother's happiness but I wasn't sure what she wanted would make either of us happy.

Not giving in to Mother had the potential to be a catastrophe. There were things I wanted to say. They were angry words that chastised Mother for being difficult. But this wasn't Mother. Instead it was the voice of a frustrated, angry child who was confused and lost in a horrible fugue—Alzheimer's.

For a while I had forgotten the nightmare existed. I bit my tongue at the thought Cuba was her dream damn it, not mine.

Alzheimer's. I hated the word. I hated the disease. Hate was a strong word that wasn't strong enough.

Were a few more days in paradise worth putting up with Mother in a snit? Would she remember even two days from now? I couldn't force her to stay here, and I had no idea how long her mood would last. Despite my earlier thoughts, I considered grabbing an early flight out and taking the financial hit.

Common sense reminded me the trip was good for Mother, good for both of us. I had to get her back on track and guide her as quickly as possible back on the path of reality. Problem was I didn't know what had set Mother off, and until I figured that out I was left to flop around like the fish our new friend Ernesto pulled out of the ocean only last night.

"You had a good time last night, didn't you?"

Mother scowled at me. "No."

"You liked Ernesto."

"Ridiculous."

For me, memories of last night were like a balm for today's emotional chaos. We'd met Ernesto while we were pulling off our sand-crusted snorkeling gear. He quietly slipped into our lives and struck up a conversation as he helped Mother rinse her mask and snorkel. He was a local who rented an assortment of beach paraphernalia to tourists. Any time we needed an air mattress, beach ball or paddleboard he was our man. On the way to easing out of business as he turned it over to his son, he'd found plenty of time to socialize.

We quickly found out that Ernesto was a socializer. Only twenty minutes or so into the conversation he'd invited us to a family barbecue.

That evening we were treated to chicken cooked over an

open fire. It was unlike the anemic chickens I was used to at home. These chickens had obviously lived a very different life. They were bigger and far tastier. The spices were unidentifiable but combined with the wood smoke, it was the best barbecued chicken I'd ever had.

We weren't the only visitors there. Besides Ernesto's family, there were a few other Cuban families. Later we all moved to a hard-packed sand area on the edges of the beach where Latin music beat a rich flowing rhythm against the steady rush of the waves pummeling the shore. Couples took to the sand in bare feet in a fluid gyrating dance that transposed heat and humidity into a sensual message that flirted with the boundaries of how far one could go with children in attendance. That dance took it all to the edge. Yet it was harmless fun with everyone laughing, and in the end, clapping and joining in. Mother shed her sandals and dug into the sand with gusto. She learned the fine art of the salsa with little hesitation, encouraged by the roars of approval of Ernesto and his family.

But that had been last night. A new day had flipped with the old and a completely different Mother faced me.

"Cassandra Lynn, I don't know why we're here or what you have planned, but it's time we get home. My house plants are dying and I've missed Mass."

Mass? I knew I shouldn't ask but I couldn't help myself. We were alone on that section of the beach as Mother stalled a perfectly lovely walk. It was a strange way to announce that lucidity had just taken a stroll down the beach.

"Sunday was yesterday, Mom. What's the big deal about Mass?"

Sometimes I was just her kid, not her friend or even her caregiver and as such, those were the times when I hit it completely wrong.

"Mass! Cassandra if you thought to go to Mass yourself instead of this heathen existence you live."

Heathen existence? I was no heathen. I was just spiritually conflicted.

"Don't you want to see the dancers this afternoon? It'll be a good show."

"No. Take me home," she demanded. With her tiny stature

and sunburned nose she looked more like a child having a tantrum in a grocery store than the mature woman she was.

My mind was playing through the possibilities and turning up zeros on how to re-route Mother in her current mood. Sometimes she locked into those things and it almost took a landmine to blast her out. I had an aching little fear it was one of those times.

I remembered the expeditions that were advertised at the entrance to the hotel. Maybe that was the answer. Certainly, talking to Cisco, the clerk in the gift shop might pick up Mother's mood. She positively loved the man and if he could distract her, I might be able to book a tour that might take her mind off thoughts of ending the trip prematurely.

"Cisco," I greeted our new friend not twenty minutes later. I looked over to ensure Mother was occupied. She was busy looking at rings in the far end of the gift shop. I made a note to check her fingers and pockets before we left the store. Ever since the card incident I'd been paranoid and watched her like a hawk any time we entered a store.

"Cassie," he greeted me. We seemed to have become a favorite among the staff and especially Cisco. Mother remembered one thing about Cisco—bracelets. She loved the bracelets he sold and insisted we stop by the store two and even three times a day. The shop was the first place I knew to look if the unthinkable were to happen—if I lost Mother. So far that hadn't been an issue, but I'd read the literature and knew the possibility, terrifying as it was, was there.

Cisco frowned as he came out from behind the counter. The shop was empty except for the three of us and Mother was occupied with the bracelet shelf.

"Don't worry," he grinned. "I take a head count every day." He nodded to the bracelets Mother was now busily trying on. "Ten dollars for any two. For you, maybe a deal." He winked at me. "How can I help?"

"We're having a bit of a bad day. Mom wants to go home." I hated that part of the disease, the part where I found myself relying on other people. They were people who in my previous life would have remained strangers. I wasn't a person to bond with resort staff. I wasn't even a person to stay in a resort.

My world was one I barely recognized and yet I'd adapted in a frighteningly short period of time. "I thought maybe a diversion would get the idea out of her head. We're not scheduled to leave for another four days."

I looked over but Mother was still occupied with the bracelets. She hummed softly under her breath as she slipped one over her wrist and then another. I knew then that I'd be leaving the store at least ten dollars lighter. Maybe more.

"There's a tour going into Banes in an hour. Let me check if there's room."

"She'll refuse to go. She doesn't want to miss the plane. She still thinks I've booked her on the next flight home. In fact, she told me that she's going with or without me. I'm really scared she's not going to agree to any excursion."

"Maybe." Cisco shrugged. "And maybe not." A crafty expression flitted across his face.

Cisco was an amazing man. I'd learned he'd trained to be a doctor and now worked at the resort because the money was better in the tourist industry. It was the same for many of the resort workers, well educated in careers such as engineering and like Cisco, they waited tables, tended bar and collected tips from foreigners. A good education was available to almost everyone in Cuba. It was what they did with the education that I had a hard time digesting.

"I'll tell her the bracelets are manufactured in Banes. She can watch the craftsmen at work."

"Craftsmen? Really?"

"No." He shook his head. "But her fixation with the bracelets gives me some hope that she might just change one fixation with another."

"You're brilliant."

"Creative problem solving, I like to call it."

Five minutes later he'd even presented Mother with a brochure of the tour to Banes. He gave her that beautiful smile that was so common in Cuba and Mother was willing to agree to anything.

"I can hardly wait." Mother did a little jig on the spot and the bracelets, three of them, jangled and clattered. The tortoise shell colors sparkled and reflected shades of purple, green and blue. They were really quite pretty.

"Thanks," I whispered to Cisco on the way out the door.

He shrugged. "I shall pray it works."

I was glad someone was praying for us. Seemed I was becoming more and more dependent on hope and prayer with each passing day. And I was depending on other people's beliefs because I seemed to have none of my own. It was a disquieting realization I refused to dwell on.

Banes turned out to be a great success. Mother's jangling bracelets only reminded her once of Cisco's little white lie and that was on the bus when she enthusiastically blurted out how happy she was to be able to see her bracelets being made. I glossed over that statement and pointed out the rolling hills and farmland that the road wound through. Forty minutes, three hitchhikers, an emancipated cow and a bevy of school children later, and she had completely forgotten the bracelets.

Outside our window, Cuba was lush woods that opened onto fields that were still plowed by oxen. We passed more than one group of school children with book bags slung over their shoulders as they headed for home after a serious day of study. Their uniforms were pressed and their white shirts and blouses glinted in the early afternoon sun.

"Aren't they darling?" Mother said with her hand on the window.

"They are," I agreed, but then I was a firm advocate of school uniforms. Discipline I'd always thought. But then what did I know? I was skimming along the edges of middle-age and I'd failed in the progeny department.

"Cassandra Lynn, you're not listening."

"What? I'm sorry."

Banes. It was nothing like the resort. Banes was travel as it was meant to be. That was as soon as we got off the darn tourist bus and strode out on our own.

I brought myself off that high horse fairly quickly. I was with Mother and leaving the tour was not an option.

We spent an amazing day amidst streets that were surprisingly easy to navigate and mostly clear of the clutter of traffic. The old world mansions were listing and broken remains of languid decadence and looked oddly like a rusted version of nineteenth century Europe rather than twenty-first century Cuba.

The housing wasn't the only dichotomy. The nineteen-fifty and sixty-era vehicles were everywhere—and in pristine shape. They weren't a surprise. We'd studied travel guides before we came here and we'd seen them along the public road by the resort. While it was all new for Mother, it was the horse-drawn buses that shocked both of us. Two horses were pulling a long carriage lined with a bench on either side. The carriage was full with at least twenty people.

"Oh my." Mother put her hand to her mouth. "I can't imagine."

My camera was in my hand but I was slow on lifting it for the picture. I was still getting over the fact I was watching a horse pull a cart with a platform that looked rather like a large sleigh on wheels. "A taxi," I breathed.

"Bus," Mother corrected. "Take the picture, Cassie."

"Right, of course." I snapped the picture, one of many extraordinary things we were to see on that trip.

By the time we got back to the resort, Mother was exhausted. "We must do something like that tomorrow."

"Tomorrow?" I imagined she would mention the plane immediately after that. Despite the intent of that day's trip, I was never quite sure what to expect.

"Yes, tomorrow. I love it here." She curled her bare toes and snapped her flip-flops against her heels.

"Fidel," she whispered, stood up, and spun lightly on her toes. "Cassie, I think this deserves a drink."

So we sat on our balcony in the quiet time before supper, and shared the warm evening air and a cocktail. It was one of those moments that I will remember always.

Chapter Thirteen

March 7

We'd been home for three days. I knew Mother was glad to be back. We both were. This morning, I had spent time in the basement again, immersed in the diary. And, desperate to acquire memories before it was too late. I'd dug through a box of what I thought was only knickknacks when I found a small packet of letters. Except for one, most of them weren't of much interest. But I held the one in my hand. A letter Mother had written to Aunt Alice, dated the year after the last diary entries.

I had to read the letter twice as I swallowed past a lump in my throat. My grandmother had dementia before she'd had the stroke that ended it all. In the end she hadn't known my mother's name. All of that was a revelation. It was painful to read and yet it bound me so much closer to my mother knowing we shared this common ground.

Sunlight streamed across the kitchen table. The days were finally starting to lighten even though the snow had yet to show any signs of leaving.

"Another few weeks of winter, Mom."

"Hmmm." She said through a mouthful of toast, her hair was rather disheveled and one elbow was on the table.

The phone rang and I instinctively knew it was Russ.

"How was it?" he asked before we'd even got through the first hellos.

I'd sent him an e-mail to assure him we had gotten to Cuba safely and a note after that and nothing more.

"Exactly what we needed. And bonus, no snow," I said

with a laugh, an attempt to keep this light.

"Your mom had a good time?"

"Yes, I think she did. If you can believe it, she took me snorkeling."

"You?" He laughed a sound that seemed to come from deep in his gut, genuine and true.

"No lie. Fear of water and all, I went."

"I'm impressed."

We chatted for a few minutes about the trip and how well Mother had done before he got down to business. "I phoned to let you know you won't be seeing much of me the next week. I'm working overtime—one of the guys badly cut his hand in a home-carpentry accident. He won't be at work for a while."

"Can't someone else fill in for him?" I tried to keep the disappointment from my voice. For seeing Russ was the one bright spot in returning home to the snow and cold.

There was a pause at that. "I suppose. But …"

I guessed he felt better being the one to cover the shifts to make sure they were done right. He'd been that way as a youth, driven to be the best. "You're a bit of a perfectionist aren't you?"

"Not so much anymore," he disagreed.

"A workaholic then," I guessed. "Although I suppose there's nothing wrong with loving your job."

"Guilty as charged. One of the perils of being a bachelor. But this won't be long—this week, part of next and I'll make sure others are filling in."

"Good." I cleared my throat and decided to just say it. "I missed you."

"I missed you, too," he said.

We chatted about other things after that. For that bit of intimacy had been more than I guessed either of us was ready for.

A few minutes later, after I'd updated him on Cuba and he promised to drop by on his next day off, we hung up. I turned to Mother who was lining a row of crumbs along the side of her thumb.

"What do you want to do today?"

"Okay."

Maybe she hadn't heard what I'd asked and maybe she had, I was never sure. I hit the on button on the coffee maker and turned around. " Mom?"

"I still have your old skates, Cassie Lynn. I presume you've obtained new ones."

"No, Mom, actually I haven't." I thought how it was interesting that her vocabulary seemed to ebb and flow rather like the days and hours, and even minutes. Good, bad, good; one never knew what it would be.

"Why ever not? Renting is a waste of money."

"I haven't skated in years."

"Let's go skating." She smacked her hands on the table and stood up.

"Why, Mom?" As soon as those words had left my mouth I wished I could have retrieved them. I should have said no. That might have ended it all.

"For fun."

It was a crazy idea. I considered Mother's age and condition. I stupidly reminded myself Mother had always been agile. So it wasn't a stretch, not really. Besides, skating was something she'd managed to do every winter. In fact, only last year she regaled me with tales of her skating escapades.

That was last year. The diagnosis that had begun this year had changed it all.

"It's good exercise and it's fun."

About as much fun as having my wisdom teeth pulled, I remembered thinking. Instead I said, "I don't have a helmet."

"Cassandra Lynn!" Her hands were on her hips and she scowled at me. "Live a little, will you? One day you will get old and stupid like me. Take a chance."

"You're not stupid," I said that weakly without the emphasis needed to convince her of her mental ability. And on the skating issue, I was beginning to lean toward yes. You could call me nuts. But I'd read that exercise was the best weapon against dementia — that and attitude. A happy person was less likely to progress into a mental fog. Of course, none of that was proven but I was willing to forego our safety for Mother's happiness and health just on the off chance it was a sound theory.

But skating? Crazy.

Crazy. I couldn't stand even thinking about that word for it brought to mind what was happening to Mother. But Mother wasn't crazy. She was only losing her memory and eventually her identity as a person and …

"Let's do it," I said before reason would change my mind.

"Let me get your skates." Mother was up and heading for the stairs.

I followed. There was no way she'd remember she was after skates by the time she got to the basement.

"You remembered," I muttered surprised, as she confronted me with two pairs of skates in hand.

One hour later Mother was whizzing by me on her second pass when I had only made one circuit of the outdoor rink.

"What's wrong, Cass?"

"Nothing. Just nothing," I muttered as I tripped and righted myself for the fourth time. It was taking me a bit to get my sea legs.

"Like this," Mother called as she glided past me.

I gritted my teeth and struggled after her. I failed miserably. Unlike me, Mother was all poetry and ease on ice.

"Mom, wait."

I wobbled and came close to meeting the ice up close and way too personal.

"Cassie," Mother giggled. "I'm a better skater than you. Can you believe it?"

I could believe it. Despite my love of armchair sports, Mother had always been more athletic than me. But instead of giving in graciously, no, I had to let my pride get in the way. "Race you." I pointed with a wool mitten-covered hand, baby blue, completely not my color—to the other side of the rink. The outfit for Dell's baby had become mitts for me. It made Mother happy at the time and I was always all for that.

"One, two, three." And we were off before my rational mind could tell me how absolutely ludicrous racing a senior with dementia might turn out to be. Insane, racing on ice through what remained of a prairie winter, and balancing on steel blades. I knew she had slight balance problems to add to the insanity of it all but she was wearing thick winter gear that kept her well padded. I hold that in my defense. That and her happiness at that point were really more important than anything else.

My rational mind shut completely off as I raced, just me, the crisp ice beneath my blades and Mother whizzing past me like the elegant athlete she had always been. Her arms swung in just the correct tempo at her sides. Her progress was effortless, unlike mine. I was panting and churning those skates like it was all in the effort and not done with any amount of grace. I was focused on the finish line right up until the moment I hit that ridge.

It was a painful walk home. I was sure my knee would swell to melon-size by the time I got there. Mother assured me it was nothing. I would be fine. I thought she even said something to the effect I should stop whining. What happened to mother-sympathy? I didn't even consider the traitorous thought that she might have forgotten. It wasn't true.

What was true was the next morning my knee was seriously bruised and I had a limp, but had avoided major injury. Last night's skate had me looking at Mother with fresh eyes. Over the last few days I'd had time to think about all that I'd learned of Mother from the diary and that one letter. It's hard to explain but I suspect we've all felt a moment when our parent suddenly takes on another dimension,—fellow human being on this planet—that spins us on a whirlwind ride.

I went to her, put my arms around her and gave her a hug. She had followed the path I found myself on, and while neither of us would have chosen it and we both went at it in our own way—we both knew what it was like to watch a parent disappear in front of our eyes. I wasn't alone in this; I had Mother.

I let her go reluctantly with a final squeeze and reached for the coffee.

Mother looked at me with a rather puzzled expression and I saw there was a splotch of something that looked somewhat like raspberry jam on her sleeve.

"What month is it, sweetie?" she asked as if that question was a normal addition to what had gone before.

"March," I replied.

Mother took a bite of toast and chewed slowly like I hadn't spoken. The neck of her nightgown was buttoned in a zigzag manner that left large gaps and exposed part of her collarbone. Her housecoat was completely missing in action. I could see from the faraway look in her eyes that the discussion was over.

"Cassie, could you reach the cream while you're up?"

I handed the cream to her and reached for the coffee. Mother delicately wiped her mouth with a napkin and stood up. "Helen is picking me up later this morning."

I stopped in mid-swallow. That was the first I'd heard of it. I made a mental note to check with Mom's closest friend, Helen.

Turned out Mother was bang on with the Helen date, and the two of them left a little over an hour later.

Chapter Fourteen

Fifteen minutes after mother left, I was outside shoveling like a mad woman. Somehow the activity calmed the despair that seemed to hit me at odd moments, it was like premature grief, and I really didn't want to grieve for her before she was actually gone.

The shoveling helped. But it was tiring work, even for me and I'm not a small woman. Big-boned, mother always said. Another thing I didn't get from either of my parents. My father, at least the man I had called father, wasn't short. He was built reed-slim with bones that weren't considered enduring.

I was breaking a sweat and the sun was gleaming hot on my neck even as my thumbs began to freeze in my wool gloves. From the corner of my eye I saw a glint and flash that made me look up as the hard snow cracked under the weight of a vehicle. Russ's SUV was pulling into our driveway and my heart, I hated to admit it even then, did a small skip. I literally didn't breathe. Instead, anticipation hung in my chest like a raw and aching, or maybe whimpering was more appropriate, beast. The door opened and I recognized the figure getting out. I had known it was him before then.

Russ.

"Hi, Cassie," he said as he opened the gate like it was normal for him to appear unexpectedly.

I leaned on the shovel and wished I could have ripped the tasseled toque from my head. It was far from my best look. I wished I was dressed slightly better, that I was wearing makeup that … I stopped such ridiculous thoughts right there. I had more serious things to contemplate.

"What's wrong?" He took the shovel from my now limp hand and dropped it to the side.

I'm so mixed up. And those words almost came out. I stared at Russ horrified I had come so close to spilling my unwanted emotions at his feet. Despite my best efforts, tears filmed my eyes.

Bless Russ, he never said a word. Instead he just wrapped his arms around me and I burrowed into the depths of his down-filled parka. His parka was slightly damp when I sheepishly pulled away.

He reached into his pocket and pulled out a tissue.

I blew my nose. Could I be any more unappealing?

He leaned down then and kissed me. His lips were warm against mine and took away some of the winter chill of both the weather and my thoughts. His hands cupped my cheeks as he reluctantly, or maybe that was my imagination, let me go.

"Do you want to talk?" His voice had that soft edge that gets me every time. I imagined he was the best interrogator the police force had. Who wouldn't tell him everything?

I shook my head. "Thanks, Russ. I'm sorry, I didn't ..."

"Don't apologize. You've taken on a load that many people would run from. A tear now and then is nothing." He took the shovel from my hands and jockeyed it from hand to hand. "Look, Cassie I have to say I admire what you're doing for your mother. And any time you need me, call."

"I can't do that. You have a life." I shrugged. "I'm not much of a friend. What do I ever do for you?"

"Don't underrate yourself, Cass. I love your company, simple as that."

"I love your company too."

Silence ticked, a second, two ...

"You're looking good. Tanned, I mean," he said as he faced me, one parka clad arm bent as he leaned on the shovel. "How's Mother now that you're back?"

"Fine." I paused deciding what to say, what not to say. "I'm glad we did it. I don't know if we'll ever do a trip like that again. But she loved it."

"Where is she?"

"Out with a friend." I looked away.

"She's worse."

It was a bald statement but I'd discovered Russ doesn't tend to beat around the bush, as Mother would say. He also seems to have that uncanny ability to just know. He hadn't seen either Mother or I since we returned and yet he knew.

"She is," I admitted. "It's progressed faster than I anticipated."

"Do you have her in a trial?" he asked quietly as if he had been to the doctor with us, and privy to the secret there was really nothing they could do except a trial.

"Not yet," I admitted. I wanted to throw myself in his arms again. It was ridiculous. I'd been strong all my life and now I was acting like he was my knight in shining armor. "We've only been to one appointment. We're due for the second next week. He mentioned a trial. Mother wasn't too excited in being, as she put it, a pig of any sort."

Russ laughed. "Your mother is amazing. It's too bad this had to happen." He made a half-hearted attempt to take another shovel full of snow before turning to me. "Would you like to go for an early lunch?" he asked in that quiet husky voice of his.

I'd already told him Mother was safely with her friend Helen and not due back until after lunch. The idea of going somewhere without Mother was mostly inconceivable and now suddenly doable.

"I thought I wouldn't be seeing you?"

"Yeah, well I took your advice. Another of the guys is filling in and I'm officially off duty."

He began to shovel the back half of the sidewalk. For a minute there was only the quiet scrape of the shovel against ice coated concrete.

"Let me help you," I said and ran for the second snow shovel. For the first time that day the world seemed slightly brighter. We had the walk shoveled and the drive cleared and we were sitting comfortably in a popular bistro not thirty minutes later.

"I never thought of you becoming a police officer." It was an occupation I don't remember anyone in our graduating class considering.

"I didn't until I realized that professional hockey wasn't going to be for me."

"Why not? You were drafted weren't you?"

He gave a brief nod, staring distantly at the posters behind the bar before giving me his full attention. "I was drafted in a later round and ended up playing for LA's farm team. Great weather but I missed the snow. Plus, I only saw one big league game in two years."

"And ..." I coached, sensing there was more.

"I came home—went to university and applied with the City Police and here we are."

"Here we are," I murmured. And realized how different we were. I loved to travel, get away from the snow and cold and Russ, his passion was grid-locked to snow, cold and ice.

"I can't believe we've both hit thirty-nine and neither of us has been married. Especially you, Cassie," he said as we waited for our orders.

We sat on high stools, the old-style counter swept in front of us. I imagined swinging my legs but I wasn't feeling that upbeat.

"I'm divorced," I admitted as I took a quick chug of coke like it was fortified with something stronger than excess sugar. I'd always hated to admit that fact, divorce. "We were both too young."

"Divorced." He shook his head.

"What?" I frowned at the way he reacted like he was disapproving. I knew I was heading for that high horse of mine—another Mother expression. And as she said, once I was there, it was near impossible to get me down.

"It's not unbelievable. Lots of marriages end up in divorce." I don't know why I felt the need to justify. I'd never felt that need before. But there was something about Russ. I wanted his approval like I'd never wanted anyone else's.

"I can't imagine what man would divorce you."

Did I mention how much the new Russ was growing on me?

I blushed and I swear my heart rate speeded up just a touch. When I looked at him, he was smiling at me with a satisfied kind of smile. Like he'd gotten the reaction he wanted.

He smiled easily and passed the saltshaker. "For your fries and good luck." A chair scraped behind him and he swung around. "Sorry," he said as he turned back around.

"Hazards of being a cop. You're always on duty," he said as if there had been no break in the conversation. "I came close to marriage once." His brown eyes darkened. "Turns out she couldn't stand the prairie or this city. Me, I love it."

"One strike and you're out?" I asked quizzically. I couldn't imagine why no one had snapped him up. Tall, good-looking, well-employed. I almost smiled at the thought. I was thinking of him as a commodity more than a flesh and blood man.

But those thoughts only brought me to the growing attraction I felt for him. I shifted uncomfortably. For as much as I'd had those kinds of thoughts about Russ, my head kept telling me it just wasn't doable.

"How are your parents?"

"Enjoying the hell out of Florida," he grinned. "Since Dad retired five years ago they haven't stopped. Cottage in the summer, Florida in the winter and between that, a cruise or two a year. I'm lucky if I see them at Christmas. In fact this Christmas was kind of special, the whole family including Wade had Christmas at the cottage."

"Wade," I repeated, remembering his brother as a thin, pre-pubescent boy. "What's he up to now?"

"Overseas mainly consulting in the oil patch."

My phone rang. "Cass, it's me, Helen. I'm in the hospital emergency with your mother."

"What's wrong? What happened?"

Beside me, Russ had pinned me with nothing but concern and solid dependability in his brown eyes. He shifted his stool closer as if his physical proximity would give me some solace.

"She may have broken her wrist."

It was six hours later before we learnt the truth. Mother had a sprain because she'd tried to shove her arm into a vending machine and panicked when she thought it was stuck. She twisted her arm at an odd angle to get it out and was clutching it to her chest when Helen found her. Helen had only managed to get the how of the incident out of Mother. The why had long been forgotten.

Russ was there for the entire ordeal and insisted on chauffeuring Mother and me home when it was all over.

"I'll pick up pizza," Russ offered once we were home.

"Delightful," Mother enthused. She twisted to look at Russ. "You're a good boy."

"Thank you, Mrs. McDowall."

"Jess. Just Jess," she repeated. She looked at her watch. "I'm starved."

Russ took our order for toppings and headed out the door. It was too bad, I thought, as the door shut behind him. He was too reliable, too predictable and no matter how hard I tried, I couldn't find asshole pinned anywhere on him. He was definitely not my kind of guy. That was the problem. My twenties had been dotted with men that were more boys in men's suits. I'd married one of them and divorced him when I discovered he was better at flirting with other women while spending my money than he was at loving me enough to make a marriage. My thirties had been a dating wasteland.

"I really like that boy," Mother told me when Russ had left.

"That's good."

"I think he'd be good for you," Mother persisted. "You really don't know a good thing when you see one."

"Sorry Mom, no. He's a friend. That's it." I knew Russ Thomas was a gem of a man. I could even admit I wanted him. But I also knew that the timing was all wrong.

"You'll see," Mother chuckled. "One day you're going to admit I was right."

"Maybe," I said just to shut her down.

"He's the cat's meow," she said and winked.

I walked away. Sometimes you just had to. After all, Mother had her opinion and I had mine.

I scanned the yard that sparkled under a sky bluer than anything I have ever seen on any of my travels. The sun was sending shards of light sparkling from the mounds of snow. The temperature was only fifteen below zero. Tolerable for a prairie winter day, not so tolerable for a winter that was beginning to beat on the edges of a spring we'd all longed for.

As I looked out into that bleakly beautiful landscape, I came to another realization. I couldn't do this alone and I didn't have to. Russ had already proven that to me. But I needed more. Mother needed more. We needed, it might be an old-fashioned term, but we needed community.

Somehow reaching out to others was appealing. Her friend, Helen had reminded me of that. Maybe it was because I no longer turned to the women I had considered my close friends. I had heard from them occasionally these last months but my world wasn't theirs and I'd noticed lately that conversations had fallen flat. My world wasn't Russ's either, not the world of Alzheimer's despite his experience with his uncle. But somehow, and maybe because of that, he not only understood, but made everything better.

The door shut and I turned around to face Russ.

"The pizza is on the table." He stopped. "What's wrong?" He didn't wait for an answer. Instead he came over and put his hands on my shoulder. "You can't do this nonstop. It's taking a toll. Maybe I could take you out—there's a show you'd love…"

"Russ," I said cutting him off. I would've liked nothing better, but that wasn't going to happen. "I'd love to, but I can't. I have to be here for Mom."

He frowned.

"You're not alone, Cassie. I'll be there for you every step of the way if you'll let me."

"Russ, I can't …"

He hauled me against his chest and kissed me. His lips were soft and then hard, hot with passion. Feeling his strength, his heart beat against mine, my breasts rocking against his chest and it was all too much. I wanted him. And nowhere in my life was there room to have him.

When he let me go I just stood there—shell-shocked, my heart pounding in a good way.

"And not just as friends," he finished. "I want you in my life, Cass."

"We have nothing in common." That was a lie. We enjoyed many similar things, hockey being one of them, time together in high school, another, a hometown—the list went on. But, I said thinking of my broken marriage and pushing away my feelings of never wanting to leave his arms. What I said and what I felt didn't match—not at all. But my circumstances screamed I couldn't have him. I had Mother.

"We have a lot in common. For one, you love your alone time."

It seemed an odd thing to say considering I'd just run through my own list, a list that was slightly more comprehensive. But I was willing to play along—spin this out just a little, see where it went. At least now, in this moment—outside of that, I was still running scared and overwhelmed.

"So do you," I said, and the words almost came out involuntarily.

"That's one of the reasons we'd be good together. Neither one of us is interested in being conjoined at the hip like some couples."

"You can't think of me like that, Russ." I shook my head.

"Like what?"

"In a romantic situation. It's never going to happen." And as final as that statement was I knew by the look on Russ's face and how I felt when I looked at him, that neither of us believed it.

He took my shoulders in a firm grip, drawing me closer. "Damn it, Cass." He kissed me again. This time it was a firm almost rough edged kiss that I only wanted to reciprocate. Instead I shoved back and away from him.

"No." I shook my head. "You want kids eventually and my window for that is closing." I was grasping at reasons. Throwing facts out that we'd never discussed and making presumptions that issues even existed.

"You're wrong there, Cassie. Kids aren't a make or break deal."

"I have Mother." It was my clinching argument.

"And I respect that. But you can have more than that."

This time when he kissed me I leaned in and gave back whole-heartedly, opening my mouth to his and tasting him like I'd only dreamt of in the long nights of these past months.

I wanted him and yet … Sometimes his persistence was grating even while his presence was something I relied on. His kisses? Well they were just more of what I shouldn't have. I longed for him and when he offered what I wanted, I retreated.

I didn't know if I was coming or going in those days—another Mother expression that was a bang-on match.

Russ left shortly after that, not staying to eat with us. He took a piece of pizza with him. I don't know what that meant. If he was angry or even if he'd given up. The latter broke my heart. I spent the next half hour agonizing about the rightness of why I couldn't have Russ.

But I had to face the truth and what was important. My needs came secondary, at least that's what I believed. What I knew was Mother was taking my time. She was rapidly getting worse. I could see the changes in her almost from day to day. Even though I knew it would happen, somehow I waffled between accepting and not accepting it was all leading to an end and I would lose my mother.

I was tired of facing that truth but it didn't seem tired of facing me. I sat for a long time with my head in my hands. I didn't cry or wail or anything like that. I just sat. I don't know what I thought or if I thought anything.

For once I just was.

Chapter Fifteen

April 4

There is no God.

It was an odd thought to wake up to and not one I completely believed. But I'd been struggling with getting my spiritual house in order for some time. It had all come to a head these last months living with Mother. So with a full plate struggling through the narrow straits of Alzheimer's, I added spirituality to the list. I never do things in half-measures so to add to all my other questions, the issues with Mother—all of it, I now questioned my very reason for being. I knew that if I didn't, I'd never come to terms with what was happening to Mother. But I suppose the reality of why I woke up to that thought was because yesterday I'd had the thought I could bargain with God. That's rather a difficult thing to do, bargain with an entity you weren't sure you believed in. I was desperate for any kind of trade-off that would make Mother better or at the least slow down the decline.

It was a quiet breakfast. Mother was no more talkative than me. Later, I settled down in front of the computer—my mind was all over the map. Now, I was researching the possibility of an online class and finally finishing that long ago, prematurely ended education. I'd veered slightly in my thoughts on that. For a mid-life career, psychology seemed appropriate.

"Mom?" Everything was too quiet. The refrigerator breathed little electronic gasps behind me as the motor kicked in. But otherwise, the house was silent.

I found Mother barely coherent in the living room. The pills she still held in her hand told one part of a terrifying story. Too terrifying to go back over those moments. I will only go to where I handed the terror over to someone else after I drove like a maniac straight to the front door of the Hospital Emergency and blocked the entrance to any and all as I carried Mother in.

I was so frightened that I had a hard time letting her go. It took a stern look from a doctor and a gentle nudge from a nurse before I backed up from the stretcher. It was overwhelming. I never want to go through that again. I never want Mother to go through that again.

Mother had her stomach pumped.

I felt like a negligent parent. I didn't have it in me to be responsible for a human life. The best I'd managed so far was a canine, and while that had turned out all right, it still wasn't good training for caring for one's Mother.

It should never have happened. It was those damn pills. There were a variety of pills she'd been prescribed at one time or another—one in particular, sleeping pills. I wasn't sure how she reached them unless she pulled out the stool I'd tucked into the far back of the closet. *Out of sight, out of mind,* I'd thought at the time. Again, I was wrong.

"I can't believe this happened," I said to the doctor, nurse and anyone else who would listen. This time it was a nurse. "Mom just didn't remember. She wasn't depressed, suicidal or anything like that."

"I never thought she was," the nurse replied. "But you might want to consider putting the pills out of sight and out of her control."

"I will. I did. I ..."

As I'd watched Mother disappear down the sterile halls, I prayed she wouldn't be frightened. It had taken all of my will not to run after her. But I realized as I wrestled with my emotion that for once it was more about me needing her than her needing me.

"Why am I so stupid?" Are the first words she said when I saw her after the procedure. "I just wanted a mint."

Even though it wasn't the first time she'd called herself stupid, that time those words broke my heart. She was not stupid. She was a smart woman. She was my mother, and I loved her. And yet we could not deny her memories and intellect were sifting softly out of both of our reach.

"Maybe it's time to see about one of those trials."

"Guinea pig," she whispered and her eyes fluttered as she began to fall asleep.

"Guinea pig, Mom," I agreed. "But a darn cute one." I gave her a kiss on the cheek as she fell into the innocent realm of sleep.

Mother stayed overnight that time. Eventually I went home. I slept little and finally gave in to a cup of tea and an old black and white movie. I couldn't tell you what the movie was about.

I do remember that Bette Davis played in it and Russ showed up somewhere in the middle. He was in his uniform. I guessed he had driven by and seen the living room light on—I didn't ask. That led me to guess he'd done it before—driven by, checking on us, on me. All those crazy words I'd said to him before about not wanting a relationship, about not wanting him, they'd been words I wish I could take back. But there was nowhere to begin back-shoveling the sludge I'd spewed out as my life had crumbled around me. With every crumble he'd been there, and I knew it. He'd been there and I'd wanted him to be there. I couldn't imagine my life now without him. And I couldn't stop saying words that might drive him away.

"I don't have time for anything but Mother," I said while my inner self screamed to shut up. "I don't know if I ever will." Despite all I'd said, Russ stepped over it all. He manned up when I had only let the potential of us down. I've never been held so tenderly in a man's arms—ever.

"I'm failing her, Russ."

"You've doing everything you can. Don't beat yourself up over this."

"It's just so frustrating there are no answers for how to deal with these behaviors." My eyes burned dry but I was still too upset to consider sleep was what I might need.

"What about the latest trial."

"I'm hoping," I said simply. "Really hoping that there'll be one for her soon."

He kissed me gently on the forehead while leading me to

the couch where I snuggled against him. He kissed me again, this time on the lips but still soft and gentle. I wanted more. My pulse raced with desire and my skin was warm where it pressed against his shirt. My barricades to romance were slowly softening, possibly crumbling, as every day my reality changed. The truth of it was he turned me on, especially in his uniform and especially knowing rather than going for coffee — he came to me.

But, despite those feelings, it had been a trying day. I nodded off minutes into his visit and woke up to the sound of sirens in the distance and the quiet hum of the refrigerator. There was a blanket tucked around me. Russ was gone but he'd left me a text message that said he'd be in touch first thing tomorrow and he added an emoji — a heart. My heart skipped at the sight. And it was early that morning before I finally fell asleep again.

Russ phoned me as I was having my coffee the next morning.

Speaking to him not only gave me the courage to face the rest of the day but reminded me I needed to reach out to others, my friends I'd neglected. I phoned one of my girlfriends and the conversation was flat. She was sympathetic but not very empathetic. I listened to her rendition of how someone she worked with had a mother with a similar issue. At least similar to her, to me it had absolutely no relevance. I ended the call quickly.

Thankfully, discharging Mother ran surprisingly smoothly. Immediately after that, we headed straight to the neurologist's office. We'd had the appointment weeks ago and I was glad. Somehow, his abrupt been-there attitude was something I was looking forward to.

Not Mother.

In the foyer of the building that housed the neurologist, a foyer that streamed winter sunlight, my stomach clenched and Mother's fingers dug into my arm.

"Shouldn't we go home," she whispered.

"Soon, Mom. We're going to see the doctor."

"No!"

Mother might be forgetful but I had no doubt she was still

the queen of scene. I had to convince her to keep going and it had to be her choice. I fumbled for a reason. "I have a doctor's appointment," I lied. And, good old Catholic guilt swept through me like a toxic breeze.

"A doctor, you?" She stopped dead with mother-worry plastered across her face.

"It's nothing. A standard check, that's it." I opened the door and put my hand to the small of her back to encourage her inside. The waiting room was full like it had never been before and disconcerting as there were so many in that room that stared back at us with vacant eyes. I closed my mind as I found a seat near the door as if we were both prepared to bolt.

The fact that these people were only varying degrees of the stages Mother might face had me drawn like people are to an accident. I couldn't stop myself from looking, if only briefly. Beside us a man hummed a nondescript tune, his grey hair piping straight up on one side. Kitty-corner to the hummer was a middle-aged man who held the hand of a petite man with a few sprouts of hair who stared vacantly ahead while crossing and uncrossing his ankles. But it was the woman across from us that seemed to have caught Mother's attention. She was a fairly large woman, husky, Mother might have said, and she held a doll as gently as she might have held a real baby as she rocked it back and forth.

"Why on Earth, Cassie Lynn, is that silly woman holding a doll?" Mom's voice hovered somewhere between a whisper and a normal speaking voice.

"Shh," I warned her. A mistake I knew even as the word slipped from me.

"I will not shush. Cassandra, is that any way to speak to your mother?" Her voice rose and a few people glanced over at us.

Across the room, the doll-holding woman began to hum as she rocked.

"Jessica Jane McDowall," the receptionist's voice broke through whatever else Mother might have been about to say.

Despite our down moods, the neurologist was in his usual state of good cheer.

"Shall we check your memory, Jessica Jane?"

"Just Jess."

He breezed right past her name as he always did and began to ask Mother questions. He had her drop from one hundred backwards by sevens.

No problem.

"I want you to remember these three words, Jessica Jane."

"Just Jess," mother said in a rather gripe-filled voice.

"Apple, television, pen."

"Apple," she repeated.

He held up his hand. "I'll ask you them all later."

"What day is it?"

"Thursday," she replied without hesitation. "And hot."

It was actually a cool spring day. The snow hadn't even completely melted.

"Do you know the year?"

She looked at him and then at me. I wanted in the worst way to blurt out the year and contradict the fact that it was hot.

He asked her to repeat the words he had said not two minutes earlier. She shrugged and spun the pencil.

"How many words did I tell you to remember?" he encouraged.

She shrugged again. "Five. But I don't remember which ones."

He spread an assortment of objects on his desk a pencil, notebook, and a bright red miniature toy truck. He swept them away and asked her to write something about her day.

Mother sat for a minute with the pencil in her hand and wrote nothing. The neurologist asked her to tell him how many objects he had placed on his desk for her to look at. After giving him a blank look, she told him two. He nodded as if that was correct and asked her what they were.

Again, she looked blank. I supposed she'd say she didn't know. I must say it was disturbing to see how far Mother had gone downhill since the last visit that had only been weeks before.

Mother pursed her lips, looked thoughtful and told him there was a brush on his desk. Her eyes lit up as if that were correct and then she was on a roll, mirror, chalk and a telephone she added. She smiled brightly, folded her hands in front of her and sat up straighter.

"That's fine," he assured her. "Now can you finish writing something about your day? Just a sentence will be fine."

"Ridiculous," she muttered and picked up the pencil anyway. It took her a minute before she began to write.

Silence sat uncomfortably in the room as we waited. When she dropped the pencil the neurologist took the sheet from her and thanked her as he pressed a button I know summoned the nurse to take Mother away.

He looked at the paper and pushed it aside.

I could see even upside down that Mother had written her name—Jessica Jane McDowall, twice on two separate lines.

"I can't believe she overdosed," I began. "It was an accident. I ..."

"I'm sorry," he interrupted as he leaned back. "It's tough, I know. My father was hospitalized three times before he died. The last time was because he drank detergent."

"Detergent?" I squeaked feeling relieved somehow I wasn't alone in this and panicked there was yet one more commodity to be locked up and another thing I hadn't thought of.

He nodded gravely. "Even considering what I do for a living I couldn't be on top of it all the time. You can't take everything away from them but you need to keep them safe at the same time. It can be a real juggling act."

I nodded at that. That was exactly it.

He ran a finger along his desk. "She scored considerably lower this time than she did the last. I'd like for you to consider a trial."

"Definitely," I agreed, remembering Mother's words in the hospital.

"And I'd like to see both of you again next week. Right now there's nothing in the works that fits her as well as the one that will be beginning shortly. I'll have the information by the end of the week."

When we left the office, Mother turned around once to give a second look to the doll-rocking woman.

"What a beautiful baby," she announced to the world.

That was the last bit of reality we could stand for one day.

I took Mother to a movie after that, a Disney movie that had none of the subtleties Mother might not get.

We indulged in coke and popcorn with extra butter and laughed our way through it all. After the movie, I held Mother's hand all the way to the car.

She skipped like a little girl.

It was just the two of us and that was all that mattered.

Chapter Sixteen

April 11

"I have the information about the trial I told you about on your last visit," the neurologist said.

"It's moving quickly, isn't it?" I whispered.

He said nothing. That was what he tended to do when I was right. Instead we went over the details of the trial. It involved Mother taking a pill a day and checking in with him on a regular basis. It was a second-phase trial and as such it had already been tested on people for dosage, toxicity and such things. That it was second-phase made me feel better, like there was hope. He also mentioned he believed Mother might have temporal lobe dementia. He'd determined that from some of the personality changes I'd mentioned and how quickly the disease was progressing.

"Either way, the trial may slow the disease," he replied. "While your mother has deteriorated quickly, we can't accurately predict how fast the disease may continue to progress."

The man had a scary tendency to read minds.

"But the drug won't do her any harm. Whether it slows her disease, we can only hope. So far there's been a forty percent success rate."

"Stopping?"

"Slowing."

We discussed the requirements, extra visits, and adverse reactions. He handed me a sheaf of papers before he went on to the next issue.

"She'll start wanting to walk more and more. It's one of the hallmark symptoms of the disease," the neurologist warned. "We'll run another MRI later and possibly confirm if this is frontal or not or if there's some sign of infarctions."

The reference to the MRI swished right by. Whether you called it Alzheimer's or something else, I was losing Mother. Whether the disease struck front or middle brain, the end result was the same.

"… locks."

"Pardon me?" I missed everything else he'd said. I had never been so bad at paying attention.

"I'd suggest you alarm the house and put locks on any exiting gates."

It took me a minute to digest that information. "Locks? Why?"

"So she can't get out."

"That's outrageous," I gasped. "I'm not keeping her under lock and key."

"I know it's difficult but I've seen many caregivers broadsided by a lost loved one. One day they're good and when they're not—the day always arrives without warning." He twisted the pen in his hand.

I shook my head. Mother didn't usually walk alone and the few times she had it was just to go around the block for coffee with Helen.

"It might head off any problems if you start going for walks with her on a daily basis. Besides, it's good for her to get stimulation and physical exercise. For some reason exercise has been proven as one of the most effective methods to slow down the disease." He cleared his throat. "Did your physician give you a prescription for sedatives?"

I told him the name of the sleeping pills.

"Keep them on hand. You may need them should she begin to get agitated."

"No, never." I shook my head thinking of the hospital visits.

I almost broke at the look of sympathy in his eyes.

"I make it a point in my work Cassie, never to say never. Sedatives are a last resort but sometimes a lifesaver for the caregiver and even the patient."

I shook my head but he wasn't done.

"More than likely you'll require additional help at one time or another. You may now."

I know I was stone-faced when I looked back at him. We needed no help. If Mother were here she'd say the same.

"Is there anything you want to ask?"

My mind was still whirling at the thought of the extent of potential behavior changes and the reminder that Mother would forget her past and even more of her present. And my thoughts edged tentatively to what I had known for a long time—one day she might even forget me.

There were times when all of it was just too much.

"She's good much of the time." I wasn't sure who I was trying to convince. But it was true. It was just when she wasn't that caused the problem.

"Excellent. Still, you might start giving thought to long-term nursing care. For the future."

I sat up and my stomach did this tight little gurgle-like flip.

"There are only a few places that take advanced dementia patients."

"A nursing home?" It had taken me a minute to catch up to where he was going. "No!"

"Indeed."

I hated when he went into that pseudo-sophisticated style accent of his and yet I truly liked the man.

"I just want you prepared for that day. Nursing care isn't a death sentence."

We agreed to disagree at that point, and he scheduled another appointment.

Still, his talk of nursing care had me feeling slightly bristly for the rest of the day.

"Cassie?" Mother looked at me with questions in her beautiful blue eyes.

It was one of those days when Mother was a little less with it than normal. I knew she sensed something was wrong but she'd lost the words.

"I'm just a little down today, Mom."

"Ice cream."

"You're right," I agreed. There are some simple truths you

learn in childhood you should never forget. Ice cream was one of them. I squeezed Mother's hand and her eyes smiled back at me.

"Ice cream makes everything better."

And that day, it did.

•

The next day found mother and I out for coffee at a coffee shop that was *the* shop to go to. Its coffee was really not much different than the coffee shop's down the street, but their name was gold and Canadians queued up across the country.

"Two coffees," I said to the teenage girl with the bright red bob that clashed with her sullen expression. Her lips were pursed in a rather pissed yet expectant look but her eyes skated right across us with something that looked rather like disdain.

"Double-double," Mother piped up pushing closer and a little ahead of me. She held up two fingers. "And a double dip." That meant coffee and cream times two and a chocolate donut, double coated with chocolate.

It was all a ridiculous, lemming-like affair, this addiction to one coffee shop, I thought. And utterly brilliant, the business side of me was reminded.

I looked around. The small tables were full, covered in a sea of chattering people. There had to be fifty double-doubles that went through the till in the last ten minutes between the drive-thru traffic, the walk-ins and what was already here. The place was a gold mine.

We sat down at the one vacant table in the room.

"You'd be good at something like this, Cassie Lynn," Mother said unexpectedly as if she could read my thoughts. Her elbow was tucked neatly at her side, and her purse was set firmly on her lap. Her attention never veered from me.

"Cassie!" Mother set her coffee down with a slight smack of the cardboard that caused the coffee to slosh and a few drops landed on the table. She pulled out a paper napkin from the stainless steel, utilitarian stand and wiped up the mess. Then she stood up and walked over to the garbage in the far corner where she deposited the napkin. When she came back she carefully took out an outrageous pile of napkins, folded them, and put them in her purse.

"Mom!" But it was too late. I'd watched the whole event nonplussed yet fascinated like I'd arrived at the scene of an accident. I glanced at the now empty napkin dispenser. "You can't take those."

"Why not?"

"They don't belong to you, that's why not."

"Ridiculous."

I gave up. I knew that rational conversation was over and I had just become a partner in a napkin-filching incident. Was there a penalty for such an act? Was I morally culpable because I hadn't wrestled Mother's purse from her clutches and retrieved those napkins? I suspected I just needed to forget the whole incident and be more vigilant next time.

What I didn't expect was a return to normal conversation.

"You should have gone on to university."

"I did," I reminded her. I had quit five classes short of a degree.

"You should have finished," she chastised. "You should have gone into business for yourself. You would have been good at it. Like your father."

"He was good at business?"

"Amazing. Anyone with his talent wouldn't stay here long. Besides, he couldn't. His visa ran out."

"He was foreign," I breathed, sensing finally there would be answers.

"Latino on his mother's side. Cuban on …" She stopped, her eyes on a toddler jumping on and off the bench two seats to our left.

"Latino? Cuban?" I turned my pasty white hands palms down. I look nothing like someone who had Latin blood. Except, my thoughts veered to my full lips. "I'm half-Latina? Cuban?" Why hadn't she said something on our trip? Was that why Cuba had come to her mind? Why she suggested it of all places? The questions reeled one over the other. "Am I half Cuban?"

"Cassie Lynn, you come out with such ridiculous things."

Mother laughed and handed me a napkin as she pushed away her empty coffee cup.

I wiped my mouth dutifully. It had always been Mother's silent sign, handing you a napkin, that something was amiss, some crumb or stain had been left around your mouth that must be dealt with.

"Mother. Who was he?"

"Let's get going before the lunch crowd arrives." She stood up as she said that.

The questions were just piling up. I was terrified in the end I'd be left with nothing but questions.

Chapter Seventeen

There's an old saying about when everything is running too smoothly, there's trouble around the corner. That's not how it's exactly worded but that's the gist of it.

There's truth to those words for two weeks of good luck and easy sailing ended with the microwave being carried out in a body bag.

I blame myself. I was in the yard and left mother in the house on her own. Actually, I was out in the garage only meaning to be there for a minute or two when my phone rang. I had a good eye on the house and yard so I pretty much knew where Mother was at all times. It was a friend I hadn't spoken to in ages and somehow time slipped away from me. Problem was, time slipped away from both of us.

"Cassie!" Mother was flagging me with both hands over her head as she jumped up and down on the back lawn. Smoke was streaming out the kitchen door.

"Mom!"

We were like two parted lovers in a bad movie, both racing to the other. Mother swerved, spun in a pirouette that would have made any ballerina proud. Then I was chasing after her instead of running to her.

"Mom. Stop!" I yelled and hollered a second time, but Mother didn't hesitate. She was heading back into the fray with or without me.

"Jessica Jane!" I tried her given name, as if we were strangers. Sometimes that worked. Not this time.

The kitchen was choked with foul-smelling smoke. The door to the microwave was hanging open and two charred specimens of what might have been the chicken breasts I had planned for supper, smoldered on the glass tray.

"Cassandra Lynn, look at this mess." Mother was standing in front of the microwave with her hands on her hips.

I was only temporarily relieved to see she wasn't in danger, nor was the house burning down. My relief was only a blip in time. Mother wasn't one to remain on the sidelines. She reached toward the microwave that was still billowing smoke.

"No!" I choked, coughed and lunged forward. I was determined to physically pull her back. I should have known that wouldn't work when she danced out of my reach. Mother wouldn't be forced. I firmly believed some days psychology was a field created solely for me with regard to my mother. Some days it wasn't easy and other days it failed. I really needed a course in mother management. Mother was a tough case. It might take a whole series of such classes before I was up to speed.

"Mom, c'mon." I stepped between her and the microwave. Let's go outside. It's a beautiful day."

Mother continued to wave her hands over her head, futilely trying to get the smoke to clear.

I finally convinced her it was better outside. I pulled the plug on the microwave and still kept a firm grip on Mother. I then ushered her outside with instructions to stay as I set up a fan in the kitchen and opened windows to start getting the smoke out.

"Shouldn't we check on that smoke, Cassie?" she asked at least seven times in the next hour. I'd already put in a call to our insurer and lined up an agency expert in preventing smoke damage. In the meantime there was nothing to do but wait for the smoke to clear. And while I waited, I finally pieced together the story.

Mother had decided to turn on the microwave to thaw the chicken breasts that I'd left on the cupboard. Then, she came outside and I could see her putter away in the garden. The thing of it was, I had no idea about the chicken. I assumed they were still on the counter not in the microwave.

My phone rang and it was Russ.

"I'll be right over," he said once he'd heard what happened.

"I just finished a workout and I'm not that far away."

My heart pounded at the thought—of Russ and of how being near him made me feel like a woman. A woman instead of a caregiver.

I knew I was blushing but there was no one who would notice. There was no denying it, I was falling for him. It was the worst time in my life for any of this to happen. And yet, the boy from my past was now the man who'd arrived when I needed him most. I'd never counted on anyone like I counted on Russ. But my feelings for him went much deeper than that. So deep that I was beginning to be afraid of where it all might go or if it could go anywhere at all.

"Cassie." His face was a mask of concern when he arrived. He glanced at Mother who was paying neither of us any attention, and hugged me.

"Russ." I sank into his hard dependable frame, my arms around his neck. "Thank God."

He tilted my chin and bent down and kissed me hot and deep. I clung to him, my fingers creeping to the dark curls that flirted just over his ears. I knew he was ready for a haircut. His hair was just long enough to begin to curl; he never let it get longer than that.

I let go and ran a hand through my own hair. I knew I looked a mess for I didn't have the same grooming discipline Russ had. I didn't have any of his discipline. Hadn't since I'd moved in with mother. I'd been winging it ever since.

"Cassie, you're amazing."

It was as if he saw someone different, not the me who was a mess. There was something soft in the brown eyes that locked with mine and when he bent again and kissed me, his lips hot against mine, it took everything in me not to be lost in that kiss. Moments like these, I had to avoid. I knew that. Instead I thought about them often.

"Your mom is okay?" he asked as if nothing had happened between us.

"Over there picking snapdragons."

He gave me another kiss, light this time. I kissed him back, drawing that kiss out. Knowing I needed so much more from him. More than I'd even admitted to myself. I'd been lying to him and I'd been lying to myself. I couldn't say any of that. Instead, I locked my arms around him and didn't let go.

"Cassie?" There was worry in my name. "Are you all right?" he asked against my lips.

I only shook my head and held him tighter. This time the kiss he gave me was not one of comfort but one that promised so much more. One that offered life and hope, and love. I wasn't sure what I'd ever done without him.

When I finally pulled away I felt like I could face an army or at least the disaster of the kitchen.

Russ. He was everything I needed.

Chapter Eighteen

May 8

Mid-week I thought of Russ. It had been over a week since the micro-wave had almost burned the house down. I'd cleaned up, dealt with insurance and gotten the kitchen back in order. Other than that, there'd been nothing happening in my life, just the same old day to day. I missed the company of someone my age. If I were truthful, I missed him. He'd been working nights and I knew that made staying in touch difficult when he was sleeping when I was awake.

As if conjured by my thoughts, the phone rang.

"What are you doing?" he asked and carried on before I could answer. "I have three tickets to the races."

"Races?" Every doubt I had about everything in my life was in that one word.

"Car races. There's a track just outside the city." He laughed. "I know it's not your thing but I think you need a break. Something different and your mother might enjoy it."

"My mother?" I squeaked.

"She had some interesting comments the last time we saw a souped-up car on the street," he said cheerfully. "Besides, it's a great way to spend a brilliantly warm spring day. C'mon, you'll love it. It's a new experience."

Russ really didn't have to spend that much time convincing me.

A few hours later found us sitting on benches, sucking in exhaust and basking in sunshine to the roar of the cars on the track.

"Do you suppose he's upgraded his ..." Mother stopped with her fingers on her lips and her eyes sparkling. Forgetting words was normal now and she waited for one of us to fill in.

"Trani," Russ said. "Yep, bet it's got the latest powerglide."

He got into details then that I couldn't have cared less about. What I couldn't believe was Mother knew anything about the inner workings of a racecar.

There was something for everyone that afternoon. Even I enjoyed the experience that included something I hadn't had in a long time—cotton candy. But what I remembered most was Russ's hand on mine as Mother got out of the car.

When I turned to him, he leaned down and gave me a kiss that seemed to last just a little longer than all the others that came before.

"Come in," I invited him. "Coffee?"

"I'd like that."

Mother was already heading up the sidewalk, moving quickly toward the familiarity of home.

"She's beat," I said with a smile as if I were talking about my child rather than my mother. It felt that way tonight and not in a bad way—but in a comfortable, easy way that in this moment in time, I'd come to accept. As long as mother was happy and safe, that was all I wanted, all either of us wanted.

I unlocked the door and Mother swept past me.

"Goodnight," she said with a lift of her hand when we were all inside.

I knew she was off to bed.

I followed five minutes later only to make sure that she was all right. She was tucked in and already her eyelids were drooping. I gave her a kiss and turned off the light. I could hear a soft snore before I'd taken more than a few steps down the hall. I'd check on her again later before I went to bed. I always did. This time I shut the door firmly behind me, assured that her sleep was so sound that nothing would awaken her.

Nothing.

And that thought led to another: Russ. All thoughts of coffee were forgotten.

He was in the living room. All six foot three inches of toned muscle and easy personality. I had to push the thought of bed from my mind.

"Would you like to watch a movie?"

"I could think of other things I'd rather do," he said with the hint of suggestion lacing each word.

That had me turning to face him only to find myself in his arms.

He bent down and before I realized his intent, he was kissing me, his lips soft and hard at the same time, his tongue offering hot, passionate caresses against mine. I clutched his shoulders, pushing myself closer forgetting all the naysaying of my past.

He made a sound; it might have been my name, it might have been anything. All I knew was I was tight against him, feeling every bit of him. Knowing he wanted me every bit as much as I wanted him only crushed every barrier I'd built.

I couldn't remember the last time I'd had sex with anyone. But even this one embrace, just seconds in I didn't have to guess where this was going. Where both of us wanted this to go.

He pulled away from me, looking into my eyes as if all the answers were there. His voice, deeper, gruffer than usual, "You're okay with this?"

"Beyond okay," I said as my hand arched over the rounded tight fit of his jeans against his butt. My hand slipped under his shirt feeling hot flesh. And my heart pounded as I drew him down, sliding slightly ungracefully to the couch.

"I want you, Cassie. If we do this—I'm not walking."

I wasn't sure if the fact that he wouldn't walk meant that he was asking me to be his girlfriend or he wanted something more. My hand slipped under his shirt, feeling the heat of his skin.

His lips were on my neck, his hands … The thoughts couldn't be, couldn't compete with what was happening. His hands were in places … I could find no return. As my clothes slipped into the dusky room and his followed, my doubts vanished as well.

Soon there was only Russ, the moment, and a pleasure that took me to the stars and back—and there again.

And again.

It was a night that neither of us would forget— a night I would remember through all the grief I knew was yet to come.

Chapter Nineteen

May 16

"Mom. You don't want that."

"To water the plants."

We were arguing in a back alley, hanging over a dumpster. If I could have projected forward to that moment, I would never have imagined it. But there we were, Mother enraptured with her latest find, and me trying not to pull her physically back before she stuck her hand into … Well, who knows what.

It all began with walking through the alleys that Mother loved. She found them more interesting than the street. It was quieter back there as we strolled together. It was relaxing until Mother acquired the new passion for dumpsters.

Dumpsters are not my friend.

I learned that the day Mother removed her first find. A bright red plastic jug with black marks and a dented spout whose original purpose was obscured by a stained and mostly removed label.

"Plants," she said and smiled.

"We have a perfectly good watering can. Put it back." I put my hand on her arm. I'm not sure what I planned to do, maybe a sneak attack and pry the offending container from her hand. Maybe I was attempting to ground her in reality with that touch on her arm. "It's garbage."

I knew as soon as I said what I did, it was the wrong thing to say.

She hung on to the container, shook my hand from her arm and reached in with her free hand and pulled out a worn and semi-deflated soccer ball.

I hovered somewhere near her left shoulder, while I helplessly fished for a solution to the new dilemma and tried not to breathe as the rotted remains of food and who knew what wafted up to me. I hunted for a diversionary tactic but I was drawing blanks on brilliant strategies. I had to settle.

"Look, Mom," I said and pointed down the alley. "Isn't that Helen?"

She looked briefly before her attention veered back to the dumpster.

I held my breath. "And she's with Russ," I added, thinking there might be a better success rate with higher numbers. It didn't seem to matter. She was only slightly interested in my diversion populated by imaginary sightings.

She glanced at me, dropped the soccer ball and held on to the jug. Apparently it was a keeper.

"I think Helen is waving to us." It was just another lie to add to the thousand or so I was already responsible for.

Finally she turned away, still clinging to the jug.

"Do you want me to carry that?" I pointed to the jug, praying she would relinquish her prize.

She handed it over and I took it gingerly aware of the slime that clung to one corner. I waited until her attention was on the stink weeds flowering behind a neighbor's fence before I tossed the jug into a cluster of weeds on the opposite side. I didn't care if it was littering. I wasn't taking that jug home with me.

Mother was raised to be frugal. Everything could be reused according to my grandmother, and now I supposed those teachings were coming back, memories of the past. Wasn't that what the neurologist said? When the present failed us we went to the past?

Sometimes I avoided the back alleys and thus the endless fascination of the dumpster. But I could only avoid the alleys so long because Mother pulled my hand every time we passed one. And, they made her happy. I couldn't deprive her of that because she was already deprived of so much. To see interest light in my mother's eye again, well, I'd put up with a mountain of smelly garbage for that.

I don't know how many dumpsters I'd seen the inside of over those days of dumpster addiction, but Mother began stopping at every one. At first I was humiliated and furtively glanced around to see who might be watching. But like every repeated behavior, after a while, no matter how bizarre, it becomes the norm. I'm embarrassed to admit that once or twice I spotted treasures before Mother. I couldn't help myself. You didn't see the joy on her face.

Later that week we were on our usual walk, only that time I hesitated at the alley. I don't know why, intuition, maybe. But Mother was pulling at my hand and I allowed her to take the lead. That was before I realized what her lead entailed. The dumpster mid-alley was chock full of smelly goodies that had Mother in a half lope to get there.

"Mom, no." I thought of what germs might be in that fetid pile. I always tried to steer Mother to the cleaner dumpsters— if there was such a thing.

Mother ignored me. She was happily wading through the over-stuffed dumpster. She chortled as she came up for air with a sweater in her hands.

"Mom, that's garbage."

"Perfectly good." She held the sweater out in a gesture that only meant I should try it on.

"No." I stepped away from the rotted mess of refuse that was trickling into the alley.

She shook the sweater and a bit of black plastic drifted to the ground. She shook it again like a matador.

I tried not to grimace at the broken bit of macaroni that slid off one sleeve, and my eyes flitted to the fly that buzzed by Mother's left ear.

"No." I shook my head.

Mother dropped the sweater. But she wasn't done.

An oversize pink jersey followed and I silently cursed the people who could throw perfectly usable clothes away. Perfectly usable clothes that tempted Mother in ways I couldn't understand. I resisted the urge to rip the soiled garment from her hands. I had no tolerance for that dumpster; it stank and was just nasty.

"Mom, let's go home."

"Okay." She dropped the sweater and took my hand.

Sometimes, it was just that easy. Problem was I never knew from one moment to the next which way she'd swing. I upped my pace. Mother was almost running to keep up, but I didn't want her attention to lock on another dumpster. No matter how happy it made her, that day I'd had enough.

At home I pulled out one of Mother's big band CDs and put it on. I cranked the volume like the music would blow the memory of that walk from every corner of the house.

Mother's face lit up as Tommy Dorsey's band kicked into high gear. She held out her hand.

I took it without a second thought.

She led and she did it well. She could have danced with a goat, she was still that good. Even her balancing issues seemed to disappear.

"Slow down, Mom," I gasped after twenty swirling laps of the kitchen.

She looked at me, twirled me around with a laugh and then let me go and did three spins for good measure. The dance we did was not one I could name and not one that fit the music and it didn't matter. I collapsed on the cool linoleum with Mother and we laughed. What we were laughing about I couldn't tell you. It just felt good to sit side by side and laugh, her laughter propelling mine and vice versa.

Chapter Twenty

May 30

With destiny taking me forward like an unmanned rocket, my lack of beliefs nagged at me. My time for spiritual discovery was limited. If I was losing my mother, I wanted to know before I lost her, who or what I was losing her to.

I was already going to church, truthfully, taking mother. But whatever the reasons for being there, they weren't helping much. I wasn't acquiring any blinding insight on life after death, if it even existed. I suppose sacrifice wasn't enough. Maybe I actually had to believe in the religion in which my childhood had been steeped.

Everything was confusing.

Me.

Mother.

Mother was remembering less and less, and I was struggling to figure out what to do to keep us both moving forward, both engaged in life and both sane.

"Mom, where's your Bible?"

She shrugged.

"I want to start reading the Bible," I began to explain. But I wasn't so sure I did. I just wanted to begin—somewhere.

"Ridiculous." She turned back to her game of solitaire.

She had a point. The last time I'd looked at the Bible it had been high school ethics.

I spotted the Bible on the lower shelf of a side table. I picked it up gingerly. Just having it in my hands made me reconsider my approach. It was thick and intimidating—rather like *War and Peace* but with a much wider influence. I set it down with a promise that I wouldn't completely ditch the idea.

Meantime, Mother slapped the Jack of Spades on the Queen of Clubs. Outside, darkness had settled and we were in that grim morass between supper and bedtime. We didn't go out after dark. We hadn't since the time we arrived home and it was dark outside. Mother got out of the car and then refused to leave the safety of the garage. I spent over three-quarters of an hour trying to convince her to leave with every reason I could think of for why it was safe to do so. I finally turned on the outside light to the garage and rushed to the house to turn on the outside light I had forgotten to turn on earlier.

Then, for good measure, I even turned on the decorative lights that bordered the lawn. It was only then Mother emerged from the garage, but she clung tightly to my arm the entire way. Once we were in the house she insisted on turning on every light and making sure all the locks were engaged.

Mother hated the outside darkness. She wasn't scared in the house, even with the lights off. But the outside, that was a different matter. I never figured out exactly where that fear came from. I suspected it was a simple matter like maybe the darkness disorientated her. I had it scheduled on my list of questions to ask the neurologist at our next visit.

Meanwhile, every evening we were locked safely in our house as soon as darkness began to descend. At first I found it rather confining, almost scary in a way like we were under lockdown in a prison. Eventually I got used to it as I suppose you can get used to anything.

Some evenings I used to get things done around the house. The cleaning duties that often didn't get done in the day I scurried around to complete. And Mother, well she had her own nightly rituals. Every evening she hauled out a deck of cards. She used the same old deck of cards, smooth and ratty around the edges. I tried giving her a new deck but those were familiar and she refused anything new. I assumed it was the change. Whether I was right or wrong it was hard to tell. I tried asking Mother.

"Good enough," she said shortly and pushed the new deck aside.

I supposed that after my ninth or so attempt at changing up the playing card situation, even Mother was tired. She often headed off to a too-early bedtime. She'd begun to find refuge in sleep and would sleep twelve or more hours if I let her. And, I hated to admit it, sometimes it was a relief not to be on duty and I didn't always discourage her retreat.

Somehow my mood crashed after that. It was one of those nights that brought me down, trashed me, rolled me around and made me struggle to see there was any hope at all. And I couldn't even say that anything had happened, not anything different from the norm. That's just how it was. Some days you could handle reality and other days reality broadsided you. That's how I was feeling when the phone rang.

"Cassie."

Russ's voice alone was a pick-me-up.

"I was just thinking of you," he said before I could say a word past hello. "I've got my hands on a movie I thought you'd like. Mind if I come over?"

"Sure. But I'll warn you I'm bad company."

"That's why I'm bringing my own entertainment," he said cheerfully.

He was there twenty minutes later, and in thirty we were sharing the couch and a bowel of popcorn. The movie was perfect. It was a comedy with one of my favorite actors. And when the credits finally rolled I had to wipe the tears from my eyes and for the first time in a long time, they were good tears—laugh tears.

"It's getting tough," he said as he took the empty bowl of popcorn and set it on the coffee table.

That was the thing about Russ. He had the ability to head for the gloppy, sticky heart of any problem. Me, I'd rather avoid it—all of it. Nothing changed if you talked or even prayed about it. I already knew no amount of pleading with my shaky God had changed anything.

He took my hands between his. "I wish I could help, Cassie."

"No one can." *Not even God,* I wanted to say. He didn't answer requests—or maybe he did and I wasn't on the list. "I started going to church with her."

"I'm glad."

That wasn't what I'd expected. I knew Russ wasn't a churchgoer. In fact, he'd declared himself a contented agnostic before he'd graduated high school. Not long ago, he'd hinted his thoughts on religion had evolved more into a belief in a higher power that could be housed by no religion or house of worship.

He squeezed my hand, drawing me closer to him. I could feel his comforting heat, the hard muscle of his chest.

"Religion isn't simple, is it?" I asked. They were big questions and not something that would be solved in a single sitting. "I suppose it's not just where are we going but why are we here."

Another too-big subject but I had thought about it especially after Mother's revelations about giving up her dream.

Russ sat silent and let me talk.

"Maybe our passion is why we're here? Like you with hockey?" I asked and it was a relief to slant my questions to something I might be able to answer.

"Maybe," he said with a frown.

Everyone had a passion, or if they didn't, there was much talk about finding one. Mother's had been dance. Russ's was hockey. Mine, investing. We had all modified our dreams in one way or another to mold to whatever curve life had thrown us.

"You know—I still love watching a good hockey game," I said.

"You always were a rink rat," he agreed looking obviously confused at the turn in the conversation.

"That was years ago," I admitted. "Now it's TV all the way. No hard benches and cold rinks for me." I crossed my legs and looked him in the eye. "Why'd you give it up? You were on the farm team, playing hockey. Professional. They were paying you to do what you love."

Silence kind of sat uncomfortably in the middle. I leaned forward and he leaned back.

He ran his fingers through his hair. "I don't know, Cass. I guess maybe that's something I've always struggled with. Pride. I couldn't downgrade my dream. I wanted to play in the

THE TEARS WE NEVER CRIED 141

NHL not on some obscure farm team."

"If you weren't one of the best you weren't playing?"

"Exactly."

"But you play on a rec league now."

"And I'm the best player they have." He laughed but this time it was rather disparaging.

"I imagine you are."

He shrugged. "Okay, maybe I do like being the star player. But it's a ritual every Tuesday and Thursday night whoever can make it is there. Sometimes I think it's more about the friendship than it is about the game."

"Like family," I whispered.

"Exactly. A crazy kind of family, but after all that's what family is all about, people you care about."

"I don't know who my father is," I blurted.

"What?" he said turning. "I thought ..."

"Tom." I shook my head. "We all thought. He's an obvious choice as he was married to Mom and I called him Dad. But Mom told me months ago she had an affair. From the little she said, what was clear was I'm not his." I shook my head. "I should be sad about Tom. But I'm not."

He took both my hands in his. "This was the first you've heard of it?"

"Yes. Just before we went to Cuba. She was in Toronto alone for New Years the year I was born. That's where she met him."

He squeezed my hand.

"Is it for sure? I mean that Tom isn't your father and ... Do you know his name?"

"No, not fully. Mom won't or can't give me full details but she's outright stated about the affair, and that I'm not Tom's child. That was pretty clear even though she only said it once."

"But is it true?"

"I think so, Russ. Something in my gut tells me this is the truth. I'm not Tom's."

"Not wishful thinking."

I shook my head. Russ knew what I thought of the man who'd walked out on mother and left the two of us alone. I'd mentioned my disdain of the man when his name had come up the first time he'd taken me for coffee. He knew that Tom had left without a word to me and never come back. "After she outright said I wasn't Tom's child she hinted that my father is Latino. She refers to him as Fidel."

"Do you want to find him?"

I nodded and I don't know why but I began to cry.

"Ah, Cass." He put an arm around my shoulders.

My heart thumped as he twisted, his face a little too close to mine.

He kissed me, his body hot and hard against mine. But we could hear Mother through the crack I'd left so that her door was not completely shut. She wasn't sleeping easy tonight not like she had in past nights. The reminder of the restlessness of her sleep made intimacy beyond a kiss not an option, not that night.

Still, just having him close was enough. By the time Russ left, my equilibrium, my confidence, my very soul had returned. I knew no matter what happened, I could do this.

Chapter Twenty-One

Despite a rocky entrance into spring, June was beautiful that year. The pseudo summer-like days melted one into the other with temperatures that made one want to do nothing but lounge on the deck.

"What do you think about having a party, Mom?"

Mother swirled a dainty circle on one toe, her arms spread out and her skirt twisted in delicate folds around her ankles. "That would be lovely."

I was surprised. I hadn't expected that. So why had I floated the party balloon out there? It was hopeful, possibly wishful thinking on my part. I had been prepared to produce the party card again and again, coaching her through one negative response after another in the hopes of eventually convincing her that it was a good idea. It meant everything that Mother had been receptive.

"This weekend," I suggested. "The weather is supposed to be gorgeous."

"Root beer."

"Okay, Mom. Root beer." I couldn't expect totally rationale answers all the time. But in light of everything, we'd have root beer. Obviously it was another early memory that had just shadowed Mother's murky thoughts.

"And rum and coke," she added and grinned, taking my hand. She made me twirl that time. "It'll be fun, Cass." She dropped my hand and danced her way across the yard leaving me to plan the event.

I knew right off there wouldn't be many people. Just an informal gathering of the people I had come to count on these last months, Mother's friends and of course, Russ.

Saturday came quicker than I anticipated. Even Mother was bubbling with excitement although she kept asking me what we were doing. I patiently explained. She nodded happily and twirled every damn time. At least a dozen times before I lost count.

By three o'clock in the afternoon we were both more than ready for company that didn't involve each other.

"Doorbell," Mother sing-songed and looked at me to get up and answer it.

Mother wasn't into answering doors anymore—or company. But the barbecue had shifted her company aversion paradigm. I had no idea why but intuition had told me it would. I supposed no one would know the real reason, not even the neurologist. On a whim I'd initiated the barbecue and on a whim I'd invited him too. It seemed only fitting, as he had been such a support for both Mother and me.

"I'd love to, Cass. And I'm thrilled that you asked. Most of my patients don't think of me like that, a friend."

"We'd be lost without you," I told him.

"I can't stay for long but I'll slip in for a drink. Probably earlier than later."

Henri was the first to arrive. He was widowed and one of those men who was just more comfortable with women than men. While he wasn't gay, he was what I'd call slightly feminine. Strangely enough he brought another man, Albert, with him. I didn't have time to consider what that meant. Maybe I had been wrong about Henri all along. Not that it mattered. He was a friend and whoever Albert might be, he seemed like a nice man.

The neurologist was next. Even dressed down, he was dressed up. He looked smaller than usual even though he was exactly my height, five foot nine. But his white tennis shoes and Bermuda shorts seemed almost preppy and out of place.

"What a fabulous yard," he gushed.

That surprised me, I hadn't thought of him as a gusher. But everything aside, I liked him. And like everyone else he was different outside of the confines of the place of his employment.

"Jessica Jane," he enthused like he had missed every

moment she was out of his sight. "Good to see you."

He took Mother's hand like she was an old friend and the two of them grinned at each other like school kids.

Five minutes later Elvis swung into *Blue Suede Shoes* and Mother's eyes lit up. The neurologist put his drink aside and held out his hand. "Shall we dance?"

"Yes," Mother replied.

And the two of them danced around the lawn with surprising agility. After two iced teas, the neurologist left, leaving Mother smiling and waving as his car pulled away.

The neurologist. Alphonse. He had been the most mulled over invitation to that small gathering. Now it appeared he had turned out to be one of the best. For Mother it had sealed her confidence in the man I considered our lifeline. Lifeline and the neurologist were pretty much a mantra in my thoughts.

Outside I watched Henri's friend Albert corner another of Mother's friends, Eleanor, who looked pained.

"Turnover in the end zone," I heard Albert say in a voice full of passion for the sport. I grimaced. One thing I knew about Eleanor was she hated sports. I dived in hoping to save the situation.

"Albert, have you met Helen?"

He shook his head and I led him none to gently by the hand over to Helen who regularly went to football games and watched any and all sports on television.

"This party was a great idea, Cass," Russ said as he came up to me, a drink in one hand that was also juggling a loaded smoky on a bun. Your mother seems to be having a good time. I've never seen her so animated."

"I didn't know how it would turn out," I admitted. "But everyone has been so good to me. I just wanted to have a party for all Mother's friends and support network."

"I know what you mean. Strange isn't it? They're an older generation we would never have considered partying with except for—" He blushed. "Well you know."

I knew what he meant. Except for Mother's dementia. It was something neither of us wanted to mention on a hot summer-like day with nostalgia in the form of Elvis rocking in the background, and drinks in hand.

"To good friends." He raised his glass and we clinked the glasses together each taking a long drink as our attention went to the gathering. We were silent for a minute just watching Mother swirling amidst people who mattered in her life.

"Where did you get these?" Russ broke the solemn moment as he motioned to the smoky. "They're the best I've tasted in a while."

"They were Helen's idea. She suggested the Ukrainian Deli."

"Excellent. And your mother, she really got into this. I'm glad, Cass."

"Me too. I was kind of scared how this might turn out." I looked around at the dozen people scattered in our backyard. The warm evening air drifted around us, and wafted the tantalizing smell of smokies and burgers through the yard while Elvis crooned some of his earlier tunes. "It's like I'm collecting memories."

"If that's the case. You're doing a fantastic job."

"I'm making the best of a bad situation."

"You're a warrior, Cass. There are not many women who would move in just to keep their mother in her own home out of a …"

"Stop, Russ." I knew what he was going to say, nursing home. "I'm no more warrior than you. It's just that I love her so much. I couldn't see her going to one of those places. And you know, the hardship is not being with Mom." I shrugged. "She has her own guilt to deal with. She had to place my grandmother in a home and I don't think she ever got over it. I couldn't do the same to her."

"I know that, Cass, I mean not about your grandmother." He lifted one shoulder, the sun glinting off his hair, "That you'd do anything for her. That's what makes me admire you even more."

He was making me blush.

"You know." I hesitated to say this, maybe because it made our relationship more intimate than it could be. "You always have my wing. Thanks."

He chuckled. "Well, if that's all I get for now, consider it done. I've got your back."

"Wing," I corrected. "I couldn't do it without you," I said and I meant every word of it. But it seemed the more he was around, the more I realized I needed him in other ways.

"Cassie," he said gravely. "Some day we have to talk about us."

Despite my thoughts, my logical self kind of fled at that notion.

"I don't know why I never looked you up. Maybe time has a way of getting past us. Maybe I thought you were only a school boy crush. I realized when I saw you again after all those years that you were the one for me."

"Russ, no. I …"

"Don't say it. I know now isn't the time. Not here, and not while you're taking care of your mother. But someday."

Only the music and the chatter of other voices drifted around us for quite a few minutes. What Russ said had struck a nerve in me. I might not have agreed with the beginnings of our relationship but I knew that in any other circumstance I would have said without a qualm, that Russ was the man for me.

I couldn't contemplate that now for all the essence of my being had to be directed to Mother. For now, she was my everything. But I was beginning to put more consideration into the fact that all of this, my time with Mother, would end, and it wouldn't end well.

"I can't imagine her gone." I ran my finger along the edge of the lawn chair. "I keep hoping it's all a bad dream. If I give up enough maybe the cosmos will accept that in exchange." My voice hitched and I had to concentrate to get control. This was no place to lose it. "Silly, I know."

"Don't," he said softly. "You've got to live in the moment. That's one thing you can learn from your mother. Look at her."

Mother was twirling around the yard in perfect time to a song I couldn't quite name. And she wasn't alone. The music was Mother's choice and already she'd encouraged a few of the women to shed their shoes and dance barefoot on the freshly cut lawn.

I laughed the first time I saw her do it. The second time I hauled out the camera. No matter where Mother's new lack of inhibition came from, it was contagious.

Chapter Twenty-Two

June 20

I don't know why my thoughts are all over the map. Maybe it's nerves. I know that's what Mama would have said. She blamed many things in life on nerves or in some cases, a lack there of. She never accused me of not having nerve. She accused me only of being just a touch too impulsive. Maybe she was right. I know I did marry Tom without adequate consideration, I believe she said a year or two after the deed was done.

I married, I suppose, because I was a few years away from thirty, which was old in those days to still be single. I was an only child and Mama had told me often enough of wanting grandchildren. Instead I was wasting precious time she always said longing to dance. And I did dance, through my twenties while working part-time at paying jobs. But somehow I was affected by the pressure to get married, maybe it was a combination of what I thought I should do and what wasn't happening, my dance career. I don't know. I used to think of it all often, in the early years before Cassie.

Sometimes I think of how things might have been if it had only been Cassie and me, if I had never married Tom. Would I have bundled her up and pursued my dream? Would I have taken up that offer to perform a dance routine evenings in little theatre? And what would have come out of that? I only imagine bigger opportunities. All pipe dreams I know, but sometimes I think about what might have been. Maybe when Cassie is grown up I'll consider getting involved in the arts. In an amateur capacity of course.

I've always wanted to be a professional dancer. Even though in the end I was only fooling myself. Mama always said I was good at that. What I wasn't good enough at was dance. I didn't make the cut. And everything that followed after that, Tom, the mistakes I made with him … I have to admit that now, my marriage was bad but I think maybe it wasn't all Tom's fault.

I had opened Mother's diary that morning with anxious fingers. It was like coming home to a world that felt oddly unknown and yet strangely comforting. It was Mother's world and it was a place where I was only a visitor.

I thought about Mother through the years. No matter what she said, she'd been good. But I know in the arts, good isn't the only factor. There's opportunity that meshes with fierce competition. It might have only been a case of wrong place, wrong time.

As I thought back over what she'd written I don't think after her marriage ended she was sad—at least I hoped not. Maybe her dreams had changed as she'd aged, as all our dreams do. Maybe it was as simple as that. I closed the book and stood up. I wanted in the worst way to talk to her. And as the chances of that were now remote, I took her shopping instead. Thirty minutes later found us in a bookstore and twenty minutes later we ran solidly into a problem.

"Cassie."

"Yeah, Mom."

"Are these books free?"

"No, Mom. This is a bookstore. The books cost money. See." I flipped the book I held around to where she could clearly see the price marked on the back.

I was looking for more information on Cuba. The country had intrigued me in our short visit and I thought poking deeper into its history would be an enjoyable pastime through the long evenings when we were cloistered in the house.

"Ridiculous," she announced on seeing the price. "Costly," she finished.

"That's the price of books these days, Mom."

Mother's pricing seems to have settled somewhere in the mid-nineteen-eighties. She was forever amazed at the price I was willing to pay for things.

Her attention shifted to another shelf. She began to flip

through a coffee table book as I turned my attention back to the history shelf.

I was in luck and found two books. One that was written by a former Cuban national and focused mainly on the revolution. I was more thrilled about the second book, a history of the country that dipped back even further to its Spanish influence. For someone with no interest in history, my interests seemed to be changing. We poked around the bookstore for another forty-five minutes before I thought we might be pushing our luck on Mother's attention span.

It wasn't until we were out the door with my purchases under my arm that I saw Mother had two books in her hand. They were pocket books she had tucked under her right arm and with her sweater hanging loose over her shoulders, I'd failed to see them. Apparently, so had everyone else. No buzzers had gone off and no floor walkers had spotted her. I don't know how she did it. I suppose I'll never know. But what I knew then was a sense of panic we'd just been branded thieves.

"Mom! Where did you get those?"

It was a redundant question. I knew where she'd gotten those books. From the bookstore we had just left. She had hovered just behind me as I'd paid for my books and followed me out the door. She'd never gone nearer than ten feet to a till.

"You didn't pay for them." There was a pain that was more a dull ache somewhere in the vicinity of my left upper ribcage. I wasn't sure if it was panic or something more serious.

She looked at the books in her right hand. She held them up and her eyes lit up. Her cornflower blue eyes were wide and innocent, and every bit as surprised as I was. Fortunately, she was missing all of the horror I was feeling. One of us had to remain calm after all, like Bonnie and Clyde, we might be running for it. I'm ashamed to admit that was my first instinct.

"Mom, we have to take them back."

"No."

She took a step away from me as if I meant to take her books away from me then and there. I have to admit the thought was there. But there were a lot of thoughts, and I wasn't sure which one I would act on. The whole situation was completely unprecedented and unfortunately, unexpected.

"What did you get?" she asked with surprising interest.

"Cuban history," I said and briefly forgot the immediate problem as I shifted the books, hiding titles.

I remembered the third book in my hand, *The Caregiver's Guide to Dementia*. I hated the title and I had it tucked beneath the other two. It was a book to read like I had read many as a teenager, out of Mother's sight. I didn't want her to see that book because it would be like waving a red flag and reminding Mother of the nightmare she had to battle every day. The other book, I also had well hidden, something about spirituality and the modern woman. I wasn't sure if I was ready to go down that road.

"Mom, you have to take the books back."

"I will not. I want to read about Cuba. The only man I loved was from there."

"What?" It was the only word I could say as I stared at her in shock.

"You heard me, Cassandra Lynn."

And I knew because her eyes had taken that angry sheen that was becoming disturbingly familiar and her words were flat and without any compromise—that there'd be no more words on the matter, any matter.

I bit back the questions and filed what little information she'd just provided. I needed to address the situation. "Mom, give them to me, please. We have to at least pay for them."

I gently took an edge of the books but her grip wasn't loosening. Short of ripping the books from her hands, I wasn't sure what to do.

"Okay, let's go back and …"

"I want to go home."

Her lips were pursed in that thin line she had when she was annoyed about something. Her eyes glittered and I knew she was pissed. I was getting nowhere. So I led her to the car, stolen books and all.

I got her settled and scooped up the books that lay in her lap. I was lucky, because she didn't notice me do what she might have considered a dastardly deed.

I was feeling that sweet edge of relief a little prematurely.

I knew when her eyes met mine that she knew what I had in my hand. What I was threatening to take from her.

"Give me those back, Cass." Her voice rose and her cheeks began to flush.

"They're not paid for."

"They're mine."

Before I could get out of her reach she had both hands on the books and she was wrestling me for them. I could overpower her. That was never a question. I wasn't going to that place.

"Mom, wait here. Don't move." I gave up control of the books and hoped that my word might be good enough. After all, who was crazy enough to return to a store without merchandise and attempt to give that store money. Surely they'd believe me. I took a picture of the books and their barcode in the seconds before mother swept them out of my reach. I hoped she'd stay put. She seemed to like the car and previous experience had shown she was content to sit inside and wait for me. Except those times I had her in view.

I was taking a chance and feeling slightly queasy about it as I locked the car. I had already thought slightly ahead as I'd parked her in the backseat with the child safety-lock on for good measure.

I jogged across the parking lot with what I'd done to Mother, locking her in the car, at the front of my mind. I kicked the jog into a run.

I'm not sure how many people would go to those lengths of honesty. And I had to admit that I'm more like Mother than I imagined. Whether that was a good or a bad thing I had no further time to contemplate as I was hit by a blast of over-air-conditioned air that threatened to freeze parts of me well covered.

I headed up to the front counter empty-handed and debated what I'd say even with the pictures. I veered and headed for the shelves where I picked up two identical copies of the books Mother had in the car. Then I jogged back to the counter. Time was a premium. Mother was alone in the car and who knew how long the child safety would work. Mother might have the capacity of a toddler but every once in a while her lucidity came back for long enough to make her dangerous.

It took quite a bit of explaining and a request for a manager blared over the intercom before anyone seemed to make heads or tails out of what I was telling them.

I may have been labeled crazy that day. I couldn't have cared less. I walked out of that store proud to be my mother's daughter.

•

Later that evening I spooned us both out ice cream with chocolate sauce. We ate the first serving, and I was spooning more in my bowl even as mother began to nod off. I put the ice cream in the freezer as I heard her head down the hallway, the toilet flush and her bedroom door close. She'd gone to bed.

I pulled the bowl back out and dug into the ice-cream. With ice-cream, I was like an alcoholic going for the drink they promised would be the last but never was.

The doorbell rang and I stopped mid-scoop. I opened the door to a uniformed Russ.

"I just wanted to check in on my way to work." He frowned and took an uninvited step in. "Cass, what's wrong?"

I think my eyes were watering. Some days it just seemed like too much. I shook my head and managed to mutter that nothing was wrong, not really. He had his hands on my shoulders and folded me against him. We stood like that for a minute maybe two before he let me go but not before bending down and offering a kiss with no passion, nothing but a promise to be there. It meant more to me than any other kiss I'd ever received from him—even those hot with passion. At times like this, all I needed was someone to lean on and Russ not only promised me that, he delivered. It was everything.

"Thanks."

"No thanks needed," he said as he lifted a strand of hair from my cheek and his lips warmed a soft dance against mine.

I was feeling much better when I shut the door to a draft of cool air and Russ's broad shoulders heading down the walk.

Better?

That was a lie. I felt like I could face the mountain again. I could do this.

I took a deep breath.

When I checked in on mother after he left, I found her asleep. I went back to the kitchen and washed the remains of my now melted ice cream down the sink. I didn't need a weight problem to add to my troubles.

Chapter Twenty-Three

I asked Tom to leave over a month ago. His being gone, even with money tight, is the best Christmas present I could have. I need nothing more and Cassandra is still so little that a new doll is all it takes to make her happy—that and her Christmas sweets.

I signed up to be a hospital volunteer. It's something I've been meaning to do for quite some time. Now Cassie is spending Sunday afternoons at the library in a children's program so it works out perfectly. The first day I was assigned to a ward where there are many chronic and terminally ill people. I only hand out snacks, smiles and a word or two. I didn't think it would bother me like it does but I've never faced so much death nor have I seen so much acceptance. It makes me feel like I have faced few obstacles in my life in comparison to others.

Then a few weeks later:

I find myself putting on my old dance music. We've progressed from the tango to other steps. Someday I'd love to learn the salsa. It reminds me of Fidel. So many things remind me of him. Especially, of course, Cassie. He would have loved her if he'd known. But he could never know. And now, of course, he's gone.

July 11

Mother was gone.

It was late afternoon and a collection of hours that I will never forget.

"Stay in the yard," I remembered, calling after Mother. She

had been antsy again so I'd thought that roaming around the backyard would be good for her. She always stayed in the yard. And I had no doubts she would that time. The neurologist had said people like Mother would eventually have an insatiable urge to walk and he'd been right. He'd also said they would forget their boundaries. I had thought he was wrong. Again, unfortunately, he was right.

I was so sure, right up until that day, that Mother wasn't a wanderer. The outside world was beginning to frighten her. And I hated to say it now but that was my trump card. I knew she'd remain in the area where she felt safe.

I should have been smarter than that. Her behavior had changed numerous times in a short period of time. I think early summer was one of the most trying times. That day in July certainly was.

I remember looking out the window and seeing the grass in need of cutting, the scraggly hedge in need of trimming and the non-existent garden. I realized then what was missing in my view of the yard: Mother.

I remember running out the door and stumbling as panic had all systems on alert and jangling in a discordant variety of directions. I remembered stuffing that panic back where it belonged. There was still the possibility Mother was in the front yard or had even made a short trip down the alley. She wasn't there. She wasn't with any of the neighbors either.

"I've lost Mom," I puffed into the phone. I'm surprised I could even puff, that I could still breathe. The panic had just relocated itself and was firing off in every nerve ending. The phrase—I didn't know if I was coming or going—was taking on a very real meaning. Somehow I knew Russ would know what to do. Me—I'd lost all sense of reality right after I realized I'd lost Mother.

"How long has she been gone?" Russ followed that question with a few others and soon had all the relevant information I hadn't thought to volunteer.

"We'll find her, Cass. I'll report this. In the meantime, get a hold of anyone you know who would be willing to help search." He then gave me details on how I should divide the neighborhood into quadrants and once that had been exhausted expand the search. He also suggested I call Leah. He said more firmly than I had ever heard him, that there was no way I should drive in my condition.

I didn't question what he meant. I was swirling in a black fugue—panicked.

"One more thing—transfer her landline to your phone. If anyone has found her we'll have both numbers covered."

We disconnected after that.

"Mom," I whispered. "Please be all right."

I took a breath, picked up the phone and began calling. The seconds ticked dangerously that day as I rallied outside help.

"Helen, I've lost Mom." It was no time for intros or soft-soaping a conversation.

"Tell me what to do," she said without hesitation.

I assigned her one of the neighborhood quadrants that Russ had outlined.

It was ten minutes later when I'd exhausted the list of people who were near at hand and possibly close enough to Mother and me and, of course, physically able. It was a sadly small list I realized as I put my phone in my pocket.

We were all out looking that day a collection of her friends and mine; Helen, Georgette, Leah and Henri. There was no need to mention Russ. He assured me if Mother was anywhere in the city I needn't worry; we'd find her.

"She's alone. Someone could mug her, take advantage …"

He took me in his arms then and just held me. "She'll be fine. We'll find her."

I clung to his words. They were what kept me sane through the long hours that followed.

The police checked in immediately, and a car was soon scouring back alleys beyond the quadrants Russ had drafted.

And Russ, after the first check in with me, voluntarily placed himself in the position of police liaison despite the fact that he was on holiday for another two weeks. I learned that day that public transit and taxi service all linked in to police broadcasts for missing persons.

The sky was clouding three hours later and Mother was still missing. The forecast was for a severe thunderstorm. An hour later, darkness had settled along with the storm. By that time she'd been missing for over four hours. I promised myself I'd do more. I'd be more generous, more understanding and definitely more patient. I'd do anything if I could just find Mother.

"She's scared of the dark," I whispered to myself as I glanced furtively at the premature darkness imposed by the storm, and Leah drove us down one street after another. Russ was right and maybe for different reasons on why Leah should drive and I shouldn't. It was easier to have a driver and a spotter. Besides, I was in no state to drive anything. I was pretty much ready to be committed.

"Do you think she would have made it this far?" Leah asked. She had both hands gripping the wheel and she was showing some signs of stress in the little grooves that were forming by the corner of her mouth.

"You should have called me long before this," Leah chastised.

I knew I should have but I also knew that Leah wouldn't understand. I couldn't go out with her or my other friends, not unless I brought Mother. I hardly saw that as an option. Our day-to-day lives held little in common. Yet, in a crisis, I knew she was one of the few people I could count on.

"I'm sorry, Leah. Mom's taken all my time these last few months. I know that's no excuse for not giving you a call or text."

"I'm sorry too," she said. "I should have called. It wasn't about me after all. It's about you."

I smiled gratefully. She didn't have it quite right. It was about Mother, but it was the closest we came as friends to understanding my situation.

Mother.

I was terrified for her as thunder cracked and rain began to slash the windshield. An elderly elm tree waved in the wind that was gusting in angry spurts.

"She was only wearing a housedress and slippers." The housedress was something that had belonged to my grandmother. I don't know where Mother had found it but she'd refused to take it off since.

"We'll find her, Cass." Leah patted my knee as if that would be enough to make everything right. "I hate that this is happening to you," she said as she gripped the wheel and scanned the road. "I'm almost glad my parents died before …"

"Don't even say it, Leah." I cut her off. "We'll find her. We have to. She'll be fine. I can't lose her, not yet." I had a death grip on the door handle, ready to jump at the first sign of Mother.

My phone rang thirty minutes later as we drove through yet another dark street and Leah efficiently barked street names and I checked them off on the map. My hand shook as I answered.

"Do you know someone by the name of Jess McDowall?" A woman's voice asked after making the proper introduction that I immediately forgot.

"You've found her," I blurted and then realized in my fugue of near hysteria that the statement made no sense. "My mother. An older lady wearing a dress and slippers. She may be confused."

Leah pulled over and stopped as she heard my side of the conversation.

"I believe it's her," the woman replied softly. "She gave me quite a scare. Arrived unexpectedly at our front door and insisted that I let her in. She just told me her name and I was able to find her listing in the phone book. She hasn't said much more than that since."

"Thank you," was all I could say but my heart was in each word.

It was only a ten-block drive or so to the address I'd scrawled on the map. But it took us over fifteen minutes to get there when we got lost in a loop of cul-de-sacs. When I finally hopped out of the car, I was faced with a man who made my solid frame look puny. He rushed over to me and I resisted the urge to back up. But I stood my ground. I wasn't backing up for anyone. I would have wrestled dragons, never mind this man if he was all that stood between me and Mother.

I vaguely registered in the rain-damp darkness with thunder cracking overhead, that the house was bracketed with at least two emergency vehicles.

"She's in the house," he said simply and moved aside.

I think I thanked him. I'm not sure. I know I rushed up to the front door to see an interior ablaze with lights and uniformed people. Two police officers for sure and someone who looked like they might be ambulance personnel. I don't know why I assumed that. I was registering everything in a confused state that was kind of a half-throttle muddle.

I make my way through the kitchen, vaguely noted the well-loved furnishings and chipped linoleum, and hoped Mother hadn't mentioned the clutter on the counter. She hated clutter. Besides clutter, the small kitchen was also full of official-looking people, another policewoman who smiled as pleasantly as the first, and a policeman who took up more than his share of the kitchen. I guessed it was a slow night and could only be grateful that it was.

One of the policewomen came briskly toward me her gun and handcuffs registering first, her smile second. "You're her daughter?" It was more a statement than a question. I'm sure even she couldn't imagine anyone else looking as panicked. I was the odd woman out in that little tableau of officials and somewhere in the bowels of all that business was Mother.

She pointed with a traffic directing like swing of her left arm. "She's in the dining room."

And there, I came face to face with Mother.

She smiled at me, her arms folded and her legs crossed. She had a cup of tea in front of her and across from her was a dark-haired woman in an outdated navy tracksuit with red piping down one sleeve. She had a relaxed expression on her face like it was normal to have a drenched stranger in for tea.

It came to me in a rush, more clearly than it ever had before, what Mother meant to me. She was irreplaceable. She was the one person who had my back no matter if she agreed with me or not. I couldn't remember a time she hadn't been there, when I hadn't loved her. I had come so close to losing her. And yet I hadn't. She was still there with those beautiful eyes and that eat-me-up smile. She hadn't left me yet.

"Mother, thank God," I blurted and rushed to her.

She held me off with one hand raised. "Really, Cass."

At other times I know that sentence would have been

finished with "… don't be so effusive." But those times, the times of Mother's ability to use words was gone. I may not have mentioned that and maybe it's not the time to mention that, but Mother was once a collector of words. She thrived on the *Reader's Digest* vocabulary test she reviewed so many times that she was never wrong on any word featured during her few decades of subscribing.

In that moment nothing mattered. Mother was alive. Mother—she just smiled. It felt so good to know she was alive and well. I had come so close to losing her.

By the time I got through getting the report from the police, Mother was annoyed I had taken so long and was ready to go home.

"She's all right?" Leah asked as I steered Mother to the vehicle.

I could only nod.

I opened the van's back door for Mother.

Mother struggled to even lift her foot. I boosted her from behind, both hands flush on her bony butt. Finally she landed on the seat with a grunt that merged with a frustrated giggle. She patted down her hair and eyed me like I was the one who had been all the trouble.

I looked behind me. I was tempted to go back and thank all those wonderful, dear people from the homeowner on down, who had saved Mother. They were people whose names I still didn't know. I was terrified if I left Mother for one moment she'd exit the van and head for parts unknown. The humid post-storm air closed around, me and in the distance lightning sparked the sky and thunder rippled softly. That made up my mind. I wouldn't lose her again, not tonight. I'd send an appropriate thank you tomorrow.

"Thank you," I said to the two police officers who watched from the sidewalk.

"Hurry up, sweetie," Mother called from the safe confines of the vehicle

I shrugged and opened the passenger door where I let out a tense breath and resisted the urge to rest my head on the headrest.

"Seatbelt, Mom." And I don't know why I bothered.

"Ridiculous," she said flatly. Her cheeks were pale and her mouth sagged.

I knew just by the way she had wobbled on the sidewalk she was well past her physical limits. In fact I'd been terrified through the entire search that we'd find her stretched out on someone's front lawn in the driving rain unable to walk another step. Of course, I was more terrified we wouldn't find her at all.

Leah put the key in the ignition. I waved one last time at the police and assortment of others on the sidewalk and we were off.

I resisted the urge to keep waving.

Behind us, stretched out on the seat, Mother began to snore.

My phone rang.

"You've got her?"

It was Russ.

And it was his voice that flipped the switch on my mood like no other voice could.

"I just picked her up. I thought that's what the police did."

I knew my tone was sharp and I wasn't sure why. Maybe it was because I hated relying on anyone and now I relied on everyone. Maybe it was a mixture of panic and fright. My hands were shaking as I reached for a tissue to blow my nose. We'd found her only, in the bigger scheme of things, to eventually lose her again. Who was I kidding that I could dodge a nursing home? I was so tired I didn't know how I would see this to the end, how I was going to keep it all together—keep us together.

Leah looked over with a puzzled look. I dodged eye contact.

"She's okay?" Russ danced easily around my tense tone and bitchy comment.

"Exhausted but otherwise okay." I took a shaky breath almost glad he wouldn't play the misplaced blame game. Mother could have died and that thought haunted me.

"Cass? It's not your fault," Russ said.

I sniffed and blinked.

"Quit beating yourself up. There's only so much you can do."

Leah put one hand on mine, the other on the wheel. "We have your back," she said quietly. "None of us could do any better."

Tears were running down my cheeks then as, in the back, Mother snored loud enough for two.

"Thanks," I whispered to Russ while smiling through tears at Leah.

"No problem," Russ said as if nothing had happened. "I've notified the others. They're all heading home."

"Thanks." I repeated. The word was so small in comparison to all that had been done that night for Mother and me. No matter what would happen in the future, I had this moment, friends to rely on, and Mother who was safe.

"Don't thank me," Russ said while beside me Leah only returned my smile. "I'll see you in ten minutes or so."

I disconnected with a sense of relief. We wouldn't be alone that night.

Russ.

That's just the way he was—reliable and irreplaceable.

Chapter Twenty-Four

I needed to keep Mother safe and I needed to be able to track her.

Russ and I had discussed the situation into the early hours after the horrific evening of looking for her. Russ had come over. It was well past one in the morning before he left for home. But in that time we'd hammered out a plan of action. Step one involved getting some sort of monitoring device that Mother could carry on her. That was my mission today. Step two was locking the yard down by affixing padlocks to every gate in the back and rigging the front door so that Mother couldn't open it. I didn't like the sounds of any of it but I knew I had no choice. The alternative was unthinkable.

Via Internet, I explored tracking options and finally hit on a fantastic little number they were using on children. Problem was it seemed to be manufactured and exported strictly by a Chinese company. I couldn't find any North American dealers, at least online. I ended my Internet search and started going through the phone book. It was on my fifth call that I hit it lucky. An electronics store that carried the latest in tracking your child. A GPS empowered child's watch. Fortunately for me, Mother had small wrists. A large child's watchband would easily fit her.

"Let's go shopping, Mom."

"No."

"It'll be fun."

She was at another stage, one of continual resistance. I tried to cajole her in those one-syllable words I'm becoming so familiar with. Simple and few were the words she reacted to best now, especially when she was showing signs of resistance. The dementia book I'd purchased only weeks ago was my guide post marking every step of the path neither of us wanted to take.

"Staying home."

"C'mon Mom, I'll buy you some jelly beans."

Her face lit up at that.

We spent a good hour browsing the electronics store and speaking to the sales clerk who couldn't have been more than nineteen. Despite my doubts about his abilities all strictly based on my prejudice in regard to his youth, he seemed to be on top of the GPS situation. He even had a suggestion or two about monitoring the device for exactly the purpose I was considering—keeping Mother in view at all times. I looked over—she was enthralled with the phone display.

"This model will probably do the trick," he replied as if it were common news to have customers wish to track their confused parents.

I doubted if his parents were anywhere near the age where that might be a problem. I wondered if he'd remember should he ever be faced with such a situation. Of course, by then, a GPS would be long relegated to the world of obsolescence.

The option he showed me was fairly utilitarian without even a scrap of color that might entice a child or Mother.

"It gets a range of seven miles."

I would have preferred more. I don't know why. I know Mother can only walk five or six blocks. Although she beat that record last night when she walked over two miles. It was still a long way from seven miles but I preferred over-cautious and safe.

We discussed some of the other options and then I called Mother over.

"Mom. What do you think of this watch?"

"Plain."

"It is but it won't overpower your bracelets."

She frowned at me. She'd forgotten the Cuban bracelets she jangled as she lifted her arm and tentatively touched the watch. She'd forgotten either that she had the bracelets on or the meaning of the word *overpower*—possibly both.

"You can wear it in the yard."

"To work."

"Exactly." I'm thrilled that she laid the trump card. Of course I planned to rig the watch so she couldn't get it off. The last thing I needed was to find the GPS watch on the lawn or in the garbage or any number of other places where she might put it.

"We'll take it," I said.

Ten minutes later, the wristwatch was on Mother's wrist and the instructions and warranty were in my purse. I even turned around and gave the clerk a little wave. We all waved. I wasn't sure what that was about. I think that the exuberance on my part was really relief to have one safeguard dealt with. Mother, of course, was imitating me, and the sales clerk—well, he was more than likely glad to see the end of us.

•

That night after mother had fallen asleep, I began the search for the elusive man who might be my father. I'd begun that in the provincial death records and discovered both to my surprise and my dismay, finding one man named Fidel with no birth or even death date, was not an easy task.

There was a soft knock at the door and I peeked out even though I knew who it was. The sun had already set but I could see his familiar shape even in the shadows of what light remained.

Russ.

I opened the door. He stepped in and hugged me immediately, cupped my face and had me on my tiptoes as he kissed me long, hard and hot.

"I missed you, Cass," he said in a throaty growl against my lips.

"I missed you," I said as I separated from him long enough to close the door. "Mother's sleeping."

"So I hoped."

He was wearing jeans and a T-shirt, and even dressed down I knew he'd get second looks. He could wear anything and ace it. I wished that I'd dressed slightly better than the sweats I was wearing. But I'd been working out earlier and I hadn't planned anything more than a night on the couch.

"I thought you were on duty."

"Nope. I'm off beginning a few hours ago and through the next few days."

I offered him a beer, which he turned down.

Only then I told him what I'd found, or more aptly what I hadn't found when it came to the search for my father.

"Too bad you didn't know what year he died."

I lay with my back to his chest, my legs on either side of him. My right thumb traced patterns on the palm of his right hand. "Or what year he was born."

"Any chance your mother might be able to tell you some of that?"

"Maybe," I said. "But it will be tricky asking her. It depends on the day."

He frowned. "And you may upset her."

We talked back and forth, moving off that topic and starting another. And as the night thickened, the words became less, the actions more. And soon we were onto something completely different as his hands began to work their magic. And as I flipped, repositioning so that we lay chest to chest I felt my reward. He was hot and hard beneath me and now it was my turn to start the magic.

It was hours before we called it a night. Daylight was already streaking outside and hope had arrived back in full force after a night of passion.

Chapter Twenty-Five

July 18

Sometimes I feel like I should burn this diary. It's all drivel anyway and will mean nothing to anyone more than it means to me right now. It's only a way to get my feelings out so I can turn a smiling face to Cassie in the morning.

That's not a good way to live.

I need to change that and I suspect the only way is getting back to what I love best — dance. Oh, I don't mean quit my job or anything, we need that to live, Cassie and I.

Volunteer work, using my dance to help others. Maybe not now while Cassie is little but later.

Heavenly days, it's been hot this week. I think both Cassandra and I are feeling a little house bound. But without a car it's not easy to get around town with any speed. The bus schedule is terrible. I suspect one of those civic officials has messed with it again. I bet they've never been on a bus. I'd like to get down there and give them a piece of my mind.

Instead I've considered it may be time to get a driver's license. I ran the numbers on purchasing a vehicle and think I could afford a secondhand compact if I sell my wedding rings. They didn't mean much, other than a bad memory.

I considered selling Mother's pearls. But, I couldn't do it. Couldn't bear to part with them for they link me to my heritage, to generations of women who came before.

This time when I set that little book down I found myself wiping my eyes. Nothing had been easy for her.

It was blistering hot that day and I guessed a thunderstorm would roll in to finish the day. The heat and humidity were starting to get to me. Outside there was a heavy silence except for a slight breeze that tousled the overgrown dogwood. As I considered that the bush needed trimming, I realized I hadn't heard Mother's familiar humming as she watched TV. I dropped the ladle on the new electric stove and rushed into the family room. Her chair was empty!

My heart did that small flip of panic that seemed to always chauffeur in disaster.

"Mom!" I shouted at the top of my lungs even though it was a small house. But the television was loud and Mother was slightly hard of hearing. I looked into the living room where the laugh track of a familiar sitcom had been keeping me company as I prepared supper.

I'd assumed Mother was there. I should have learned by then not to assume anything, not for one minute, not for five.

I covered every inch of the main floor. I even hovered on the top of the basement stairs before something made me turn around and look outside.

I had to look twice to really believe what I was seeing. In the midst of a summer storm that was just beginning to heat up, beneath a sky heaving with angry clouds, was Mother. Lightning was already flashing and the thunder was rumbling much too near. She was in the midst of it all twirling like a prima ballerina.

There was no emotion to tag on what I felt. How can you describe when your parent becomes your child? There were many times when I could say that had already happened. But then I only slipped briefly into that role and it always had a feel of unreality. In that moment I definitely stood on the other side while the lightening flashed and like some Frankenstein-like intervention our roles reversed.

I didn't know then if it was permanent or not, but it was as real as anything I'd ever felt.

I stood in an open doorway and watched my child dance on that stormy July day as tears welled and merged with the rain that began to fall. It took a good crack of thunder for me to jolt into action.

"Mom!" I yelled. She kept dancing, and I knew she'd left her hearing aids in her drawer.

"Feels like a great clot of wax," I think were her exact words when I'd asked her why she wouldn't wear them.

"Mom!" That time it was a shriek that made my throat ache. I stepped on the deck and into the rain. I was prepared to take her in by force if necessary. Not the best choice but preferable to having her hit by lightning.

"Cass."

I remembered Mother's face lighting up. I remembered how shocked I was that she could remember the steps to the salsa. For that was what she was doing, a one-woman version of that dance we had learned in Cuba. She couldn't remember anything else, not the year or what we ate for lunch today, but she could remember that damn dance.

The umbrella she spun in one hand with all that lovely metal had me stirred up. I hate thunderstorms, and Mother with a lightening rod in her hand was not a comforting feeling. I took her by the hand, spun her once and literally pushed her into the house.

The power went out that night. That was the night Aunt Alice made an appearance. I hadn't heard from her in over a decade. She was my great aunt, an elderly woman we had lost touch with as some families are apt to do.

We, I hated to admit, had been one of those families. It wasn't that I hadn't thought of the missing relatives. The few scattered relatives, separated by time and distance, had disappeared into the fog of their own lives. It seemed hardly appropriate to call them now just because I needed them.

When the phone rang, we both jumped.

I was quick to grab it. Lately it seemed like everything might be an emergency.

"Cassandra?" Aunt Alice began the conversation. "It's been so long since I've seen you. How's your mother?"

As the conversation continued she didn't pull any punches and I appreciated that. No need for me to go through the motions of how I was. It was all about Mother. Relief flooded me. It was strange how that happened. Lately, my independence seemed to be threaded with a crazy need to bond with people I'd lost touch with.

"She's managing."

It was strange to speak to her after so long, that missing relative who was alive and well and by my calculations, close to or past ninety years-old. Only the faint scratch in her voice gave any indication of age. The candles flickered, throwing shadows against the walls while Mother hummed quietly in the background.

There was something that sounded like a cross between a snort of disdain and a guffaw of disbelief on the other end. "I've heard that she's failing fast."

How I hated that word and now how I was beginning to resent this woman who I had only been too happy to hear from a minute earlier. "She's fine. Forgetful."

"Alzheimer's," Aunt Alice said abruptly. "And a shame too. Jessica Jane had a fine mind. She could have had a career in performing arts if she hadn't insisted on marrying that fool. No offence Cassie, but getting pregnant years into a bad marriage wasn't the best idea either."

Silence drifted over the line. Aunt Alice wasn't exactly the person to go into the details of my illegitimacy, or was she?

"Look. That's all the past. I'm just phoning to say I'll be in town next week. I'll see you then." She went into a long conversation about her family and how they were doing—and wound it all up with instruction to pick her up at the bus depot the following Wednesday.

I hung up the phone with a notepad full of Aunt Alice's pickup instructions and no idea what I had or had not agreed to. I wasn't even sure if Aunt Alice was staying in a hotel or staying with us. I only hoped she had answers or that she boosted mother's spirits. I was beginning to sense I'd been railroaded by a ninety year-old.

•

"Fasten your seatbelt," I reminded Mother almost a week later. Time seemed to stand still at times and other times it evaporated.

"Why?"

"It's the law." I'd presented that argument many times over the past few months. Sometime in May, Mother first stopped wearing her seatbelt, and no amount of what I considered, reasonable discussion could convince her otherwise. Reasonable and Mother were just no longer on the same page.

"Ridiculous."

I put the car into drive and put the brake on my anger. It was endlessly frustrating and I fought daily with patience. As much as I loved Mother and would do anything for her, what I wanted most, her sanity, was rapidly slipping away from her.

Some days I didn't know who I was angry with—Mother, the disease or the fates. *The Caregiver's Guide to Dementia* said this was all normal and letting go was another step in the grief process. I'd learned the seat belt issue was one to let go. Barring a seatbelt check, everything would be fine.

Isn't that the thing about destiny? Once you think of the possibility of something, especially the remote possibility, it's guaranteed to happen. And not twelve blocks from home I saw the police cruiser. Nothing out of the normal except when the flashing lights went on and the short bleat of the siren that was a polite message to pull over.

"You're the owner of this vehicle?" A baby-faced, dewy-eyed blonde young man asked. Despite the seriousness of his uniform and his plethora of equipment strapped around his waist he looked too young for such an occupation. When had everyone begun looking so young?

"Registration."

I reached across Mother to get the registration out of the glove box.

He looked at it briefly before handing it back. He didn't look at my driver's license—instead he looked at Mother.

I followed the line of his gaze. Mother was smiling blissfully but the expression in her eyes was vague like she didn't quite know what was happening. And that's when I remembered her lack of seatbelt.

I looked back at the officer.

"Can you encourage her to put her seatbelt on?" It was inspiration that I said that. But like I said before, I was becoming used to asking for help from unexpected sources. "She won't,"

I said in an undertone. "She won't believe that it's law."

Mother was busy fiddling with the window, raising it up and down and oblivious to our conversation, which was obviously boring her.

"Alzheimer's?"

I nodded. Bless him. There were few people who caught on to Mother's situation that quickly. Maybe it was my few words combined with his training or personal experience but whatever it was, whenever it happened, it felt like we were a little less alone.

"Ma'am."

Mother's attention was on the window and the passenger window swished down and then up.

He shrugged and moved around to Mother's side. I saw he had her attention immediately.

"Am I under arrest?" she asked.

"Not this time, Ma'am but you'll have to put on your seatbelt. It's the law."

"Oh my. I didn't know." And just like that the seatbelt was on and snapped in place.

We got home an hour later. Aunt Alice would be arriving in two days, if she was arriving at all. So far there'd been no word.

I'd prepared a room for her just in case. I supposed if I were already taking care of one senior, two wouldn't be an issue.

Of course Aunt Alice was taking the bus in a two-hour journey from her home. A journey alone, how needy could she be? I imagined a woman of her age had a walker at a minimum.

"Aunt Alice is coming for a visit," I reminded Mother for at least the fifth time.

"Aunt Alice?" She frowned as if the name had no connection for her. "My mother's baby sister."

I blew out a long breath. It was a crapshoot from one day to the next what Mother might remember and what she might not.

That Wednesday I stood with Mother on the already blistering concrete waiting for Aunt Alice's bus to pull in. It was late and Mother was antsy.

She fiddled with her skirt and then her purse, opening it and closing it. Her eyes had a rheumy look about them that morning and there was that disturbing purple shadow under her eyes that suggested she might not have slept well.

But when that Greyhound bus arrived and Aunt Alice got off, somehow I knew things were going to change.

"Cassie?" she said before her foot had even hit concrete.

She was a woman who might have been my size in her prime. There was still a good substance to her. She wore no-nonsense jeans and a nylon bomber style jacket. "My, my," she grabbed me in a bear hug before letting me go as other passengers streamed around us.

"Jess. It's me, Alice." She wrapped her arms around Mother and threatened not to let her go.

We had a delightful few days. We didn't do much, just talked for hours out on the patio in the languishing still-warm days of summer.

"This is the best time," Aunt Alice said as she sipped her rum and coke.

"Crickets," Mom replied.

"I love the sound," Aunt Alice agreed.

That was how each of the days of Aunt Alice's visit ended— on the patio with drinks in hand.

It was mid-visit and mother was napping, when I finally asked Aunt Alice the questions burning in my mind, questions about my paternity.

"I love the story of Mom's trip to Toronto," I began. "I suppose after I was born that ended any trips." And in fact, it had—to a point.

Aunt Alice looked at me oddly and silence ran between us.

"She told you?"

I nodded. It wasn't a complete lie. She had told me about going to Toronto and the rest had been broad brush clues that left me picking up the pieces.

"We were all relieved when he passed."

I clenched my fist in my lap. I wanted in the worst way to ask questions but I didn't want to reveal how little I truly knew.

Fortunately Aunt Alice had just gotten started. "You didn't know him so it didn't much matter to you. I managed to convince your mother not to go to the funeral."

"She never said how he died," I said.

"Run over by a city bus." She shook her head. "Dead at the scene. Terrible but quite frankly we, my sisters and I, were relieved. He wasn't right for your mother either. The worst was he'd threatened to come out here only weeks earlier. Before he died, I mean. I don't know how but he'd heard."

Her lips pinched as if she'd said too much.

"About me?"

She stood up. "That's enough. This isn't up to me to tell."

"There's no one else," I said softly.

She sat back down.

"Tell me about him."

"There isn't much," she said with a shrug. "Not that I know, anyway. She met him at a dance. Fidel was a landed immigrant. From Cuba. At least that was what Jessica Jane told me. I never met him."

"Did he and Mom plan to marry?"

"I don't know. All I know is that years after you were born, he contacted her. Tom had already left by that point. And I think, from what little your mother said, that Fidel had only just learned of you. My guess is your mother reached out to him." She held up her hand as if fending off further questions. "I don't know, love, if he knew about you or for that matter what his intentions were."

My heart seemed to skip a beat. "What was his last name?"

She shook her head. "Your mother was very closed-mouth on it all. I saw a picture once and that's it. Good-looking man. You look rather like him."

My heart raced at that even as disappointment flooded through me.

We chatted after that but there was really nothing else she could tell me, having never met the man. The talk had brought us closer.

I was counting the days when Aunt Alice would visit again, and I told her so as I helped load her luggage back on that Greyhound three days later.

Now, I had a good start to solving a mystery that had seemed more intriguing than personal. I'd been without a father most of my life.

In my mind there were more important things in life than genetics. I also knew or hoped if I told myself that enough times, eventually I'd believe it.

Chapter Twenty-Six

August 1

It was unbelievable.

Impossible really.

It had happened again.

Mother sat on the floor with her knees drawn to her chin. The pill bottles lay around her, some with pills out, others not.

"Pills messed, sweetie."

My stomach hit the bottom of my toes.

Could this possibly have happened a second time? I was negligent. Thank God I didn't have children. I probably would have accidentally killed or injured them by now.

Who knew what Mother had taken or how many. She seemed fairly perky like maybe she hadn't taken any or not that many. Maybe they had rolled under the fridge. I got down on my hands and knees to look.

No pills there.

The phone rang and I hesitated to answer. I could see from the call display it was Russ.

Mother got up and walked into the living room like nothing had happened. She was humming and so far showed no sign of poisoning. But that could mean anything and nothing. I had to find the evidence she'd swallowed them or she hadn't.

The phone rang, six, seven and then eight times. In the other room, Mother was oblivious but fully conscious. The television was blaring and I determined she was not in danger, for now.

I grabbed the phone.

"Russ!" My voice was loud, his name staccato. "Should I

get her stomach pumped?"

"Slow down, Cass. What happened?"

I took a breath. It was slower that time even though I was forcing down the urge to race to the end of my sorry tale, rush into the living room, airlift Mother under my arm, and charge for the car. Instead I took a breath and gave him what I thought was a deceptively calm rundown of Mother's current ordeal.

"Bundle her up and get her to the Emergency."

He was telling me the obvious. But I needed the confirmation.

"How am I going to know for sure?" It was like I was running blind, like it hadn't happened before. The panic was just as fresh and mind-numbing as it had been the first time. "I don't know if she took any or not."

"There's probably no easy way of telling. Just take her to the Emergency to be on the safe side."

I knew he was right, but how could it have happened a second time? I was an idiot. I shouldn't be in charge of a goldfish. What cosmic joke made me responsible for Mother?

"Mom, what pills did you take?"

She smiled. There was toast stuck in her front tooth. "Some."

"Which ones?"

"Sweetie." Her smile would be completely endearing in any other circumstance.

"You're not supposed to touch them." I couldn't keep the anger out of my voice. But I wasn't angry. I was terrified. And I couldn't figure out how she got to them. That was until she opened her palm and I saw the key to my jewelry box that I had locked the pills in before putting them up on a high shelf. I'd hidden the key too, or at least I thought I had. Then I remembered the phone call. I'd grabbed the phone and left the key on the dresser. Had Mother been standing behind me the whole time watching the performance? Was her memory intact enough to remember a sequence of events? Apparently it was.

"It's okay. Took two pills." She held up four fingers.

I kicked myself all the way to the Hospital Emergency. Mother was already looking a little pale, or that could have been my imagination. Russ met me there and picked her up carrying her the rest of the way as I raced ahead, reaching for automatic doors.

She stayed overnight and again I found myself driving home alone. Russ had left for work a few hours ago when it was clear that Mother was stable. I don't remember much of that night except that it was long. I arrived at the hospital early the next morning to be flagged down by the head nurse.

"I'm sorry, we've had to move your mother."

"Move her?" I was puzzled and ready to jump into battle. It seemed that Mother's personality wasn't the only one that had changed. I was finding myself more assertive as I was always prepared to do battle for what was best for Mother. "What happened? Why wasn't I called?"

"I'm sorry. Normally we would have but it was quite late and ..." She shrugged. "It's okay, really. Your Mother is in a private room."

"Private room?" That alone was suspect. In a public health care system a private room was an anomaly. Patients are housed four to a room and if you're lucky two, depending on the ward.

"She began shouting in the night. She was quite agitated and the nursing staff couldn't calm her down. She seemed to think the other patient was someone named Rita."

"Her former sister-in-law," I filled in while my mind swirled through this new information.

"Yes, well. She was becoming quite vocal and had the other patient terrified. We thought it best to move her."

"She was okay after that?"

"Not really." The nurse shrugged. "We let her spend a few hours in the staff lounge. She watched television and finally fell asleep. Fortunately, it was a quiet night."

"I'm sorry." And as I said it, I wanted to take those words back. They should have called me. Taking care of patients, no matter how difficult, was their job. But Mother wasn't difficult. She'd never been difficult.

"No need to apologize."

She was right, there wasn't.

"You should have called me." I was feeling edgy and regretting my apology. There were obviously holes in their policies and that was unacceptable when it affected my mother.

"It was late."

"I would have come right down. In future, when you have a dementia patient I would recommend you call their next of kin immediately. Being in a strange environment is terrifying for them."

The nurse stood up, unruffled and surprisingly agreeable. "You're right. I'll mention it at our next meeting." She then showed me to Mother's new room. It was in a corner, a sunnier, more open room than the one I had last seen her in. Mother was sitting primly on the edge of the bed, her back to me. It was good to see her up and obviously feeling better.

The social worker showed up an hour later. It wasn't a surprise. Mother had overdosed not once but twice after all, and that combined with her dementia was like a red flag for help. I had known that visit was imminent even if the nurse hadn't warned me earlier. But as the young woman knocked softly on the door and I noted her youth, I was sure there was no help she could give us.

"It's a big job," the social worker began. She'd already introduced herself as Nadia. Her soft brown eyes were set in a squeaky clean, peaches-and-cream face that looked like it hadn't cracked thirty.

What could someone so young know about any of this? I couldn't focus on anything but her age.

"How old are you, sweetie?" Mom asked the question that obviously was bothering both of us.

And I hated that *sweetie*—that special endearment meant just for me—Mother now shared with another.

"Twenty-seven," she said without missing a beat. "I know." She held up her hands, palms up. "I've been practicing for two years. But anything I don't know, I'll find out for you. I promise."

Mother grinned and took my hand and I knew she was won over. She was tired though. Her usual spunk was gone and weariness was edged in her silence.

"Home care might be beneficial." She smiled at Mother. "You like company?"

Mother looked at her blankly.

"Can we speak in the hallway," I said as I saw Mother's eyelids droop. "Why don't you get some sleep, Mom?"

"Home care?" I repeated once we were safely in the corridor.

"Someone can come in so many days a week and help you with various tasks. You have to remember that you're no use to your mother if you burn out trying to do it all."

"We're managing." It was an outrageous statement considering the circumstances, Mother in the hospital and all. "I just don't know if she'd allow a stranger near her."

"Look, I'll give you my card. And I'll be in contact in the next few weeks. Meantime, give it some thought."

I promised myself that Mother and I were in this together, the two of us. We didn't need anyone.

When the phone rang that night, I knew who it was. I didn't need Russ either. I let the phone ring through to voicemail.

•

One week later

"Did you ever contact the social worker?" Russ asked.

Days ago I'd admitted to him that the home care option was available. He'd gently prodded me in every conversation since that revelation, but I'd turned the option down. I'd even spoken to the social worker the other day and assured her everything was fine.

"No need," I assured him. We talked about mundane things after that and as always, I felt less rattled when I hung up.

"You know my feelings on it," he said. "You need help." His hand gently covered my mouth as my lips formed words of protest. "Forget all that. You need some fun."

My heart skipped. The contradictory homecare situation pushed to the side. I loved his ideas. I loved that he was here. There was pretty much nothing I didn't like about Russ. I deliberately dropped from love to like. I wasn't ready for a more long-term commitment than I already had—Mother. Or, at least I kept telling myself that.

"The weather is supposed to be hot tomorrow and it's my day off. Let's go to the beach."

"Mother isn't easy these days."

"I know, but we'll keep it simple. Fish and chips on the

beach for supper. A stroll around cottage country. Nothing more than that."

I blew out a relieved breath at the thought that it didn't mean me wearing a bathing suit. Despite the walks with Mother, I'd gained weight that summer. It wasn't something I wanted to contemplate—the extra weight and my natural aversion to exercise. Dancing with Mother just wasn't burning enough calories to beat my new craving for ice cream.

"What time?"

"Ten o'clock. I'll pick you up."

"Perfect. We'll bring bottled water and sunscreen."

"You're on." He ended the conversation on that cheerful note that had me humming for an hour after.

Chapter Twenty-Seven

The next day I pulled out a sundress and swung around to show it to Mother.

"What about this?"

Mother nodded and I left her to get dressed.

"You look fantastic, Mom," I enthused minutes later, took her hand in mine, raised it over her head and gave her a high five.

She smiled like she'd just been crowned royalty but she looked great in the summer dress that was oddly reminiscent of that beautiful confection she'd lifted from a hotel room in Cuba. With azure hues rather than yellow, it was perfect for Mother. She did a little twirl and took my hand.

"I love the beach," she breathed in a voice that was thinner than it had once been.

I loved that she remembered we were going to the beach. I'd told her over thirty minutes ago, well past her usual memory record.

Russ arrived right on time. Just a few minutes before the time he'd told me yesterday. That was Russ, never late, never too early.

Mother was beaming. There was something about Russ that just clicked with Mother.

"You look beautiful." He took her hand as he helped her into the car but his eyes swept over us both. I tried to look nonchalant even as my cheeks flushed and Mother, well her smile upped a notch and she pretty much smiled and hummed the entire twenty-minute drive.

"You didn't bring a bathing suit, did you?" Russ asked me

as we turned off on the last leg of our short journey.

I grinned and shook my head. "I thought we'd just walk along the beach and stop for fish and chips like you suggested." I glanced at him. "Did you?"

He smiled and shook his head.

An hour later we were strolling along the beach. We watched the water-skiers, laughed at the antics of the beginners who stuttered on shaky legs and crash-landed more than they stayed up. I fondly watched Mother as she stopped and started, bending down to pick up this trinket in the sand or that. Mostly she picked up small stones. The beach wasn't the smoothest, and every once in a while she found a real treasure like a hair clip. By the time we left the beach, Mother's pockets were full. I offered to help her carry them with the intent of disposing of her finds in a nearby trash can.

"No!" She swerved around me as if I planned to wrestle her to the sand and steal her treasures.

"Okay, Mom." I threw up my hands.

Mother sidestepped me as if I were a poisonous viper. But a minute later she was holding my hand and skipping beside me.

I looked up at Russ and smiled. It might be strange to most people but that was my new reality and there wasn't anything strange about it. It just was.

After Russ had gone to the takeout counter to order our fish and chips, things got bad.

"Home," Mother demanded.

"We're going to have supper first," I assured her. "Then we'll go home."

"Now." Her hands were on her hips and her bottom lip was close to protruding. "Cass," she said much too loud. "Home. Let's go home." There was a whine in her voice.

For a moment, a small bubble of panic cut off rationale thought. I didn't know what to do. If this was an indication of the future, then even a day at the beach couldn't end in an easy or even predictable manner. My heart sank. I took her hand, meaning to sooth her but I was feeling prickly myself and maybe those feelings transposed to her.

"Ahhhh!" she screamed and heads turned. She sounded

like I had just broken one of her delicate fingers.

A middle-aged woman whispered something to the man behind her. They both swung to stare at me. Another woman looked like she was about to intervene in what I assumed they all saw as elder abuse.

"Mom. Quiet, please," I pleaded. I dropped her hand and tentatively touched her arm. Touch often seemed to calm her. Not today. She lurched away from me and clutched her arms beneath her bosom. She shuddered and her face was scrunched up so tight I could barely see her eyes.

I hadn't felt that helpless since the day she was lost.

She was hiccupping and there were tears running down her cheeks. "Home," she repeated.

"Okay." Why hadn't I given in sooner? I handed her a tissue and she knocked it to the ground.

"Why, look who we have here. Jessica Jane." It was Russ behind me. He had a note of surprise and was carrying our meals balanced precariously on his forearm and right hand but his attention was on Mother.

Mother looked up at him and something changed in her expression. It was like he brought with him a touch of reality.

"Jess," she whispered.

"Jess. I'm glad to see you. I didn't want to be eating my supper alone. Fish and chips sound good to you?" His voice was almost boisterous in its good humor.

I just stood there, like a giant stump. Helpless. Desperate. Praying what he was trying to do worked.

Already the others in the lineup had lost interest in us. Apparently they had determined that we were neither persecuting nor beating defenseless senior citizens.

Ten minutes later we were sitting at a table on the boardwalk eating supper as if nothing had happened. At least Russ and Mother were eating like that. Me, I was eating slower than I'd ever done in my life. It was pretty hard to swallow food around that unidentifiable lump that threatened to kick it all back up and out. I was so tired and so out of my depth. It wasn't Mother who wanted to go home in the worst way. It was me.

I looked into Russ's dark eyes and I saw something else that day. I saw hope and the promise of a future.

And, so far all I'd allowed myself to think about was how much he meant—now. Of how he made me feel—now.

I could easily melt into his arms. I wanted him, needed him. But always in the present. There was no future.

In that moment, I knew that wasn't true. I couldn't live without Russ. But, it wasn't the time to get into all of that. It was enough to know that this was the man I could spend the rest of my life with. And maybe someday I would. Maybe someday I would tell him or he would ask me. But for now, there was mother.

I took her hand and I took Russ's and it felt right, me walking between the two of them. At least now, today—with the sun dancing overhead and smiles on everyone's faces— this was how it was meant to be.

Chapter Twenty-Eight

August 22

"It's moving faster than I anticipated," the neurologist confirmed as I sat alone in his office. "I know we discussed the progression before but I presume there are underlying conditions, small brain infarctions possibly." He shifted and for the first time I saw he was uncomfortable. "Unfortunately, there's nothing we can do as far as prevention of the infarctions. If that's what's happening." He shuffled papers. "There's also a little understood faster progression of the disease. I believe I mentioned it before. Of course, unless you'll agree to another MRI …"

"No." I shook my head. There was no need. We'd already determined no test or proper disease name would stop what was happening. We knew, too, that no test could give a hundred-percent right name to an uncontrollable disease. It was all pointless. I looked beside me to the empty chair. Mother had left a few minutes ago, led out by a new nurse who had admired her hair. Mother was smitten immediately.

"What do we do?"

"You might begin to consider nursing care." He pulled a sheet from his desk. I took a quick look and saw the administrator's contact numbers of the various nursing homes.

"No!" I pushed the sheet back at him.

"Look, Cassie. You need a life. You can't continue like this indefinitely." He pushed himself back in his chair and eyed me. "I don't mean nursing home necessarily but someone to come in. Spell you off. You don't want to burn out. You won't be any good to either your mother or you if you do."

We both digested that as a long silence burned between us.

"I've seen the most well-intentioned caregivers never make it back from a burnout. That pretty much sentences the patient to a nursing home."

The patient! Mother was Jessica Jane McDowall, not the patient. I pushed the bubble of anger down that wanted nothing but to scream at this man that he was an insensitive boob. Maybe he was in that moment, but he was also a friend and the voice of reason that kept me from being dumped over the edge of that cliff.

"Think about it, Cass. I'd say the sooner the better. While you're still able to cope."

I stood up. There was nothing more to be said except, "I'll think about it."

I found Mother in the waiting room looking lost and alone. She looked up and saw me and her blue eyes lit up. She lurched to her feet.

"Cass, let's go home."

There was a slight odor as she moved toward me. And I realized I wasn't sure when mother had last bathed. She'd always refused to let me help. I'd heard the water run. Assumed she'd been bathing. I was wrong.

I decided at that moment to phone the Social Services contact. We needed help and maybe there was something the home care people could do. In little time, we had a worker named Anna scheduled to arrive to help.

•

One week later

"Cass!"

Mother's shriek that day would have impressed an opera singer.

I rushed into the bathroom to find Mother pressed against the wall holding a towel to her chest, even though she was fully clothed, I knew from the look on her face and from an instinctive unspoken connection between us, that she thought she was naked. She'd been discovered in her all together, as she would have called it. Nude was what the rest of the world might call it. Either way, Mother had not an extra inch exposed as her newly hired home care worker hovered in the doorway.

"Thief!" Mother screeched and relief flooded her face at my arrival. "Cass," her tone dived a notch and her lip trembled. "Police."

"I'm sorry," Anna said looking rather shook up.

Anna had been assigned to Mother less than a week ago and had already made two visits—one more of a get to know you and now this one.

I remember thinking I had never seen a woman move so fast as she backed up and out of the bathroom.

"I didn't mean to frighten her. The door was ajar and I thought ..."

"Don't worry about it." I cut her off. There was no time to worry about other people's feelings of inadequacy. Whatever it was she had to say, it could wait. Right now, Mother was all I could focus on.

"Mom, Anna's here to help you." I lightly touched her shoulder and when she didn't flinch, I pulled her into my arms and hugged her. She snuggled against me, her head not reaching my chin. Her whole body shook.

"I'll handle this. Maybe just wait in the living room."

I motioned to Anna and turned my attention back to Mother.

It was a good thirty minutes before I had Mother calmed down.

"A walk?" Mother asked once she'd stopped shaking.

"Later, Mom. We have a visitor."

"Oh?"

I knew she'd forgotten the incident and Anna. Just like she forgot my explanation that morning about the woman who was here to help her. So, I pretended like this was the first time they'd met. I reintroduced them for Mother's benefit. Anna had a magazine in her hand and looked quite comfortable as she smiled at Mother, stood up and held out her hand.

Mother gave her a rather limp-wristed handshake before her attention was diverted by the sound of the furnace kicking in.

"I'm sorry." I said it as an aside.

"No problem." She smiled. "We were both startled, weren't we Mrs. McDowall?"

Mother nodded her head but I could see the blank look.

Anna gave me an understanding look and put a hand over Mother's. "I think a walk is a good idea."

Mother nodded happily.

"Do you have a phone?" I asked.

"On me," Anna said brightly. "We'll see how it turns out. With any luck I won't have to use it."

The door clicked shut as Anna and Mother left.

I called Russ.

My heartbeat seemed to settle when I heard his calm voice.

"Cassie? Are you all right?"

"Yes," I breathed. And it wasn't a lie. The sound of his voice just made everything right. "No," I contradicted. "It is now but it wasn't ... Mother wouldn't let Anna, the homecare worker, bathe her."

"That's not good," he said his voice deep, smooth and soul-healing.

"I know," I said, my voice barely a whisper. "She's walking with her now."

"How long is she there?"

I looked at my watch. "Another three hours." I'd been offered what they called a long-stay for a few afternoons to allow Anna and mother to familiarize. Or, at least that was my take on it.

"I'm coming over to get you."

"No."

"Yes," he said and disconnected before I could present further argument.

I opened the door fifteen minutes later and my eyes met his for only a second before I was in his arms.

"Ah Cass, I wish there was something more I could do."

"This is fine, really. A hug is all I ..."

The sentence ended with his lips on mine. They were passionate and determined. I sunk into him. He was hot and hard and ...

The thought broke off and I pushed away.

Mother was worse and I couldn't do this.

"We're going out," he said as if he'd heard my doubts. "I caught up with your caregiver just down the block and told her you'd be out for the next few hours.

"Russ ..." It was a weak attempt at protest.

Instead my heart was still pounding from his kiss.

"Let's go," he said.

"Like this?" I asked looking down at my jeans and T-shirt.

"Like that," he said.

He took me to a bar a few miles from my house. It was the kind of place where pool tables filled a quarter of the floor and an ancient jukebox blasted in the corner.

"I'm going to whip your butt at pool," he said with a smile.

"Like hell," I replied. But the response was more bravado than anything else.

I think Russ knew that. He put a big hand on my shoulder and squeezed, leaned down and gave me a kiss. "For luck."

There was hardly anyone else in the bar. But it was mid-afternoon. We played one round and then two, and Russ was as good as his word. He beat me easily.

After that, he insisted I have a beer while he sipped on a coke.

"This is so good. I haven't had beer in a year." Not since I moved in with Mother.

"Don't—" His hand was over mine. "—think what you're thinking. This is your time."

"Okay," I said. My mood was still up. There was something about this dark, dank out-of-the-way bar that just made me feel happy. Maybe because this wasn't my reality. Russ had known exactly what he was doing when he brought me here.

"Another game?" he asked. "C'mon Cass—today's for you."

I'm not walking.

Russ's words all those weeks ago. A promise really, offered before that first time we made love. They were words that would haunt me until I succumbed to what he offered. I knew that. He knew that. Those words lay between us—layered, forever.

I looked up into his gorgeously sincere brown eyes and there was no room for *no*. Sex was one thing, but what I felt was quite another. I wasn't sure if I could hold out much longer. I'd fallen for him weeks ago. No matter what he'd revealed to me, I wasn't ready—yet. How I really felt about Russ, how much I needed and wanted him—that was my secret.

I knew, looking into his eyes, it was the worst-kept secret in the world.

But for now, that's how it would remain.

Chapter Twenty-Nine

September 1

I got my driver's license and that's such a boon. Now I need a car. I spotted a second hand compact in the paper the other day that fits the budget. I don't want anything too big as it will be difficult to park. Besides, with only the two of us and just running around town it will be easier on gas. I can hardly wait. It's like another step to freedom, to that new life I dreamt for Cassie and me.

It's something to be excited about despite the news overseas. There's so much hardship in the world. Another drought in Africa has taken the lives of many. I can't bear to think of all that suffering. I can see why many people remain illiterate about world events because then it's easy to think just about your life. Hearing the news only reminds me of the trivial things we waste our lives on. Dance — that's what I did for how many years? Maybe that effort would have been better spent on bigger issues.

I want so much to sponsor an overseas child. It's such a lovely idea sending money each month and corresponding over the years to aid a disadvantaged child. Like a hand from across the ocean. The option was available in the church bulletin last Sunday with a contact name and all. It hit me immediately that it was the right thing to do and it would be such a lesson for Cassandra. But yesterday the store cut back their hours. I had to give up the idea of sponsoring for now. Instead we are packing up all the clothes Cassandra has outgrown and giving them to a charity. I'm letting her help me even though the task is taking twice as long because of it. I hope someday she'll be old enough to understand why it's important to give back.

I remembered as a child wanting a new dress, and Mother saying we didn't have the money. I remember Mother telling me I was lucky to have a dress at all. And I remember something else—she taught me how to twirl as she explained how unimportant a new dress was. I remember spinning on tiptoes and thinking I was a princess. Mother had done that. On little more than inspiration, she had made me feel special. I hoped if I ever had a child, I could do the same.

The next day I reminded Mother that it was September second not so much because it was my birthday but rather because marking that milestone kept Mother focused on time and place.

She looked at me blankly.

"My birthday. I'm forty."

"My goodness," she breathed. "Let's dance."

She twisted and twirled me around the kitchen as she danced to music only she could hear. She smiled the whole time, her beautiful blue eyes alive with the joy of those simple moves. It was the best birthday present I could have had, those moments with her.

Despite my reservations about celebrating the day, I did. It was an impromptu celebration led by the doorbell and the arrival of Russ with cake and takeout Chinese.

We feasted after that. Russ was a master at drawing Mother out. He was the only person who could keep her from bolting to the family room just because he had arrived. Mother shrank from all company these days. But Russ seemed to have just the knack for including Mother and not making her feel stupid for what she didn't know.

"To Cassie McDowall, daughter extraordinaire." Russ raised his glass and we toasted.

I blushed after I took a sip and set down my glass. "I really wish you'd quit saying that, Russ. It's not true."

"Not many would do what you've done, Cass," Russ whispered as an aside for me. He dropped a casual kiss on my cheek and my heart leapt with a little cry for more.

"Best Chinese food I've had in ages," he said. "Don't you think so, Jess?"

Mother nodded and smiled. There was sauce of some kind

on her upper lip, and I resisted the urge to wipe it off. I'd learned to let the little things go.

I'd also learned sometimes the little things mattered.

That birthday celebration was one I'd never forget. Just me, Mom and Russ in Mother's little kitchen eating Chinese food and listening to Mother's favorite Frank Sinatra tunes. Memories, I stashed them up for a lifetime and that one was put in a drawer with all the others called unforgettable.

Later that evening, with mother asleep on the couch, Russ took my hand and led me outside. We stood under a star-studded sky, shoulder to shoulder, just enjoying the feel of each other's nearness. It had been a wonderful evening with memories I would savor for the remainder of my life.

"Cassie," he said. "You're an amazing woman." His palm cupped the side of my cheek. His breath was hot on my skin. "I love you." Those words were deep, almost a growl in the night.

Silence drifted between us.

I loved him, too, but despite everything I knew, everything I'd thought and even everything we'd done, I couldn't say it.

He cleared his throat, leaned down and kissed me. The heat of that kiss had me lifting off my feet, on my toes meeting him kiss for kiss.

"I want to make a life with you, Cassie," Russ said.

"No." I shook my head and disappointment sunk stone-cold and heavy. "I can't."

"Because of Jess?"

"I just can't." Despite what I said, I wanted to say yes in the worst away. I couldn't.

"I know, you're not ready," he said without looking the least surprised or even upset.

Damn Russ, I thought, but my heart was breaking inside.

"And that wasn't a formal offer."

"Wasn't ..." My mouth snapped shut. I wanted to ask what the hell else that statement was but all I could think were five damning words.

I love you too, Russ.

I wanted to scream the words, instead I watched him walk away. Watched him disappear into the warm night air. I knew what I wanted. I wanted him like I'd never wanted a man before.

I only hoped if and when I was ready, it wouldn't be too late.

Chapter Thirty

It was the homecare worker's visiting day. This was my time to relax. I was looking forward to settling down with one of my favorite authors and the latest historical romance. I couldn't remember the last time I'd done that.

I'd barely settled when there was a clash of voices coming from the back of the house—bedrooms or the bathroom, I wasn't sure. Didn't matter—the outcome was the same.

"Kraut!" Mother shrieked.

"Jess, please."

I heard Anna's voice as I dropped the book and skidded at a run from the porch to the kitchen. But I was still too far away to stop what would happen next. I heard the smack of flesh on flesh, and rage sailed through me. Had Anna slapped Mother? How could she?

Mother yelled the slur again followed by a curse.

Mother kept hollering one insult after another.

I ran the short length of that hallway, cracked my elbow against the wall as I turned the corner. It seemed the longest run of my life. I almost ran into Anna who looked at me with her hands to her cheeks and tears sparkling in her eyes.

"I'm sorry." She said to me, and dropped her hands as a defeated expression swept across her pale face where the red-imprint of Mother's hand seemed to jump out at me. "I can't do this."

"What do you mean you can't do this? I promise she'll never do this again.""

"No." She shook her head. "I didn't tell you but I've had trouble with your mother before, before the bathing incident and even after. And, then this. I don't think we're a good match." She slipped on her coat, repeating her apology as she closed the door.

I supposed I didn't blame her. There was only so much you would take for a paycheck and being assaulted by your charge, no matter the reason, might be the line in the sand. Still, my eyes filmed. How could I take care of a woman with dementia when even the professionals couldn't do it?

As the door shut behind her I was faced with Mother who looked at me with those beautiful blue eyes full of nothing but innocence.

"What were you thinking?" I demanded.

"Lunch?" she asked hopefully and took my hand to lead me out to the kitchen.

I wanted to rip my hand free and tell Mother she'd been cruel to talk like that to Anna. I wanted not to be angry but I couldn't help myself. Instead I pulled my hand free and I said none of the things I was thinking, but later I thought about why it might have happened. Anna did have a bit of an accent having been born in Germany. We had a good discussion about it, she and I, about Germany and the challenge of coming to a new country at the age of fifteen. Because of her age, she'd never lost her accent.

And Mother, she'd always been open to other cultures, languages, and races.

That was the first I'd heard of a dislike of Germans.

"Mom, why did you do that to Anna?"

She looked at me vacantly.

I knew better. I knew she didn't remember what she'd done or even who Anna was.

We sat down to our sandwiches. As I dug into mine and washed it down with a healthy swallow of iced tea, I could feel Mother's eyes on me.

"You were always so pretty, Cass."

"No Mom, that's you."

She shook her head. "A beautiful girl."

I took another bite of the sandwich.

"His beautiful lips."

Okay that made me put the sandwich down.

"Beautiful," she repeated dreamily and took a bite of her sandwich.

"Tell me about him, Mom."

"Gone. But I have you." She patted my hand and looked at the fridge. "More iced tea."

•

I called the agency again the next day to see if I could speak to Anna and offer a proper apology but I was told she had been reassigned and was unavailable. They didn't offer a replacement and I didn't ask.

Nadia called a few days later and I brushed her off. I was pissed at the system. They, with all their big promises from the neurologist to the homecare service—they had all promised they were no less than my savior. They'd not only failed, they'd ditched and ran. So Mother and I limped along without help. Once I'd cooled down, I realized I was wrong. It was only homecare that had failed. The others wanted to help me if I'd let them. I just wasn't so sure they could. And really, after what I had begun to think of as the incident, I was rather reluctant to ask for another homecare worker. Not only was my confidence in the system shaken but Mother had a reputation. She was officially difficult.

That hurt. Because I know how much Mother would have hated that. My genteel, considerate Mother who knew every etiquette rule and had the art of courtesy mastered, would never have thought to call anyone a Kraut—or assault someone.

When we went to the next appointment with the neurologist he wasn't pleased to hear the help was no more.

"You can't do this on your own. I don't care if you think you can." There was an edge to his voice that I'd never heard before. He shook his head.

"I don't need help. It's all right."

"No," he said. "It's not. I just had a caregiver admitted to hospital this morning. It was all too much. Now my patient is facing a nursing home." His eyes met mine, intense, hard brown with a hint of pain in his recently sun-bronzed face. "You need help."

He sifted through papers on his desk before continuing. "Sign her up for adult daycare. The nursing home has one, eight a.m. to six p.m. Check with your social worker and she'll be able to arrange it all."

I shook my head—determined.

"Cass. It's not a nursing home per se. It's a daycare, a place where Jessica Jane can socialize, be entertained and you can have a break. It's important for your mental health. And you don't need to do it all day or even every day."

"You may be right," I said reluctantly.

"I know I am. It's not fair to Jessica Jane either. She needs to get out and see others despite her condition and maybe because of it. It does patients good to associate with others like them. I think it brings comfort for them to know they're not alone, even if they can't put a definition on that. I believe, just my opinion mind you, there's a certain camaraderie in being around others like them that's good for their spirit."

"I don't know."

"Stimulus with others and a break for you. I think it's a win-win situation. Preserving your health which is ultimately good for your mother."

When I retrieved Mother from the nurse's watchful eyes that day, her eyes lit up at the sight of me. For the first time I could see the end without a sense of dread. Acknowledging that fact weighed on me.

I couldn't face arranging daycare that day so instead I decided on a trip. The idea came to me in a rush. I was feeling landlocked again and aching to travel. I liked to think that Mother might feel the same. I know she'd once loved travel and we'd enjoyed Cuba so much, I'd take her again if it were possible. It was an impossibility of course, but knowing that seemed to make the ache that much deeper. So if we couldn't go on the trip, the trip would come to us. Virtual travel. Mother still had a DVD player and a television that was far from smart. With my options laid out I planned to rent a travel video from the library once a week. That would give us two forms of entertainment, the trip to the library and a night watching the video.

Sunday was the night I'd chosen for the video. Actually, it

was Mother who chose Sunday. She said many months ago that Sundays were a lonely day. Here I'd been obliviously living my life last year and Mother had been alone and lonely. That was more than I could bear.

I remembered that and vowed we'd start doing something special on Sundays. It was the beginning of that ritual. I just wish I had begun sooner.

Chapter Thirty-One

September 12

Cassie is in her first school play, a combination of bad dance and stumbling lines. I was appalled at the direction that was being given to the children. I questioned the teacher and now I'm the official dance director. And it feels right in a way, giving those children a proper feel of what theatre and dance are all about. Maybe when this is done I'll look at what might be offered in the inner city. Maybe dance would be something special for disadvantaged youth.

It's strange to think of that when I'm up to my ears in young people. I know I said I'd wait until Cassandra is older and maybe I will. But the idea is fresh and it excites me. Maybe because that's all it is, an idea. For now I have the play that won't be over for another three weeks.

Last week Helen and I were able to go out on the town. It was Helen's birthday so we splurged on hamburgers and a show.

When we came home it was like weights had been lifted off me. Helen's right. I've been working too hard. Maybe that was my therapy. I still carry the burden of Mama and her last months. I can't seem to forgive myself for not taking care of her myself even though I know it wasn't feasible. Not with an unwilling husband, a full-time job and a child to care for. I know that but it doesn't make me feel any better. The outing with Helen, it was exactly what I needed. We had a good talk like we haven't had in a while. Much as I love Cassie there's only so much you can say to a child.

I promised Helen I'd go out with her again soon. And I will. I haven't felt so good in a very long time.

Later that night Russ stopped by. He was in the habit of doing that from time to time. It might only be for a few minutes but it was enough to send my emotions back from the deep end. I went from mother exhaustion to my heart pounding in romantic anticipation. I was a mess and I wasn't afraid to admit it. There was only one thing to do. I brewed him coffee.

He was in uniform and heading for the night shift. And me, I didn't see that I'd be getting much sleep that night. Caffeine kept me awake if I drank it too late at night.

"You're dodging the issue, Cass." Russ set the spoon aside and cradled his coffee with both hands. "You still haven't faced where this is going with her."

He kept quiet about the other issue—us and where that was going. I was grateful for that. I could only deal with one issue at a time.

"Cassie?" he pushed.

He seemed oblivious to how conflicted he made me feel. Or maybe he knew. There were things I never knew for sure about Russ.

"I know where it's going and I don't want to talk about it." I got up to get the brown sugar and maybe so I didn't have to look into Russ's eyes and see the truth.

"You do, that's true but you're not facing it. You've got to prepare yourself."

"Mother already made the arrangements a long time ago."

"Funeral arrangements," he said bluntly. "That's not what I meant."

I looked at him blankly, hoping, I supposed, he would stop right there. But we'd already spoken of my shaky beliefs. I'd been lazy in the spiritual side of life and it had risen up and threatened to whip my ass.

"You, Cass. What do you believe?"

"That we die and that's it."

"I don't believe it." He looked at me over his coffee mug. "You're never going to get through this if you don't figure out who you are and what you believe."

When he left that night, despite the kiss that had my lips tingling, I was almost glad to see the back of him. For much as I'd do anything for Russ, delving into my murky spiritual beliefs, or lack thereof, was not one of them. I'd already tried and I'd given up for now. But I spent an uneasy hour or two, roaming the house and not getting much done.

I knew Russ had been cutting a fine line between religion and spirituality. I knew I was lacking in both. I'd strayed from formal religion as an adult and dodged the thought of my mortality until this past year.

And even then I hadn't come to any conclusions on how this would end or why I was here or …

•

I began my long put-off spiritual journey with a rerun of a popular motivational talk show that delved into life-changing topics including spirituality. I'm pretty sure that's not what Russ meant, but I had to start somewhere, and as a newbie, I was taking kindergarten steps.

Russ stopped by later that day when his shift ended.

"How's Mother," Russ asked. He'd begun early on to call her Mother or Mom from time to time. I didn't mind really. Besides, when Mother had been more with it, she'd loved that he'd occasionally called her that.

"Not great. She's breathing shorter and heavier. I just had her at the doctor a couple of days ago and he said her lungs are clear. He couldn't find anything else wrong." I traced my finger along the counter. "She seems to have forgotten how to move her ankle when she walks."

"But she's still able to walk," Russ said that like it was a good thing and I supposed it was.

"She is, but she hangs onto my arm with both hands like I'm the only thing keeping her from falling over."

"What about you?" I could hear the concern in his voice.

"I watched a motivational television program this morning. A rerun but hey, you have to start somewhere."

We both laughed at that and when the laughter had faded he said somewhat more seriously. "So spirituality."

"Yep, the host had the guru of it on. I learned that I must find my purpose."

"You knew that."

"I did," I agreed. "But the bigger questions. Why are we all here and what happens to us after we die. You were right. I need to get my head around all of it before …"

"It's a lot to contemplate. One step at a time."

"Aren't you full of platitudes."

"What I do, girl?" He laughed before saying, "I hate to think of you alone here."

"I'm not alone. I have Mom."

"True." He cleared his throat. "Any chance I can take you out one evening?"

Finally, after all these long weeks and months, I agreed.

Two days later Russ made good on that promise. We went out for supper and to a comedy club. I hadn't laughed so hard in a very long time. At one point with Russ's hand over mine, his solid presence next to me—I wondered if it was all a dream.

But it wasn't.

Mom was home safe and Helen was on the couch nodding off when I got home. She stood up with a smile as soon as she saw us.

"You had a good time?" she asked.

"Yes, thank you so much for doing this," I replied.

"You know I'd do anything for Jess," she replied. "And for you. Jess and I have been friends since before you were born."

"Really?" I hadn't known they'd been friends that long.

"Then you knew her when she went to Toronto?"

"Of course. She went twice that I know of. I went to Toronto with her one year," she said with a yawn. "Look I'm dead on my feet. But if you need me again, just call." She looked at Russ. "Do you mind?"

Russ had picked her up and planned to take her home.

"Of course."

I heard the reluctance in his voice. He'd caught on as had I that Helen might know something. We were on the same wavelength. Maybe now when everyone was tired wasn't the time to ask the questions. But I'd be asking them soon. For Helen might know more about mother than I'd ever thought. I'd thought Helen had been friends with Mom since after her marriage broke up, not before. I'd never known she'd been in

Toronto with mother.

Toronto—the place that was the key to it all.

Or, at least that was what I was beginning to believe.

Chapter Thirty-Two

September 26

It had taken me days after Anna had quit to finally be able to help mother bathe. The process had involved trickery. The promise of an ice cream after, for some strange reason, seemed to work—that and planning the bath just after supper. I'd quickly learned the time was as important as the promise of a treat.

I came in with a towel over my arm and saw Mother was already standing by the tub.

"Mom. You're ready for your bath?"

Mother frowned and backed up even though there wasn't far to go. She was leaning against the closed shower doors with her eyes scrunched up and a slight look of panic.

"Who are you?" Her lips trembled and she hugged her arms to her chest.

I know a heart cannot literally break. I thought the term clichéd and worn until that moment. But something froze inside me, one giant ache of unreality. My chest seemed to constrict but I was still amazingly calm. This was a normal part of the disease, I told myself.

"Get away!" She made shooing movements and seemed to curl into herself.

"Mom."

She doesn't know you. The thought was foreign, like a treacherous invader had taken over my body. *She doesn't know you.* I couldn't stop thinking that. My eyes watered. I took a shaky breath. It was all a mistake.

I took a step forward and she cowered tighter against the glass panes of the shower door.

I held out my hand and she shrank away. She didn't know me. My mother had forgotten me. I never thought the time would come and now that it had, I didn't know how to face it. I didn't know if I could.

I reached deep inside to find that part of me that could divorce emotion from a situation that required only logic. There was no love in the beautiful blue eyes that stared back at me, only distrust and fear. I had to meet her head on, stranger to stranger. I was strong. I could do this.

"Mrs. McDowall," I began as I tried a different approach in the face of her obvious lack of recognition. Something ripped, some emotional well deep within me and I reminded myself that this was worse for Mother. She was lost and alone—and facing a stranger. I had to help her, bring her off that awful precipice.

It took all I had.

"Jess," she whispered, but the fright had yet to leave her face.

"Jess," I said agreeably. I wrestled the tremor from those words. "I need your help." I choked on the emotion that swept through me like an intellectual blackout. I couldn't think of what to do. I could only look into blue eyes that were wide with fright. I shoved tears to the side in search of a solution.

If there was anything Mother couldn't resist, it was a plea for help. In her prime, she'd belonged to three volunteer organizations. She hesitated but I could see her back wasn't pressed quite as tightly against the glass. I took another step forward and held out my hand. The backs of my knees quivered but that hand never shook, not once.

And she took it.

"Let's go for a walk, Mom," I said as casually as if the incident had never happened. I hoped her heart wasn't knocking as roughly as mine.

"Yes, Cass, let's," she replied and she left the bathroom like nothing had happened.

An ache settled in my gut, like an unfulfilled urge to cry. It was an ache I knew wasn't going away—not for a long time.

I mulled over the idea of talking my angst through with an outside observer, a therapist, someone who was versed at helping me, and not just Mother.

I sniffed and fished for a tissue. My stomach clenched and I wanted to curl up and cry.

My mother had forgotten me. Briefly. But it had happened nonetheless. I had never felt so shaken in my life, not when we got the diagnosis. Not even when she was lost.

It's not that I hadn't known there were two worst-case-scenarios. Mother forgetting me was only second to what was worse; I didn't want to grapple with that. I'd read enough on death and dying. What I wasn't getting the hang of was the whole grieving that came before it. I wasn't sure how to work through it. Maybe it was crying I needed more of. Or maybe I had to be thankful for what I had. I needed to enjoy these moments, breeze over the bumps and love Mother while she was here. I could do that. Live in the moment as I had vowed how many days earlier. For my sanity and Mother's wellbeing, I had to do that.

Later that week, video night had me opening the door to Russ who gave me a hug and a kiss that fell short of passion but promised so many other things. I clung to him and he kissed me again. The heat of him, having him here, was enough. It was the icing on a very strange cake when I led him into the living room and saw the happiness in mother's eyes. Standing between the two of them was all I needed. I was home—those I loved were safe and life was good.

That week our video was taking us to Spain. When Mother heard, she broke into a grin, curved her arms and did a ballerina pirouette that didn't quite get her on her toes. I did a rather shoddy spin beside her and didn't consider whether ballet music had any relevance to Spain. We were dancing and that was all that mattered.

●

"Cass." Mother's voice was quieter than it had been in a long time. A few days had passed since our Spanish video. She was slightly hoarse as she called from the edges of sleep. I imagined the voices and closing door had awakened her as I'd seen Helen out.

"C'mon, Mom." I pulled her from the chair she'd fallen asleep in two hours before. "Let's go for a walk." I was determined to keep her moving and as physically active as possible. I fingered my phone and hoped we'd make the six-block walk I'd planned, three blocks one way and three blocks home.

"Lovely car," Mother enthused as we passed a hatch-backed blue Ford. She said the same thing when we passed a Honda. Blue was her favorite color as far as cars were concerned.

It took us an hour to do a six-block circuit. Physically, Mother had deteriorated rapidly in the last two weeks. Only a week ago her general physician, the man I had once called a quack, had suggested it might be due to a combination of her age and her condition. He couldn't hear anything abnormal in her heartbeat and didn't think she required further testing.

The neurologist had been blunter. He had asked me numerous questions, all of them leading to one point. If there were something wrong, did we have a moral obligation to fix it or leave it? The questions stymied me. My heart said fix it and my logic said, well, my logic said nothing. It was in a death-grip wrestle with my heart.

The phone rang near the end of the week and Mother looked at me blankly. There was no connection between the ringing phone and a person wanting to speak to us. We were in the midst of one of our walks but even then another person, a voice from the outside, was a welcome intrusion.

"Cassie." It was Russ. "How are things?"

"We're just out walking."

"You're okay. Need anything?"

"Fine, Russ. You worry too much." But I said it gratefully.

"What's this week's trip?" he asked.

"Australia. Want to come along?"

"I'd love to but I start night shift tomorrow. Next week?"

"France," I said. "Can you make it?"

"Definitely."

"I'm holding you to that."

"You know I'll be there."

And I did. He'd been here every day, every hour he could. I couldn't see my life without either of them, Russ or mother. But one of them was leaving and I didn't have a choice.

Hours later, the lights were dimmed and a bowl of popcorn sat between us. A koala peered at us from the television. Mother chuckled and reached for a handful of popcorn. She tried to put the whole thing in her mouth and followed the half she did get in with a good slug of coke. I followed behind with a napkin and tried to catch what didn't make her mouth.

I'm not sure what Mother remembered of the show but I know her eyes lit up at the sight of the surfers.

"Crazy," was all she said.

I knew she referred to the surfers. And on that, we agreed.

Chapter Thirty-Three

October 24

"Quiet time," the neurologist had said when I'd asked him how he dealt with so much illness. "Every day I make sure I have time to myself."

"And you think."

He shook his head and laughed. "Exactly the opposite. I try not to think. And I get out in nature."

"Not an option."

"If it's answers you're looking for, I think they're inside. It's a matter of unlocking what you already know." He shrugged. "Utterly simplistic I know, but it worked for me."

We talked more about Mother and end-of-life care. It was a reality now, that Mother's time was short. I was learning to face that without railing against the fates and an unknown God.

"Thanks for the book." I handed him the book on bereavement he'd lent me weeks earlier.

"I've got more if you're interested. More of a life purpose sort of nature, finding your path, that kind of thing."

"I used to laugh at that kind of airy fairy stuff." I smiled.

"And now?" He didn't smile back.

"I'll take whatever you're willing to lend me."

I headed home that day with two loaners on spirituality. But I wasn't as ready as I thought. I let those books sit on the coffee table for a few days. A week later I had yet to pick one of them up.

•

That year October was the month that never ended. Nothing held Mother's interest. With Halloween only days away I couldn't conceive of that holiday being anything more than a nightmare. Not a nightmare in the fun way most people and/ or children think of Halloween.

"What are you doing for Halloween?" Russ asked.

"Playing Grinch and turning off the lights."

"That's not you and you know it. Look, why don't I man the door for you?"

"Did I ever tell you, you're a gem?"

"No, but I wouldn't mind if you showed me," he said good-naturedly.

And the gentle caress of his forefinger against my cheek made me want to lean into him and tell him everything I was feeling.

I told Mother our Halloween plans and she only looked at me vacantly like she had no idea who Russ was.

Despite that, I was actually looking forward to Halloween now that I didn't have to dodge the door. And when I opened the door to Russ early on the evening of Halloween, I could only grin.

"My favorite," I proclaimed as I took the pizza box from him.

"I thought you'd approve." He stepped in and shrugged off his coat. "How's our Jessica Jane?"

"Quiet." I frowned at him, determined to mask the relief of seeing him. "You're early." I ushered him inside.

The doorbell rang before I'd shut the inside door.

"Apparently not early enough." He grinned. "Some of the little munchkins almost beat me here." He pulled open the door and began the promised commitment to man the door to the trick-or-treaters.

Meantime, I got the pizza on the table and Mother settled. Russ sat with us and ate in fits and starts as the door traffic continued.

"Who are you?" Mother asked.

"Russ."

"No." She shook her head and her finger at him. "Who are you?" she repeated.

"I think she wants to know where your costume is."

Mother nodded happily. She got up in a big hurry and rushed to her bedroom. Sometimes I could only marvel at the mysteries of the human brain for when she came back it was with a wig that a charitable person might have called red, I called it burnt orange. I don't know how she remembered that one wig in the swamp of her mind, but she did.

And Russ, he took that wig from her and put it on his neatly combed dark curls with a flourish. "Thanks, Mom."

She grinned with her hands on her hips.

I just outright laughed. You'd never seen a funnier sight than Russ with that wig perched awkwardly on his head. To top it off, Mother handed him her apron to complete the outfit.

Once he had it all donned, she held up her hand with thumb and index in an okay position.

"You don't have to leave it on," I said through spurts of laughter.

Mother just shook her head and then her finger at him.

Russ wore that outfit until the last trick-or-treater left and we turned out the light.

Mother had long since fallen asleep in the middle of a movie I'd turned on for her.

"Did you sign up for university classes?" Russ asked.

It was strange how he could be so in tune. Weeks ago I had made that one failed online attempt, but recently I'd begun to think about it again. Maybe I'd mentioned that to him in random passing.

"I found a university that has online classes I'm interested in."

"Economics?"

"Psychology." Somehow helping people with dementia interested me more than the economics passion of my youth.

"That's an interesting twist."

"Psychology suits this phase of my life more than economics ever did."

I turned the TV off as Mother headed off to bed.

"How are you doing?" He asked after we'd sat there in

peaceful silence for a few minutes. His hand brushed mine in a caress that made me feel completely wanted. He wrapped an arm around me and drew me close. His fingers traced a gentle caress along my neck. I leaned into him, savoring his strength. Passion seeped into the embrace as he kissed me and his hands stroked inches beneath my shirt—consoling caresses that promised so many other things.

His lips lifted from mine and our eyes locked.

His finger combed a strand of hair from my face.

"How are you holding up?" he asked and the question put us in a different space.

And this time my answer was honest, when I told him fine.

Chapter Thirty-Four

Monday, November 7

I'm not as charitable as I'd like others to see me. I try but sometimes I'm just too tired to care like I should. Maybe it's just that some days it can be overwhelming. There is so much grief in this world. Even here where we are considered so lucky.

The soup kitchen today was troubling. A man was there who didn't seem to know where he was or I suspect even who he was. The supervisor said he was demented and I thought that was such a horrible term. Imagine someone who has lost their mind. But then as I watched him, I realized maybe it wasn't so bad for him. He didn't seem to know there was anything wrong with him. Instead he sang a childish ditty like he had returned to being a boy. It reminded me of Mama and I wanted so much to bundle him up and take him away from there, as if he had somehow become Mama. I thought I couldn't look at him when I served him but he smiled at me so sweetly I almost forgot the state he was in. Still I'd hate if I became demented, senile as Mama used to call it. That would be awful for Cassie. I couldn't bear it for either of us.

I slipped a blanket around mother as she slept and my fingers skimmed absently through the diary. The pages I flipped were blank near the end until I was suddenly stopped by another entry, one that had somehow become lost in the sea of blank pages that preceded and followed it. My heart stuttered as my finger traced words more recent than all the rest, written over fifteen years ago.

I believe Cassie's wanderlust was inherited from Mama same as me. Although she never said, I remember whenever she took me to the library as a child, my instructions were to report to her in the travel section once I'd found the books I wanted. It was the only way she could afford to travel. It's strange how things run in families — the urge to travel, the inability to make money. Although I'm proud to see Cassandra has broken that rule. She might never have a job that counts for much but she's a whiz at taking the bit she's earned and making it work hard. I wish I had that knack. It sure would be more useful than the talent I do have. Dance hasn't done more than entertain us and provide a few laughs.

And as I write that I think — is there something more I can do? Maybe handing out meals at the soup kitchen or working in the hospital is a waste of the talent God gave me. Maybe I should be thinking of some way to use my dance to help others. It certainly would be more helpful than spending precious hours thinking about what might have been.

I don't know why I'm so mired in the past. It's a bad habit or maybe even an illness. I believe that Helen suggested once that I might be depressed. I don't know why I should be. Since Cassie left home I've entered that phase where life is supposed to get easier, and it has, at least financially. But I have more spare time that I need to fill. The charities aren't enough. I think I may be facing a belated midlife crisis. And I sense the only way around that is a good dose of reality. I bought my bus ticket just yesterday and I'm going to spend some time with Aunt Alice. She brings me around like no one else can.

"Mother," I whispered, as she slept quietly in the armchair across from me. "You have no idea how much I love you." Her disease was not something inflicted on me. That I had to deal with it was nothing compared to what she had lost. That's what had torn me apart over the last year, what I had mourned — everything Mother was missing out on, everything she was suffering. I looked at her now with an ache that only wanted to make everything right for her.

The possibility that Mother had suffered from depression was a revelation, and I realized a possible precursor to Alzheimer's. I dropped the little book and ran a quiet hand through Mother's hair. I wanted to comfort her in the worst way and yet in that moment she looked more peaceful than I'd ever seen her. In the hour I watched her, I memorized every line and curve on her face. She was Mother and when she looked at me with that sweet smile, with those beautiful blue eyes of hers shining a big fat hello—there was nothing better. I wished I could tell her what she meant to me as I'd told her not frequently enough in the past. I could, I knew that. I guess what I really wished was that she would remember.

Finally, I picked her up and carried her to bed. As I tucked her in I was thankful once again for being gifted with a sturdy frame. There weren't many women who could pick their mother up and carry them as easily as I could. Granted, Mother was tiny, but she was still slightly over a hundred pounds.

"Thanks, Aunt Alice," I whispered to the absent Aunt from whom I'd clearly inherited my solid build. I bent down and gave Mother a kiss and then pulled another blanket over her. Despite what the thermostat said, the house seemed to take on a chill as the outside temperature dipped. Mother grunted, muttered in her sleep, and turned over. As I looked at her with her back turned to me, that's when I lost it. I just stood there and cried.

The phone rang and it was Helen. She'd called many times before and stopped over but it was this time that I had the courage to ask questions that nagged me.

"Helen do you mind if I ask you some questions about my father? About Fidel?"

"She told you. Oh my." She hesitated. "I don't know, Cass."

"Please, Helen. Mother can't and I need to know."

There was silence on the line.

"Look, I know she had an affair when she went down to Toronto and that was where I was conceived," I said bluntly. I'd realized in the course of a year, there was no time for anything but straight talking. While I may take a while to ask the question when I do, it's straight up. "But you went down there with her when she went the second time. Why?"

"You mean, did I know about Fidel? Yes. But I never met him."

"Why not?"

"Your mother met him privately. She didn't want me along. It was an embarrassment at the time, at least it was for your mother. She was always so proper. She was married and Fidel had to be kept secret."

"And that was the last time she saw him?"

"Pretty much," Helen agreed. "But he was in contact, off and on. Your mother didn't say much about it except when she mentioned he wanted to come west. She'd told him no."

A hint of anger rose in me as I imagined what I had missed because of the decisions of others, because of my mother. The anger settled. I couldn't be angry with her. It was too late and I'm sure she had her reasons. Mother had always done what she thought was best for me—always. I doubted if she'd failed me this time.

"He planned to come here?"

"Yes, but the poor man passed before he could follow through." She preceded to repeat what I already knew, but then I struck gold.

"He had a cousin in Cuba, maybe a few. I remember he was going to go back."

So far nothing I didn't already know. "Do you know their last name."

"No dear, I'm sorry. And I don't know where in Cuba. Except that one was a male cousin near his own age who ran tours. I think somewhere around Havana."

My heartbeat quickened at that news. It was a morsel but I'd take any crumb I could get.

Later I was curled up on the couch with an oversized bowl of ice cream held tightly on my lap. It was like my safety line in a world where reality had slipped sideways. It brought back the simplicity of childhood when Mother was fully aware of the month and year and I was not. Ice cream was a passion we both still shared. In fact, ice cream and condiments were really some of the only things she would eat without coaching. At that point there was nothing much left for her except the affection the two of us shared and the few foods she still loved.

The phone rang and for a moment I didn't get up. One ring, two, three—they weren't giving up. I was heavy on my feet, like a drunk and yet I hadn't had a drop of alcohol since last

Sunday when Mother and I shared a cocktail.

I grabbed the phone on the sixth ring.

"Cassie." Russ's voice was full of concern.

"Yeah," I muttered, feeling slightly resentful he couldn't have just hung up and left me alone.

"What's wrong?"

"Nothing." But I knew there wasn't an ounce of inflection in my voice.

"Look. I'm coming right over."

"No. Don't bother. I'll be fine."

"You sound a long way from fine to me. I'll be there in twenty."

Turns out he was there in ten. I wasn't sure how he made it that fast. But I opened the door and only wanted to throw myself into his arms. I didn't.

"You've got to do something for yourself," he encouraged as we sat in the family room and he stretched his long legs out in front of him, crossed his arms and looked at me seriously. "And I don't just mean an online university class."

"There's no time. Mother's a full-time job."

"You can take her to daycare more than one day a week."

"No."

"You need to take her to daycare more often. Mornings only if you want but you need some space." He looked at me speculatively. "And you need to do something for you. You're no good to your mother if you fall apart."

"I will not ..."

He cut me off. "Won't you?" He got up and came over to where I sat. He sat down beside me and draped his arm lightly over my shoulders. I wanted to burrow myself into him, to disappear and let someone else take over the astronomical problem that was now Mother. What was with that insatiable urge to escape? My emotions were all over the map. One day I could handle everything and faced it head-on, and other times, like that evening, I was a mess. Truthfully, that evening was the lowest I ever went.

"Maybe," I agreed. "It's just so hard."

"And you've been doing amazingly well." He lifted my chin with one finger, looked deeply into my eyes, and kissed me lightly.

"I think the sooner you get on it the better. Get her signed in for every weekday. I mean it, Cass." It was more an order than a suggestion, and maybe that's what I needed.

I was feeling slightly better. For the first time I noticed he hadn't taken his coat off, and underneath he was wearing his police-issue pants.

"You're on duty?"

"Yeah, but I was due a break." He looked at his watch. "I should get going." His gaze explored my face. "You're going to be okay?"

I nodded. "I think so." I didn't tell him what I'd learned. He was on a timer. I'd tell him later tomorrow or even the next day. There wasn't a rush. My father hadn't been in my life for a very long time and there was no hope of it now. Now it was only details to fill in the blanks of a family tree, nothing more.

"You can get through this. Just not alone." His fingers brushed briefly under my chin. His eyes locked on mine.

"I don't know if I can," I whispered and my eyes dropped to the remains of the ice cream that was slowly melting in the carton.

"Look, I'll call you tomorrow. If you haven't signed on for more daycare days, I'll drive you over to the place myself." He stopped with his hand on the door. "Promise me you'll do it."

"Promise." I shocked myself. I was desperate, and somehow my subconscious had wrestled my non-conforming conscious aside and called for help.

"Promise," he agreed and followed it with a brush of his lips against my cheek.

It was less than the passion we'd already shared. But it meant every bit as much.

Even as I thought that, he took me in his arms and kissed me again. It was a kiss that held restrained passion and promises of things to come. I clung to him, my arms locked around him like I'd never let him go. And he kissed me with enough passion to make me weak at the knees.

"I love you," he said.

And all the strength that was left in those knees evaporated. I loved him, but there was no way I could tell him yet. Not now, not with everything on my plate.

He drew back, his knuckle caressing the side of my cheek.

"Ah, Cass," he said with a thick edge to his voice that hadn't been there before; it seemed to suggest he knew exactly how I felt. He took my hand and squeezed it. "Look, I've got to go but I'll check in later. You're doing a fabulous job and you're not alone. Don't ever forget that."

"I know," I said. It wasn't the "fabulous job" I was agreeing to. The fabulous job was the support Russ gave me.

My heart raced a bit too fast, and my nipples tingled from the heat of being pressed against Russ.

"Talk to you in the morning."

He bent and gave me one last kiss.

I was feeling more than better when I shut the door to a draft of cool autumn air. Things were bad on one side but on the other—Russ loved me. I did a little twist and spin. Life sucked and life was fantastic, and somewhere in the good and bad—we all met in the middle.

Chapter Thirty-Five

November 14

There was something wrong with Mother. I woke up before dawn that morning and went to check on her. I'm not sure what aroused me, a sound, instinct—it could have been anything.

"Mom," I whispered into the darkness of early dawn.

I could hear her breathing. It was a raspy inhale followed by a rattling exhale. Her bedclothes rustled but other than that, she was quiet.

I tiptoed in and turned on her bedside light.

Nothing.

"Mom?"

I leaned over and placed the back of my hand on her forehead. It was too hot. I got a thermometer and discovered her temperature was hovering somewhere between 100 and 101.

"Mom." I gently shook her shoulder.

"Mmmm." It was rather an incoherent mumble. I wasn't sure if she was responding or if she was just reacting.

Her bedclothes were sticking to her. "Can you get up, Mom?"

Nothing. She either wasn't able to understand what I was saying or wasn't able to get up. I never found out which. It didn't matter. I needed to get her to the hospital and she wasn't getting there on her own power.

An ambulance delivered us both to the Emergency Room doors that morning.

"Pneumonia," the intern who examined her proclaimed.

"We'll have to keep her overnight at least." He shook his head. "That's only if she responds to the medication. There's a good chance she doesn't."

"And then?"

"She may not make it. Alzheimer's is a devastating disease both mentally and physically. I can see she's already physically weak. I don't know if she has the resources to pull through. We'll do everything we can."

"No." I held up my hand. My heart pounded. "Don't. No extra measures." And it was like I could hear Mother's sigh of relief at those words.

He fingered his stethoscope. "We'll keep her comfortable, that and antibiotics. Maybe that will be enough."

I didn't go home. I'd resolved since the last event I wasn't leaving Mother alone in the hospital again. As the hours wore away, Mother seemed to only get worse. I knew before the intern delivered further news in the form of his doubts Mother had the strength to fight.

I could feel the truth as cold and ugly as the ageless hospital walls.

Helen showed up only a few hours later.

"Take a break, Cass. I'll sit with her for a bit."

"No, Helen."

"Yes, Cassie. When my husband died I had no one to lean on. I vowed ages ago that I would never let a caregiver go through what I did."

"Thanks." I was saying a lot of that lately.

And so it went—Helen was followed by another of mother's friends, Eleanor. She was followed by Henri but by seven o'clock that night it was just Mother and me. She was sleeping. There was an oxygen mask over her face and her breathing was easier with just a little rattle-like puff that indicated things weren't one-hundred percent right.

At eight, Russ showed up. He was wearing jeans and a flannel shirt, and despite the country-like edge to his dress it looked good on his lanky frame.

"How is she?" he asked as he propped himself in the doorway.

"She's comfortable," I assured him.

"Do you want me to spell you off?"

"I'm fine for a few more hours. You don't have to hang."

"Try to make me leave," he said as his hand ran a gentle caress through my hair. His presence was a bolster in the hours that followed.

We talked quietly for a time, spelled each other off for supper, and talked some more. It was amazing how many commonalities we had. We never ran out of subjects for conversation. Hours passed before we finally pulled the plug on conversation and hauled out a deck of cards. That's one thing about a hospital—you lose track of the hours in a place where nothing really quiets. Call bells rang and the intercom sounded off an intermittent alert as carts rattled down the stark corridors and hospital personnel engaged in rapid-speak conferences in any available alcove. Through it all, Mother slept and at one in the morning I found myself playing Go Fish with Russ.

As the night dwindled, we tired of cards and set them aside. We talked more, me sitting by Mother, one hand sifting through her hair. Russ perched at the end of the bed, his hand resting on her foot. It was strange but that contact seemed to bring Mother into the conversation even though she had yet to gain consciousness.

Silence drifted between us. I was thinking back over the year that had elapsed since we'd met up again as adults and I assumed he was doing the same.

"Let's have another game," he suggested as silence settled and the seriousness of it all weighed in around us.

We both got up, stretched and moved to the chairs at the end of Mother's bed. He sat down, picked up the cards, stretched out his legs, and looked at me with a hurry-up, good-humored expression on his face.

I found that part of him, that ability to enjoy simple things, delightful.

As I sat down, I glanced over at Mother. The intravenous machine beeped and hummed. Mother's steady breaths were evident as the oxygen hissed through her mask.

"She'll be fine." Russ shuffled the cards and then set them down. "I'm sorry. It was a thoughtless thing to say."

He took my hand as we sat at the end of Mother's bed using her rolling tray as a card table.

I squeezed his hand and stood up. "Forget this. Let's get coffee."

He looked startled, and I didn't blame him. It was the first time I'd suggested Mother could be left alone for any reason.

"I might lose her," I whispered. "But I don't think it will happen in the next hour."

He stood up. But there was a slouch to him like he meant to sit right back down just as soon as I changed my mind. He looked at me and I looked at him. I gave him the "I'm serious" look, and he drew himself up tall and straight and stood by the door. I pulled the blanket up around Mother and gave her a kiss on the cheek.

"I'll just be gone a minute, Mom," I whispered, although Mother hadn't been conscious since the last round of medication five hours ago.

In the hospital cafeteria we hunched over the table. There was a coffee in front of each of us and silence spread between. There really was nothing to say. We both knew where this was going and there was nothing we could do. The medical system had finally pulled in the last rein and it was now it and Mother, and a matter of time.

At least that's what I thought until I met Russ's troubled brown eyes.

"She would have wanted this," I said. I fingered the cup's rim. "To go quickly in the end, I mean."

Russ covered my hand with his. His instincts were always bang-on. He knew when to talk and when not to.

"I wish I felt the same." I lifted my eyes to his and saw nothing but silent concern reflected there. Silence had somehow become the commodity of choice.

Together we went back up to the ward. I leaned hard on Russ through those long night hours.

Chapter Thirty-Six

November 15

I sent Russ home early the next morning. It was only my desire to be alone with Mother that convinced him to go, and even then he insisted I call immediately should I need him.

The neurologist even made a trip to the hospital later that morning. I appreciated that considering his work was more than likely done.

"I'll miss our visits," he said softly.

It was strange really, how the illness twisted and mutated lives and allowed me to become close to this man. We were friends in an odd, short-term kind of way. I didn't know if our friendship would survive once Mother was gone. I blinked at that thought and looked away.

"She loved seeing you, Alphonse."

It had been ridiculous to call him by anything but his given name since long before he'd danced at Mother's barbecue.

"I wish all my patients were as endearing."

His hand trailed on the metal bed rail as if he wasn't sure how he should act or what he should say as Mother breathed gently through her mask and the oxygen whispered through the line.

He had been my lifeline for so many months. Had I told him that?

"We can't thank you enough."

"It was nothing more than my job."

"Your job and then some."

I felt odd standing there facing him with Mother's bed

between us.

"You know, in all the years of my practice I've never become involved with a patient or their caregiver like this. You became a friend, Cass. You and Jessica Jane." His hand dropped lightly to Mother's forehead in a brief touch before he dropped his hands to his side. "You're unforgettable."

"Thank you," I whispered and I said it for both of us, me and Mother. And then I walked around Mother's bed and hugged him. It was an awkward hug and he stood stiffly in it. But it was my way of thanking him, for being there, for making time, for doing what we paid him to do and so much more, for being a friend. I probably wouldn't invite him to another barbecue; he wasn't that type of friend. But when we'd needed him, he'd been there.

When he left, we were alone. The nurses had obviously gone through this many times before. Other than making sure I had everything I needed they had withdrawn to their station and to the rooms of other patients, patients who still had hope and as such, needed nursing care.

I took Mother's hand—it was chilled and I chaffed it between both of mine hoping to force the circulation. I reached for a blanket and tucked her in, slowly folding the pink wool around her shoulders. The blanket softened her now taut features. She sighed and seemed to snuggle deeper.

There was a relaxed and calm feeling in the room. All the peace emanated from her.

I instinctively felt the imminence of her last breath. Her eyes were clear and she pulled me to her. As I shifted her oxygen mask and leaned over to kiss her, it was she who kissed me, a feather touch, on the cheek. There were no last words, only that last brush of skin against skin, a reminder of a love that had lasted a lifetime.

I smiled softly.

You were a difficult birth, Cassandra Lynn.

It was the echo of memories that made me smile. She'd told me the story of my birth many times. From what I knew, she was more considerate about her dying than I ever was over my arrival. I know that I'd not only false alarmed her twice and caused her to call a cab for the ride to the hospital—a whole unnecessary ten dollars out of her pocket, but that then I'd had the nerve to take the better part of the day to arrive. I'd had half the obstetrics floor in an uproar when on arrival I decided that breathing was optional. All-in-all I was a troublesome delivery.

Not so with Mother. Hers was the perfect exit. It seemed rather irreverent to think of it that way but I couldn't help it. It was exactly what Mother would have wanted. In fact, that's exactly what Mother had said only a few short months ago. I'd closed my mind to any words of her departure then. I remembered them clearly now.

It was funny, the thoughts that went through your head at a time like that. There was no procedure manual; it was as if thinking irreverent thoughts became a coping mechanism. For there really weren't a lot of other options. Breaking down and crying tears that never ended was one option. I don't know how emotionally helpful that would be. Besides, I couldn't cry. I wasn't ready. Instead, I sat and held Mother's hand and blessed her as she had so often blessed me with stories that all began with, "Remember the time …"

I had just gotten up to the year she had almost drowned me while teaching me to swim. That was when the nurse entered the room. I swung around, but I still clung to Mother's hand.

The nurse frowned and strode briskly over to the opposite side of the bed. She took out a stethoscope and listened.

"She's gone." The nurse confirmed a fact that I had known for over fifteen minutes. It had taken me that long to pull the call bell. "You should have called sooner."

She scurried around, adjusting the headboard and then glanced at me. "I'll give you another few minutes."

I nodded as she gave me a sympathetic look before leaving the room.

When I pass, Cassie, I plan to do it with dignity. No wailing and moaning on your part either.

I remembered Mother had shaken her finger at me as she'd said it.

I'll go out quietly and not before I'm darn good and ready.

She hadn't spoken about dying again. It was the one and only time. But she'd done it exactly as she'd threatened. If I hadn't been so damn sad I would have been happy for her.

I brought her diary with me to the hospital. Accidentally really, it was tucked in my purse where I'd put it the last time I'd read it. I loved having it here—a part of Mother. Except for a small exception, one year in her life that told me so much about this woman I loved. I opened it wanting to read her words while I could see her—just one last time.

I wasn't there for Mama when she died. It's a gift that few people receive, to be there when a loved one dies. I think even in dying there's a gift many of us aren't willing to give. I've seen many a soul die when a loved one leaves the room. Almost like they want to spare them. In my days pushing that cart full of juice and snacks through the hospital and sitting with patients who seemed to have no one— there was only one that allowed me to stay when they took their last breath.

I feel strange writing this. Maybe because Mama's death is still fresh and I'm full of memories of my own childhood. I wonder what Cassie will remember when I die. I made mistakes, Tom being one of them, but never did I make a mistake having her. I was sure of that from the beginning. What kind of childhood did I give her? I tried to give her the best.

I stopped reading right there as I leaned over and kissed her cheek that was soft and still so warm that I couldn't believe she was gone.

"You did, Mom. You gave me the best and more," I whispered as I stroked her hair.

When I left, I think I was numb until I got to the parking lot. Even then I curled over the steering wheel, my eyes hot and dry—and from somewhere I couldn't name came a mournful keening more ache than sound.

When I got home, I walked into that empty house and all I could think to do was phone Russ. I told him matter-of-factly what had happened. I also told him I would be fine. I needed to be alone.

"You did everything you could. Few are that lucky," he said.

Somehow those blunt words took the edge off my bravado. My voice broke and I fought tears that burned and didn't fall.

"I'm hanging up now, Cassie. I'll be over."

His arms were soon around me. His solid presence offered more comfort than any stale words ever could.

"She did it her way," I said with a sad smile as I looked up at him.

"*My Way*, Frank Sinatra?" he asked with a smile.

I nodded and hummed a shaky melody.

Chapter Thirty-Seven

November 19

Numb.

That's really the only way to describe it.

I couldn't imagine life without Mother. It had been Mother and me for so long. We worked as a unit. Even when Mother slipped completely off the rails it was still us. What was I going to do now?

"It's a celebration of your Mother's life," the priest had assured me as he took both my hands in his.

It was all I could do not to beg him to please ditch the standard service, the rote prayers and tell it like it was.

"You'll say a few words about her? Who she really was?" I knew I couldn't. But something should be said and this priest had known her for years. Who better than someone Mother had revered. I'd already given him enough information to fill in any blanks he had, but it turned out he knew Mother pretty well.

"No worries," he said. "I'll do Jessica Jane proud today."

"Jess," I said. "Just Jess." I blinked a couple of times at that, but fortunately the tears stayed a film that only blurred the edges of my eyes. Vaguely, I heard the priest's whispered condolence before he moved on. I had no idea what he said. It wouldn't have mattered. Condolences were only platitudes gone wrong.

I was relieved when the service began. I had to thank Russ for his suggestion in regard to the music—a last-minute decision he had offered somewhat hesitantly. I could see why—a polka band that played hymns. It was a crazy idea but they were every bit as good as Russ had assured me. Mother would have loved it. I know some of her friends did. Eleanor swayed to the beat and at the refrain everyone joined in and sang. Near the end someone began to clap and soon others followed. I even saw Henri give Albert a little spin.

The spirit of Mother seemed to dance through the church. I found myself swaying to the music. I shocked myself when I instinctively began to clap with the others.

The music and the participation were the bright spots in the service. That, and what the priest said about Mother. His sermon made it clear who she was, how she'd loved life, and how she would be remembered. Just Jess, dancer, mother, woman extraordinaire. While he might have gone a bit over the top, Mother would have loved that part, too—the theatrics of it all. She certainly knew how to pick her priests. I'd bet he was the only one in the city up to such theatrics.

The moments after the service passed in a blur. I remembered assorted relatives and friends, even neighbors, taking my hand and giving it that squeeze as if that made everything right. Others, who I hadn't met, who claimed to be friends or fellow parishioners of Mother's, also were in the line to give me their sympathy. How I was beginning to hate that word.

I don't remember what they said or even their names; it was a blur. Even those I'd met before were lost in the sea of faces. I supposed that was the purpose of the register book, although I'd balked when the funeral director had insisted on it. I didn't know if I wanted to store any reminders of Mother's demise.

"You did everything you could and more," Russ assured me as he took my hands in his when the condolence lineup had dwindled away. His hands were large and warm. It was strange the things I remembered, the ones that registered, like so little had done through the whole funeral process.

I nodded while thinking what Russ had meant to me over the past year. How he'd offered support and patience. The commitment that he'd offered and never pushed pulsed between us. With Mother's remains only feet from me I was realizing more than ever that this man was a keeper.

It was an awkward moment as I pulled my hands free. Even

though Mother would have been cheering all the way, it was more than I was ready to consider.

In the end I left Mother's funeral with all those words and thoughts left unsaid. It wasn't the time or the place for anything but a fog of grief. I went home to a house more hollow than I could ever have anticipated.

Russ called me only hours later.

"I don't think I'm up to seeing anyone," I said to his offer to come over.

Twenty minutes later I was in his arms crying like the baby I hadn't been in a long time.

Mercifully, Russ did exactly the right thing. He never once told me it would get better. He just held me. And right then, that was all I needed.

•

A few days later I went through a box of Mother's things that had been tucked in the back of her closet. I'd already packed up her clothes for charity. I felt alone and *fragile* was the only word that would describe my state of mind. But I knew I needed to do this—alone. Something in my heart told me that there was something else here, something I needed to know. My mind slipped to the mystery of my father. But I knew that secret had died with Mother.

I wiped the back of my hand across my face, dashing a stray tear across my cheek.

But when I opened the lid of that box I wasn't prepared for what I would see. A clutch of letters and a photo. A man whose lips looked much like mine. A man with dark hair and a solid build. And, a man who clearly had Spanish heritage. I picked up one letter and read. Love threaded through the words. Then I read another. Tears streamed down my face, but my heart felt full and light at the same time. It was as if part of me had been revived. I had found my family. The family that should have been.

I pieced together the story of my biological parents' short love affair, of my mother's indiscretion on that trip to Toronto when she'd fallen in love at first sight. They'd exchanged letters after that. My father had been born in Cuba and immigrated to Canada. But other than a sporadic letter—three to be exact, he'd never followed up with my mother and from the letters, it seemed she hadn't told him about me.

I Googled him after that, and found the same sad news, he'd died years ago. It was exactly as Aunt Alice had said and Helen confirmed—run over by a Toronto city bus. In his obituary was only a list of distant relations—no wife or children. No one. Maybe it had just been me. Now, I was officially an orphan, but at least I knew who both my parents were.

My hands shook as I took the box, tucked under one arm. This was part of my history I'd take with me going forward. I'd been born out of love. It was a long way from where I thought I'd been—with a father who'd walked out on us. This father, I knew would have stayed—had he known.

I picked up the phone.

I needed to hear his voice.

I needed Russ.

He didn't leave that night. I wouldn't have let him even if he'd wanted. He lay on his side with me spooned tight against him and I told him of my plans. He didn't offer to come. He knew.

We lay together like that—quiet, the night hours ticking away. Only as daybreak broke the darkness, did we make love.

Chapter Thirty-Eight

December 5 - The Present

It has been a year since it all began, almost to the day. I brush my fingers over the smooth little box that holds just a bit of Mom's ashes.

At last, Cassie, I'm free.

I can hear her singing Etta James at top volume.

Mother.

I have to do this alone. It was how it had all begun and how it had to end. Me and Mother.

Russ is the only one who knows what I'm doing. He has been my rock through it all, even drove me to the airport. He made sure I had everything, and if he could have walked me onto the plane, he would have.

As it was, he'd demanded he be kept in the loop every step of the way, and I'd dutifully called him to let him know that I'd landed safely. And, when I return, he promised he'd be there to pick me up. I'll be looking forward to that. But now this is just me, me and Mother.

I spirited some of Mother's ashes away. It might be a lot of things. Illegal for one comes to mind. I don't care. I carried her ashes through security checks and international borders to Cuba where there were so many good memories of my last days with Mother. It was here, that I knew she would want to be. And if it had been feasible I would have brought all of her—the entire urn. But air travel and their tight rules and not knowing how the Cuban authorities would react, I had brought a token instead, something I could take that would not attract attention. It was here the man who was my father was born. And it was here Mother's heart remained, in the memories of the one man she loved.

Mother would have loved the idea of some of her remains returning to Cuba. She would have loved her funeral, the polka hymns and the tribute after that when Russ poured both of us a rum and coke and we toasted her. She would have loved it all and if she could have, she would have danced at her funeral.

I chuckle for the first time in a very long time as I picture Mother dancing.

Russ's voice filters through my thoughts and reminds me it was never just Mother and me. Russ was there and the others, all those new friends and even some old. They'd all been there and will still be there for me. Damn Russ. It's not the others I'm thinking of as I hold Mother's ashes and think of how short a life really is.

He's a keeper.

I swear there was a giggle that seemed to drift across the dull roar of the waves that sounds oddly like Mother. I finger the string of pearls around my neck and think of those who have fingered them before me. My thoughts slip from my past and forward.

I've made Russ wait long enough.

While I might have underestimated him in my youth, I would never make that mistake now. It was bad enough I'd lost Mother. I couldn't imagine losing him. I know he'll be waiting for me when I get home. I think the kiss I gave him before I left told him everything he needs to know.

You'll be fine, Cassie.

I know she's right as much as I know oddly, it's Mother's voice I hear in my head. She's here guiding me. Call it strange. Call it crazy. But, I know it's true. Just as I know the answers to my origins lie here in Cuba. I will find out answers about my father—learn more about him and my lineage. But I also know that this trip is not the time. This is Mother's time.

Besides, one thing I've learned since I officially became orphaned was who my father was isn't as important as I'd thought. I knew his name, Jose Fidelis Perez, and that gave me a background, a stronger heritage. But even before I knew,

I'd had so much more than that. I'd had Mother and anything I got in the future was gravy. It wasn't that I didn't want to learn, only that I wasn't in a rush. I'd come back another time. Hopefully, with Russ. Together we'd track down the cousins I now knew existed, and maybe learn more about the man who had fathered me, about my heritage—and about even Mother.

It was something to look forward to rather than something that was missing in my life.

I silently toasted the love that my mother had known no matter how briefly, and snuffed out the candle of imagination on what might have been. I'd had it good. I'd had Mother.

The waves are crashing in today, driven by an off-shore wind. I know this, too, Mother would have loved. I fantasize she is watching from wherever it is she has gone. I refuse to think of her as dead or that there's nothing more. I believed that once, in a great nothingness after we died. But now I know there's something more, much more. My new self is short on details, but she's still evolving.

I'm free, Cassandra Lynn.

Mother's voice is as clear as if she was standing beside me. For a moment I think she is. She twirls in a gentle spin, her arms wide and the sun dancing off her white hair. She twirls like that in my memory for a good minute before I let the image go.

"Goodbye, Mom," I whisper, and open the box as the wind curls and lifts Mother's ashes, and scatters them out to sea. I cry as my feet begin to seek out the comforting rhythm of the Salsa. I dance until the light begins to fade. Every once in a while I look up as I search for another glimpse of Mother.

It wouldn't hurt you to laugh once in a while, Cassandra Lynn.

Watch out world, Jessica Jane is everywhere now.

I couldn't help but laugh and spin not once but twice. Because you know what? I'm pretty darn sure it's true.

"Señora! Un momento por favor."

I swing around, spinning on one toe, an unconscious movement really. But exactly what Mother had taught me to execute anytime a dance required a spin. I push a strand of recently dyed auburn hair from my eyes. I'm face to face with what Mother would have called a gorgeous Cuban man.

"¿Si?" The language felt rather exotic, even that one simple word in Spanish. What could he possibly want? The question is all that stood between a dark-haired beauty and me.

He is beautiful. And my thoughts on Russ aside, I still appreciate beauty.

He points out to sea where ribbons of setting sun are shifting crimson and yellow across the water. "It is incredible, is it not?" he asks in a gruff voice with soft edges. An older woman comes up beside him. He lays his arm casually across her shoulders and looks down at her fondly before turning his attention back to me. "My mother wants to know if señorita would share supper with us. We are cooking lobster."

This is a Cuban tradition, at least for those who live on the southern shores—inviting tourists to eat home-cooked lobster. The tradition is a way for locals to make ends meet by adding an extra chair or table to their home kitchen. I smile slowly. It's a risk, but life is a gamble and I'm ready to dive in.

That's how my new life began—on a rock-strewn beach eating lobster with an attractive man and his mother, and Russ waiting thousands of miles away.

I laughed more than I have in almost a year. Their stories are amazing from tales of pre-revolution Cuba to the antics of tourists they'd met. It is all told in a slightly self-disparaging way. The mother's stories are told in Spanish and repeated in English by Miguel, who had many to tell of his own. I reciprocated, regaling them with tales from the funny side of life with Mother. I know Jessica Jane McDowall is laughing at the retelling.

I promise myself that night, as the first stars come out and I take my leave, that I will come back to Cuba, not just once as I'd first thought, but maybe many times. For not only does the country hold my father's history, but it intrigues and calls to me. It is foreign and exotic. It holds the secrets to my past and maybe even my future.

And, in a strange way, it reminds me of everything and everyone waiting for me at home.

CPSIA information can be obtained
at www.ICGtesting.com
Printed in the USA
FSHW011823180820
73084FS